Dolores J. Wilson's

Jail Bertie
and the Peanut Ladies

Platinum Imprint
Medallion Press, Inc.
Printed in USA

PREVIOUS PRAISE FOR DOLORES J. WILSON'S
BARKING GOATS AND THE REDNECK MAFIA

"Before you make it through the first chapter you are laughing out loud . . . Wilson has a talent for taking an everyday situation and making it hilarious . . . the second in the series, with more to come, I for one, cannot wait."
—*Reviewed by Inez Daylong, Affaire de Coeur Magazine*

"Dolores J. Wilson will make you laugh out loud. BARKING GOATS AND THE REDNECK MAFIA is knee slappingly funny and will brighten your day on many different levels. Lucielle Ball would have felt right at home in Sweet Meadow, Georgia and you will too. If you haven't already read the first book in this world BIG HAIR AND FLYING COWS, grab both books and give yourself a treat, you'll be glad you did."
—*Cat Cody, Romance Junkies Reviewer*

"Imagine for yourself a lady towtruck driver, one caught in misadventure after misadventure. Bertie, the lady in your imagination is one amazing lady. Dolores J. Wilson must be an incredible lady herself to have come up with this delight of a book. The characters' names are even a hoot'n a half!"

—www.Buzzelle.com

"This is an amusing slice of southern living starring a confused heroine trying to do what is right for her and for others though her efforts often lead to conflict between the general good and her personal good. Fans will root for Bertie who at times wants to say bye-bye to the pressure of her business, marriage, and parenting. The sequel to the humorous BIG HAIR AND FLYING COWS is a jocular look at small town Georgia."
—*Midwest Book Review*

Dolores J. Wilson's

Jail Bertie
and the Peanut Ladies

DEDICATION

For my children, Brian, Ryan, and Tiffany, who have turned out to be my biggest supporters and have taught me laughter is the best medicine.

Published 2007 by Medallion Press, Inc.

The MEDALLION PRESS LOGO
is a registered tradmark of Medallion Press, Inc.

Copyright © 2007 by Dolores J. Wilson
Cover Illustration by Adam Mock

Printed in the United States of America
Typeset in Times New Roman PS

Library of Congress Cataloging-in-Publication Data

Wilson, Dolores J.
Barking goats and the Redneck Mafia / Dolores J. Wilson.
p. cm.
ISBN 1-932815-63-5
1. Married women--Fiction. 2. Automobile repair shops--Fiction. 3. Georgia--Fiction. I. Title.
PS3623.I5784B37 2006
813'.6--dc22
2006012460

10 9 8 7 6 5 4 3 2 1
First Edition

ACKNOWLEDGEMENTS:

With special thanks to two terrific ladies, Vickie King and Marge Smith, who are always there with encouraging words. You're the best.

Thanks to my cousin, Marsha Tharp, who does so much to help me and always laughs at my jokes.

With appreciation and love to my husband, Richard, who makes life interesting.

Chapter 1

"Isn't this exciting, LoJ?" I asked my six-week-old baby girl. "You're going to be staying with your Grandma and Poppy, and I'll be right next door working at Bertie's Garage and Towing. That's Mommy's very own business. Some day I'll pass it on to your big sister, Petey and you, just like Pop passed it on to me." LoJ's only answer came in the form of a piercing screech loud enough to shatter glass.

Which, by the way, was one of the next sounds I heard. Tires squealed. Metal crunched. Glass crashed. As I swerved to the shoulder of the highway and slammed on my brakes, a large, fiberglass bumper whizzed by my windshield.

I let loose of a string of blue words and then instantly regretted them. Luckily LoJ was screaming too loudly to hear her mother's potty mouth. I closed my eyes, bowed my head, and gave thanks my baby and I had not actually been involved in the accident at the corner of Oak and Haverford.

Because of an overgrown cedar tree, which blocked the view of vehicles pulling onto Oak Street, the notorious intersection had been the site of at least one wreck a week for the past six months.

Dolores J. Wilson

I would know because I'm Bertie Byrd-Fortney, owner of the only towing company in Sweet Meadow, Georgia. My tow truck operators picked up every one of those disabled vehicles and brought them to the storage yard behind my garage, located a quarter of a mile from the intersection.

Several other vehicles had pulled off the side of the road, and people were rushing to the aid of those in the wrecked cars.

Once my heart rate slowed to the speed of a locomotive, I dug into my purse for the new cell phone my husband, Arch, had given me after the birth of our daughter. At the time I hadn't seen any reason to have one since I'd been born and raised in Sweet Meadow, and if an emergency arose, I'd just roll down my car window and yell to any passerby. Whether it was a life-threatening situation or just something they could laugh at me about for years to come or both, they would summon help.

But I digress. I flipped open the phone and called 911. LoJ continued to bellow in ear-piercing screams.

"Sweet Meadow Police Department," the operator said.

"There's an accident at Oak and Haverford."

"We've already dispatched a unit. They're on the way. The baby that's screaming in the background, is it in need of an ambulance?"

"No, just a diaper change and breakfast." I had gotten out of the car and was trying to unbuckle LoJ from her car seat. I juggled the phone between my chin and shoulder. Evidently the mouthpiece was precariously close to LoJ vocal cords.

Before I picked her up, I turned away from her to talk into the phone. "Sorry," I told the operator. "We are on our first big excursion alone. I'm taking her to my mother, who lives next door to my business, Bertie's Garage and Towing, just down the street from this accident.

"My baby girl's name is Lois Jamie, but we call her LoJ. Just the opposite of the singer's name. Our little LoJ has a good set of lungs, as you've already heard. Maybe she'll be famous someday, too."

"Ma'am," the operator interrupted me.

"Yes?"

"Is your head wound bleeding?" she asked.

"What head wound?"

"Well, the one you must have that's making you babble to an emergency operator."

"Sorry, I'm not hurt. Just a little anxious to have witnessed an accident on my first alone trip with my beautiful—"

Click. The line went dead.

"Can you hear me now?" I whispered as I closed the flap on my phone.

A police car sped toward us. Sirens blaring. Lights flashing. Deputy Carl Kelly skidded to a stop inches from the mangled mess. LoJ cried louder.

I took her out of her seat, cuddled her, and whispered hushed tones against her sweet cheek. Instantly she quieted. Her eyes fluttered. She drifted off to sleep. I pulled a light blanket around her and walked to the dozen or so people milling around the accident.

Carl had just taken his phone from his pocket and punched in numbers.

I was standing behind him. "Anything I can do to help?" I asked.

He looked over his shoulder at me and back at his phone. "That's great service, Bertie. I was just calling you."

He handed me his cell. "Here, tell *you* to bring a tow truck."

Just as I put the phone to my ear, one of my drivers, Carrie Sue, answered.

"Good morning, bring the truck down to our favorite crash site. I'm here waiting on you," I told her.

"Oh, my goodness. I'll be right there." Carrie Sue gasped. Since she and my other driver, Linc were in love and constantly panting around each other, I didn't ask why she was out of breath. I really didn't want to know.

A few minutes later, my two drivers arrived on the scene. They were followed closely by Mom and Pop in their red Caddy. Mom's hair sprouted the same rollers she'd slept in since I was a child. She had on a multi-colored parrot-laden muumuu, and pink fluffy house slippers.

Pop was not so well dressed. He had on NASCAR boxers, no shirt, socks pulled to his knees, tennis shoes, and Mom's chenille purple robe only half closed.

I have an affliction where my eye twitches when I am stressed. Sometimes it's the right one. Sometimes it's the left. Today it was both. The one happy moment came when I realized LoJ had her eyes closed and didn't have to witness the two deranged people rushing toward us.

Suddenly I wondered why I should suffer alone. "Wake up, sweetheart," I whispered to my baby girl. "Grandma and Poppy are here."

It took a few minutes to convince my parents the baby and I were fine and had, in fact, not been part of the mess surrounding us.

We'd already equipped Pop's Caddy with a car seat, so we transferred LoJ's tons of paraphernalia and put her safely in his car.

I watched them drive away, my heart heavy, my uterus contracting. For the first time since her birth, Lois Jamie and I were separated by more than a wall or hospital corridor. Tears streamed down my face.

"Move it or lose it." Carl encouraged me to step out of the way of my tow truck, which Linc was backing into the spot where I stood. The deputy put his arm around my shoulder. "It's okay. She's only going to your mom's. She's not eloping or anything like that. She'll be right next door anytime you feel the urge to hold her."

He was right. I was being so silly. "Thanks, Carl. I appreciate that."

"So we're good now?" He gave my arm a squeeze.

"Sure."

"Then please either help clean up this mess or get the heck out of the way."

I grabbed an industrial shop broom and began sweeping up the kitty litter Carrie Sue had spread on the anti-freeze leaking from a crumpled radiator. Just that quick I was back into the swing of things: sweeping, shoveling, and flinging car parts inside the vehicles to be hauled back to my storage yard. A smile played at the corners of my mouth. I was happy to be working.

"You're happy, aren't you, Miss Crash and Tow?"

I glanced around and found a man I'd seen around town, and I may have even hauled his vehicle a time or two, but his name escaped me.

"As a matter of fact, I am happy, but how did you know?" I

shaded my eyes from the sun.

"I can hear your cash register *cha-chinging* all the way over here. The acid fumes of boiling radiator water on a hot engine smell like money to you, don't they?"

I would have joked back with the man, but I could tell by the dark glare in his eyes he wasn't kidding.

"Sorry, I've got to get this area cleaned up." I went back to sweeping.

"Do you get to charge more per hour if the boss is on the scene?" Sarcasm dripped from the man's voice.

"Is one of these cars yours?" I swept a small pile of dirt over his highly polished shoes.

"No." He didn't move, but I did.

I scurried directly to Carl's side. Out of the side of my mouth I whispered, "Hostile bystander at eleven o'clock." I hurried on my way to the other side of the road.

Linc had taken the first car to the yard, unloaded, and had returned to hook up the second one. After surveying the site and finding it clear of debris, I got into my car and drove to the garage.

Before I started my first day back in the office, I wanted to run to Mom's and check on LoJ. A car pulled between me and my path to the house next door. The man who had approached me a few minutes before climbed out of his car.

"Mrs. Fortney." He and his dusty shoes hurried my way.

"Yes?"

"Don't you think you should do something about the cedar tree at the corner of Oak and Haverford so people coming from the south can see to pull into oncoming traffic?"

"Sir, I don't have anything to do with trimming trees along the highway, but surely you can take that issue up with the city."

"I assume *you* wouldn't want to take it up with the city, because if people had a clear view, they wouldn't wreck. And that would cut into your profit. Right?"

Of all the unmitigated gall. "Are you insinuating I would do something to cause those accidents?"

"Of course not."

"Well, I would hope not," I huffed.

"What I'm saying is that you aren't doing anything to stop the accidents because they are a source of income for you."

I looked skyward. *Lord, if this man has any more to say, please let his words lodge in his throat.* When he didn't choke, I lashed out. "Sir, I would say that's the most ridiculous thing I've ever heard, but unfortunately the way my life goes, I can't make that claim. But I can say none of it is true, and I don't intend to spend another minute discussing it with you. Good day."

"I think it's only fair to warn you I'm going to report your business practices to the city."

"Well, good. While you're down there, why don't you tell them to cut down the cedar tree you've so boldly pointed out is the precise reason for the wrecks?"

The next day, it came to my attention in rather an over-the-top way the city council had no intention of cutting down the tree at the corner of Oak and Haverford. Several cars of well-meaning citizens of

Sweet Meadow unloaded in my parking lot and formed the neatest, perfectly-organized picket line you've ever laid eyes on. I wondered if they were a professional group of demonstrators ready at a moment's notice to march against injustice or to raise awareness for a cause.

What could they be doing right in front of my business? The signs they carried told the whole story: *Bertie in cahoots with city hall. Miss Crash and Tow refuses to demand city action. Tree must go—Bertie says no.*

I lifted my gaze upward. "How crazy can my life get?" I asked God, but instantly retracted the question. I didn't really want to know if things could get worse.

The ten or so picketers pacing the sidewalk were enough foolishness for one day. I couldn't believe anyone thought I would want people put in harm's way by wrecking just so I could tow them to my shop and in the end make money. But, apparently, they did. Their signs said so.

Boycott Bertie's. Take your business elsewhere.

The last two signs were extremely interesting: *Burn your bras. Make love not war.*

"Millie! Mavis!" I grabbed the arms of Tweedle Dee and Tweedle Dumber.

Millie Keats is a member of one of Sweet Meadow's founding families. Mavis Fortney is Arch's aunt by marriage. A forty-seven-year marriage which I managed to destroy in a short two weeks. My penitence for that deed is to be in charge of keeping the two octogenarians out of trouble. That's a full-time job.

I dragged them clear of the other marchers.

"What is wrong with you two? Don't you realize these people are wrong? You know me; I would do anything to make that corner safer for everyone." I raised my voice and directed my comments to the crowd. "You know I have no control of things like that. I tow you in when it happens, but I've never wanted, wished, or caused a wreck in my entire life."

They were a fickle group. Suddenly, they turned on their leader, the man who had accosted me the day before.

"She's right," someone said and tossed his sign on the ground.

"Yeah," another person chimed in. "Let's go to the Chow Pal Diner and have coffee." Several people handed their signs to the man who started the ordeal and piled back into their cars and disappeared as quickly as they'd arrived.

"Mavis, go on home and take that old placard with you," I told her.

Millie pressed against my body and lifted her face to me. "Who are you calling an 'old placard'?"

"Please go home, Millie." I rubbed my forehead. "You're giving me a headache."

She and Mavis got into the car. Before they drove away, I motioned for Mavis to roll down her window. "Have you gotten your driver's license yet?"

"No, but I'm working on it." She laid on the horn. It blared for a good ten seconds.

"See." Millie leaned over in the seat so I could hear her. "She's mastered Horn 101. Tomorrow we're going to work on passing on a two-lane road."

I should have tackled them and taken their keys away, but right now I had bigger fish to fry. The rabble-rouser who'd started all this collected signs and put them in the back of his car.

"What did you hope to accomplish with that? You *look* like you have all your marbles, so what is the deal?"

He barely glanced my way, just continued with what he was doing. "I talked to city hall yesterday, and they say they can't cut down that tree because technically it isn't theirs to cut down. It seems it was planted on that empty corner many years ago by a lady named Tiny Byrd. Any relation?"

"Well, yes, that's my father's mother."

"Right. She planted it there in memory of her husband, your grandfather. She requested it never be cut down. So the city won't cut it down."

Grandpa Byrd died when I was very small. I'd never heard anything about that tree. It was all too bizarre.

"Who are you?" I asked the man.

"Tuten. Timothy Tuten." He stared at me like I should recognize the name, but I didn't. My brother Bobby used to be friends with a boy whose last name was Tuten, but they'd moved away when I was in elementary school. I couldn't recall what his first name was, but I knew it wasn't Timothy. And besides, that young Tuten had ears and a nose that could rival Dumbo in both cases.

Whoever this guy was, his ears and nose were very well proportioned to the rest of him. It was his ego that was too big for its britches.

"Why are you singling me out? You look far too intelligent to really believe a tree being planted many years ago was done just so it could grow up and block the view of drivers. And that my grandmother did it so I could profit from others' misfortune. Why am I the target of your hostility?"

His stern look softened, but quickly turned hard again. "All I can tell you is that I moved here two years ago, and at least once a week I'm held up at that corner because of an accident. It's my understanding that to this point no one's been killed, but it's just a matter of time. What's wrong with solving the problem before a tragedy happens?

"Something has to be done. The city has washed their hands of the situation. The property is tied up in some kind of probate battle. They've hired someone to keep the lot mowed, but he's been given orders not to touch the tree because it belongs to the Byrd family. And that brings me back to you."

He got in his car. "Do something about it before someone gets killed," he shouted and drove away.

Suddenly I was responsible for the well being of every person who drove past the corner of Oak and Haverford. Their lives were in my hands.

I called city hall and talked to Cy Linder, head of the city council. He said the same thing Mr. Tuten had said. It was on private property and the city law said they couldn't touch trees with a certain trunk diameter.

"Surely you have a law that overrides it when it poses a danger to people."

"I think they always meant to have one, but just never got around to it."

"Okay, Cy, what do you suggest I do?"

"Cut down the tree."

"You want me to get rid of it when no one else in town will touch it because of legalities?"

"I can't think of a more likely candidate to handle it than you." He whispered as if talking to someone near him. "I got to run, Bertie. Sorry I couldn't be more help, but you'll figure it out. I have faith in you."

I was in the middle of telling Arch about my day when Mavis and Millie arrived. They'd been out practicing driving and thought they'd visit for a few minutes. If I happened to have dessert and coffee, all the better.

Over a store-bought bag of cookies, I explained the problem with the tree.

"If it's your family tree, cut it down. Problem solved," Mavis said with a mouthful of cookies.

"There seems to be a little more to it. The tree is a certain dimension, and it's illegal to cut it down."

"Don't let anyone see you cut it down." You can always count on Millie to go against the law.

"How can I do that? It's a busy corner."

"Cut it down at night when no one's around," Mavis piped in. She looked at Arch. "Sometimes your little wifey is a rubber ducky short of a bath ensemble, huh?"

Arch did a vaudeville take and spit coffee everywhere. Using a paper napkin I wiped it off me. "Thanks for defending me, hubby dear."

"Aunt Mavis, Bertie couldn't do that. She doesn't know how to cut down a tree. Besides, the sound of the chainsaw would wake the neighborhood."

That wasn't exactly the type of defending I had in mind. "No, but I can mow down a husband in one evil glare." I gave him my one-raised eyebrow look which usually stopped him in his tracks, but he was laughing so hard he didn't see my stare.

"I know how to cut down a tree." Mavis wiped her mouth and smiled. "Come on, let's go do it now." She jumped to her feet and so did Millie.

"Yeah, it's dark, and there's not even a moon out there. Should we put some of that black grease under our eyes like the men do?"

"You mean like the soldiers going into battle?" Arch asked.

"No, like those big linebackers in football games. You know the ones with their pants so tight you can count the freckles on their butts." Millie used her napkin to fan herself.

"Good heavens, Millie." Arch took his plate to the sink. "Is nothing sacred with you? You're making the institution of football into something dirty."

If you're watching him from behind, when he smiles his ears wiggle. At that moment, they were flapping a mile a minute.

"Mavis, are you sure you know how to cut down a tree?" I asked.

"Sure, let's go."

Millie clapped her hands like a child. "We have a saw in the trunk. Come on."

"Why do you have a saw . . . Never mind. I don't want to know."

I kissed Arch goodbye, and the two ladies and I left.

I refused to let Mavis drive, so I drove their jalopy to the corner of Oak and Haverford. Mavis surveyed the situation. She swore she could saw down the huge tree and make it fall away from the street and land in the middle of the open lot. We planned to cut it down and leave it there for the people who mowed to get rid of it.

She made several trips around the tree. Thick branches formed the base with each layer becoming shorter as a perfect Christmas tree rose about sixteen feet into the sky. A childhood memory broke free from somewhere deep in my brain.

Grandma Byrd always said that when something lay heavy on her heart, she would tell it to the tree and everything would be better. I always assumed she meant she talked to nature. Could she have possibly meant one specific tree? Perhaps the tree she had planted in Grandpa Byrd's honor at the corner of Oak and Haverford? Did I have the right or, in this case, the obligation to cut it down?

I'd been assigned the task of keeper of the flashlight. Mavis had been steadily ridding the tree of its lower branches. She sawed, and Millie piled them aside.

"How's it going?" I asked.

"Fine. I need to eliminate enough of these branches to be able to actually see the trunk. It'll be just a few more minutes." Mavis never missed a slice of the saw.

Very few vehicles traveled along the street, but every time one did, we made sure to step into the shadows. When the sun came up, no one needed to know who had taken down the tree that blocked the view of oncoming traffic. I would silently revel with the knowledge I'd played a small part in making our roadways a little safer.

Since Mavis and Millie were both laboring with their back-breaking tasks, and I hadn't even broken a sweat, I'd have to admit I played a very small part. A full hour and a half later, the lower branches were all removed, and we were ready for the greatest tree felling Sweet Meadow had ever seen. Or in this case, not seen.

I bubbled with excitement and giggled aloud.

"Hold the light still." Mavis took my hand and aimed the flashlight where she needed the beam. "I've got to notch it right here."

Forever later, she moved to the other side of the tree and began sawing first one way then the other to form a large V in the tree trunk. I yawned several times and each time I couldn't keep the light still and shining precisely where Mavis needed it.

"You have the attention span of a goose, Bertie." Mavis grumbled. "Hold that thing still before I cut my hand or leg off, or both."

"Okay, but hurry up. I have to go to the bathroom." I'd been dancing from one foot to the other for the past thirty minutes.

"Go over there by the bushes. No one's going to see you," Millie suggested.

"If you don't hurry, I'm not going to have any choice but to go over there."

"It's going to be at least fifteen more minutes. Go on," Mavis said.

I gave Millie the light, and I walked away from the scene of the crime. When I was out of the range of a car light, should one happen by, I pulled down my slacks and started what I'd come there to do.

Cracking wood split the night air. Every muscle in my body tightened. I grabbed for the bush next to me, steadying my swaying body. I stabilized my stance before my bare behind could fall into the dirt, but the shattering sound of the tree breaking off its base slammed though my body.

"Timber!" Mavis shouted. I heard her and Millie's tennis shoes slapping against the hard ground.

I held onto the bush with one hand and used the other to cover my head. I prayed it wouldn't hurt too much when it fell on me and that Mavis or Millie would pull up my pants before the paramedics arrived.

The thud of the tree landing brought quick relief. It hadn't landed on me.

"Uh oh," Mavis said.

"What do you mean *uh oh*? What happened?"

I pulled my pants up and scurried toward the light which Millie shone on the base of the tree. I snatched the flashlight from her and followed it toward the top. It had fallen into the street. The top rested on a car.

As the beam illuminated the emblem on the side of the tree-covered vehicle, and I read the words *Sweet Meadow Police Department*, Carl Kelly's voice penetrated my stupor.

"Bertie, what have you done now?"

Chapter 2

Deputy Carl Kelly opened his squad car door and slowly emerged through the branches of the cedar tree. Millie shined the flashlight directly in his eyes, which were glazed over with a dazed stare.

"What are you deranged women doing? Trying to kill me?" His voice bellowed through the quiet night.

"We are ridding this blind corner of this tree. It's dangerous and no one at the city seems to care about it," I tried to explain.

"Why didn't you hire a professional to take it down, or at least wait until the light of day?"

If he didn't know it was illegal to cut down a tree with a trunk diameter of over six inches, who was I to tell him? But, what was our excuse?

"Well . . ." I offered.

"It's against the law to chop this tree down. So we came out here under cover of darkness." Leave it to Millie to enlighten the world. She flipped the light in my direction. "I told you we needed to grease our faces so we wouldn't get caught. You never listen to a word I say."

I suddenly had a new interpretation of *aggravated battery*. The woman did aggravate me, and I did want to batter her. Was the penalty lesser if provocation was proven?

"You're a crazy woman, Millie Keats," I yelled.

"I would say that was pretty evident. Look what I'm doing and with whom. It reeks of wacky."

Carl stepped between us. "Stop right now. The three of you get in my car. We're going to the station until I can sort this out."

He grabbed the top of the tree. With all his might, he pulled it off his car, dragged it out of the road and into the empty lot. Not an easy task, but his adrenalin appeared to have peaked. Unfortunately, Mavis tried to help by taking hold of a branch somewhere near the middle of the tree. She was pulling backward when she lost her footing, fell flat on her back, and Carl slid the tree completely over her.

We all heard her thud to the ground, but the forward momentum was so great it couldn't be stopped. Carl shined the light on her. There she was, stretched out flat. As the branches had moved across her body, from toe to head, they had caught on her clothes, pulling her pant legs up to her knees, her blouse up and over her industrial strength bra, left scratches over her face and bits of flat cedar leaves in her hair.

"Are you okay?" I knelt beside her.

"I've done funner things in my life." She reached out to Carl, and he helped her to her feet.

"Are you hurt or do you need a doctor?" he asked.

"No, I'm fine."

Carl opened his car door. "Get in."

When we arrived at the police station, Mavis was still a little shaken from her fall. "I've never been felt up by a tree before," she declared several times.

As we entered the one-room establishment with a long counter dividing the public from the authorities, and one lone jail cell in the corner, I hummed, "We're in the Jailhouse Now."

Mavis steadied herself against my back. Maybe she had a flashback from an earlier incarceration where she'd driven a get-away car for her son. I reached both my hands behind me, and she placed hers in mine. Millie followed close to Mavis. Single file, we went around the counter and marched in front of the cell.

From across the room, a light flashed. Mavis and I jumped. Millie whimpered.

Jim Ed Swain, owner of the Sweet Meadow News-Leader, hurried in our direction.

"Good going, Carl. I see you rounded up a whole gang. Wha'd they do? Robbery? Burglary?"

"Cut down a tree." Carl pointed toward a bench along the wall.

"You're not going to lock them up?" Jim Ed asked.

I was wondering the same thing, but Carl didn't answer. He sat at his desk and made me tell him step by step why we had done what we did.

"Evidently that tree belongs to my family, and people are saying I want it there to block traffic, cause accidents, and then tow them to my shop." I leaned forward. "The city said there was a law against cutting down trees of that size, and they refused to touch it." I relaxed in my seat and crossed my legs. "You can see, I was left with no other choice but to take matters into my own hands."

"Are you going to lock them up?" Jim Ed inquired again.

"Of course not." Carl stared daggers at the newspaper reporter. "Don't you have someplace else you need to be?" he asked.

"Not really." Jim Ed answered.

Deputy Kelly jumped to his feet and towered over the man. "Find someplace else to be."

Mr. Swain almost fell over a chair trying to get out of harm's way.

Millie giggled, and the man left the building.

"Why aren't you going to lock us up?" I cocked a questioning eyebrow.

"Because that law about preserving trees a certain size only pertains to commercial property. That tree was on private property. The legalities about whether you had the right to cut it down on someone else's property, well, that would be another subject if the owner was around to press charges. However, the owner is dead, and his distant relatives have been fighting about it for twenty years. The estate pays to keep the lot presentable so the city leaves it alone."

Carl picked up the phone and handed it to me. "Call your husband to come and get you three. I have a ton of paper work to fill out about how my squad car got all those scratches on its roof."

I dialed my number.

"Hello," Arch answered with a sleep-laden voice.

"Hi, sweetheart. Can you come down to the jail and get me and my accomplices?"

Two days later, when I dropped LoJ off, Pop stood behind Mom, who was sitting at the kitchen table sobbing into her hands. The coffee smelled inviting, and I really needed some, but Mom was more important at the moment.

"What's wrong?" I walked up behind her and rubbed her back with my free hand and cradled my baby in my other arm. Over Mom's shoulder I saw the front page of the Sweet Meadow News-Leader lying on the table.

"Holy cow." I couldn't believe my eyes. It had a picture of me with my hands behind my back, with Mavis and Millie trailing me. We looked like we were attached together and with the jail cell in the background, handcuffs came to mind. You couldn't see them because there weren't any, but it certainly looked like it.

The headlines read: *Deputy Captures Gang of Vandals.*

"I'm going to kill Jim Ed Swain." I shoved LoJ at Pop. Mom cried harder.

As I stormed out their front door, I heard Mom ask Pop, "Shouldn't you stop her before she goes to jail for murder?"

"Naw. She wouldn't really kill him, but when Bertie is through with old man Swain, he may wish he were dead."

I turned on my heel and raced back into the kitchen. "Thanks, Pop." I kissed him and LoJ and then bent down to Mom. "Pop's right. I always respect my elders, but Mr. Swain is going to return the favor to me."

As if things weren't bad enough, Timothy Tuten awaited me in the parking lot of the garage. He got out of his car and strolled in my general direction.

"I see you caused another wreck with your tree." He tapped his hand with the paper.

"It wasn't like that at all. What are you here for?"

"There's another wreck at the corner of Oak and Haverford. I thought I'd stop by and tell you they're going to need a wrecker."

"See, the tree is gone, and they are still wrecking." I gloated.

"That's because the speed limit on this road," he pointed at Oak Street, which passed in front of my garage, "is fifty-five miles per hour, and with so much morning and afternoon traffic traveling that fast, the cars coming from Haverford have only a few seconds to build up speed when they pull out."

"Well, I certainly can't do anything about that."

"Sure you can. You have a business a short distance from the intersection. You have the right to force the city to put up a red light. That would solve the whole problem."

I took a quick inventory of the situation. As I saw it, a traffic light was a good idea and besides, I'd already learned Mr. Timothy Tuten with the cute ears and nose would dog my every step until I did something about it anyway. Why not give it up and go straight to city hall, and give Jim Ed Swain another day of life?

"Okay, toot-toot, Tuten," I fluttered my hands in a dismissive fashion. "Get out of my way. I'll give old city hall a call right now. Have a good day."

I called the courthouse and was told the only way a traffic light could be erected was by order of the city council. I told the lady on the phone to pass that info on to the head of the council and to get it up as soon as possible.

"It doesn't work that way," the lady informed me. "Someone will have to make a proposal at the town meeting and then a committee will be formed to investigate the likelihood the council will come off the funds. It is so much trouble most people don't even bother trying to get something like that through."

"Well, I can bother. When and where do I go to present my proposal?"

"The next monthly meeting is a week from Monday. Be prepared to give them statistics and hard evidence about why you feel there is a need for a red light at that end of town."

"Can we get DOT to put one of those hoses across the road to count how many cars pass that area in a week's time? I'd like to be able to tell them the ratio of wrecks per cars passing that corner."

"We don't have one of those counters."

"Well, how would I go about getting one so I can do the survey?"

"Council's not going to come off the money to buy one." The woman actually giggled. "That would cut into the Christmas Party Fund, and it's not happening. The best way is for someone to actually count the cars as they go by. Sorry, I have to go. The mayor is bellowing for his Tums. Let me know when you get your facts together, and I'll put you on the docket to present it to the council."

Sitting at my desk, I laid out plans for gathering the council's info, and it was all looking pretty good. I would drop LoJ off at Mom's an hour earlier and go to the corner of Oak and Haverford with a lawn chair and a clipboard. As they sped by, I would personally count the cars. Surely a week's worth of statistics would be enough to convince the town. And, I had just that much time before the next meeting.

My excitement grew thinking about doing something for the betterment of the community. In the meantime, I could prove to that Tuten fellow that others' safety meant more to me than the almighty dollar.

Around three in the afternoon, Mildred Locke, long-time waitress over at the Chow Pal Diner, called for a tow truck. I'd dispatched Carrie Sue, who had been scrubbing the public bathrooms in the back of the garage for the past hour, and I knew she'd appreciate the interruption. She'd been gone about five minutes. Linc came into the office and slowly worked his way over to my desk. He didn't say anything, but his body language told me he had a lot to say.

"Something on your mind?" I asked.

"No. No," he answered a little too fast. "Well, maybe, yes."

"That's what I like about you, Linc. You're decisive."

Since he always appeared to be perplexed about most everything, it didn't surprise me to see his puzzled look staring back at me.

"You know what I mean. You're succinct," I explained.

"If it's okay with you, I need to talk about something before

Carrie Sue gets back. But we can talk about my sink later if you still want to."

I applied pressure to my temple. "No, no. That's perfectly all right. What do you want to talk about?"

He pulled up a chair. "I want to ask Carrie Sue to marry me." The poor guy flushed eighteen colors, all at one time.

I went to him and gave him a hug. "I think that's wonderful. Congratulations."

"Well, thank you." He stuck his hands into his pockets and shrugged until his head nearly disappeared into his shoulders.

"Is there a problem with asking her? Surely you don't want me to do it for you. Do you?"

"No, I can do that, but what about our honeymoon?"

"I . . . I . . . assure you that's not my expertise. You're on your own there," I stammered.

"I didn't mean it like that." Now, Linc was almost purple with embarrassment.

Not daring to speculate on my own, I sat back down and waited for him to tell me how I could help him.

"If Carrie Sue and I go on a honeymoon, that will leave you here alone to make all the calls." He looked so serious.

I wanted to laugh with relief that I wasn't being asked to tutor in a subject way over my head, but I feared Linc would turn tail and run.

"That won't be a problem. You have a vacation coming. Pop'll be able to help out some of the time. It'll all work out."

Relief appeared to roll off Linc and, if it had been a tangible thing, it would have puddled at his feet.

"When do you plan to ask her?" I loved the whole idea of romance in the air and wedded bliss.

He rose. "Tonight. I have a big evening planned." He pulled a small box from his pocket and showed me the ring. It was a gold band with a petite diamond.

"It's beautiful. Carrie Sue is going to love it." I was so caught up in the excitement of it all that I hugged my greasy employee one more time.

"What's going on here?" Carrie Sue startled us apart.

I spun around to find her standing in the squatting stance a wrestler takes just before he charges his opponent. Linc and I both began to spit, sputter, and stammer.

"It's not what you think." I took a couple steps in her direction. Evil seemed to shoot from her eyes, and I stopped dead in my tracks.

Linc rushed around me. "Mrs. Bertie was just congratulating me."

"On what? A lube job well done? I'm not near as stupid as I look."

"Of course you're not as stupid as you look." Linc shook his head.

I gasped, and Carrie Sue looked ready to slug him.

"That's not what I meant, and you know it." His deep, demanding voice captured our attention. "I wanted it to be romantic and a big surprise, but I guess now is as good a time as any." He dropped to one knee and showed her the ring.

"Will you marry me?" he asked with a hitch in his voice.

Carrie Sue's eyes welled, and she pulled Linc to his feet and jumped into his arms, wrapping her legs around his waist. Before I had time to think, her arm snaked around my neck and pulled me

26

against the mass of body parts.

Finally, I was able to back away from them. After Carrie Sue slid down Linc's body and was standing on her own, she asked, "How were you planning on surprising me with this tonight?"

"I was going to take you by ET's Donut Shop, and Elton was going to slip the ring into one of his famous holeless donuts."

"Oh, that would have been so special." She turned to me. "Why did you have to ruin my surprise? Can't you mind your own business for one minute?"

I shrugged. Some questions just aren't worth answering. "Congrats, you two." I went back to work.

Over the weekend, Arch and I went out to dinner and our next door neighbor, Barbie, sat with LoJ and Petey. Her husband, Rick was working late on an audit. She was expecting her own baby in a few more weeks and said she needed the practice. I shuddered at the thought of her "practicing" on my kids, but Arch insisted he had faith in Barbie's motherly instincts. Since I have faith in Arch's judgment, we were on our way, even as I wondered if we should set up a nanny-cam.

We went to the Chow Pal Diner for the Saturday night special, fried catfish and hush puppies. The place buzzed with loud voices, clanging dishes, and an old Garth Brooks' tune booming from the juke box. The smell of grilled burgers and French fries made my stomach growl almost as loud. Arch and I waited about ten minutes for a booth to empty, and then we slid into one in the middle of the diner.

Instead of sitting across from each other, he sat beside me. And, why not? We were on our first date since LoJ was born.

I nodded to a few acquaintances and spoke to Clyde and Peggie Morrison, who sat in the next booth. I'd opened the menu just in case there was something else I might enjoy eating, even though I would inevitably choose the catfish.

Through the front door walked my new nemesis, Timothy Tuten. His name had a musical ring.

Tooootin'! I wanted to shout, but something inside me said it was too childish to be acceptable. Did that stop me?

"Toooootin'," I yelled over the noise. He saw me, and I motioned to him.

"Timothy Tuten, this is my husband," I said.

"Call me Tim."

"Arch Fortney," he announced as he shook hands with Tim.

When I talked about the idiot who thought it was my fault people wrecked at the corner of Oak and Haverford, I wanted Arch to put a face to the name.

"Please, join us for dinner." Arch pointed to the empty seat across from us. "There's a long wait to be seated, and we wouldn't mind the company."

I kicked my husband's leg. He jumped and gave me a mean look. Tim wasn't stupid, so he quickly picked up on the fact that he having dinner with us was the last thing I wanted.

"I'd love to join you." He smiled and slipped into the seat across from us.

He ordered liver and onions, which made the experience even more unpleasant for me since I don't enjoy being in the same town with that entrée let alone being at the same table with it.

"Are you new in town, Tim?" Arch asked.

"I moved here about two years ago."

"I believe I've seen you in church." Arch dipped his catfish finger into the tartar sauce.

"Yes, I transferred my membership to Sweet Meadow Baptist when I moved here from Atlanta."

"Are you married?" Arch was really delving into the man's history.

"I was married until two years ago."

For a moment, Tim had a far away look in his eye. It almost touched my heart, but there was still that accusation I caused accidents for profit standing between me and compassion for the guy.

"Have you made any progress with the council about the traffic light?"

It took a second for me to realize he was actually including me in the conversation.

"Oh, well, not really. All next week I'm doing a count of the traffic that passes the corner and compiling stats about the accidents. A week from Monday night, I'm going to present my findings at the town meeting."

"That should be interesting." Tim shoveled in his last bite of liver and dabbed a napkin to his mouth.

"Why don't you come by the meeting and watch me in action. I might even call you as a witness for the defense."

"Bertie." Arch put his arm around my shoulder. "Repeat after me, I am not an attorney. This is not a trial."

"Thank goodness," Tim chuckled, "I have a feeling your wife

would find a way to have me declared guilty and hung in short order."

For some reason, I found that funny, and I laughed along with him and Arch.

"I'll tell you what. I might show up there, and I'll be willing to vouch for the fact it is a dangerous corner and that I personally have witnessed several wrecks in the two years I've been in town."

Tim "Toootin'" Tuten might turn out to be okay after all.

"Tim doesn't seem like such a bad guy." Arch pulled the car into our driveway.

"Maybe not, but he certainly came on like his pants were on fire at first." We got out of the car and, hand in hand, strolled up the walkway.

Suddenly, sirens blared in the distance, getting closer and closer. An ambulance made a sharp turn onto our street and came to a stop six feet from us. A police car followed close behind. I couldn't move. Arch grabbed my arm and hauled me up the stairs and through the door.

The scene we found could only be described as chaotic. Barbie lay on her back with her head toward us in the middle of the kitchen floor. With her maternity dress shoved to her waist, her hands held her thighs up. A towel thrown over her spread legs formed a tent.

Our twelve-year-old daughter peeked from under the tent. "We're having a baby," Petey said. She smiled widely and disappeared again. Barbie did a modified sit-up and screamed one time, hard and loud. The EMTs pushed by Arch and me, knocking into us with their equipment. They hurried through the living room to the mommy-to-be and underage mid-wife.

"Whoa," one of ambulance attendants said. The other two stared under Barbie's leg tent.

"Check LoJ." I pushed Arch into action. I rushed to Petey's side. I couldn't believe my eyes. A real live baby lay on a blood-soaked towel on my kitchen floor.

"Good job, young lady." An EMT nudged Petey out of the way. "I'll take over from here."

I took her hand and pulled her to her feet.

Barbie reached out. "Thank you, Petey. I couldn't have done this without you."

She knelt beside Barbie and took her hand. Only moments later, the whole house filled with the beautiful cry of a newborn baby girl.

By the time the EMTs scooted Petey and I out of their way so they could tend to Barbie, I was sobbing. I couldn't be sure if my emotional outburst was from being witness to a birth or from the fact that my sweet young daughter had delivered Barbie's baby.

Petey became a hero. During church services the following day, the mayor presented her with a key to the town and declared Monday Penelope Tam Fortney Day. That was probably the first time many of her friends had ever heard her given name. Penelope Tam became P.T. and eventually Petey, which was given to her by Arch's father.

Pete died a couple of years ago, but I'd been fortunate enough to have met him. Once in a while he visited me in my dreams which, at first, creeped me out, but lately had brought me comfort. I miss Pete, the old goat.

After church, we stopped by the hospital to check on Barbie and her baby. Rick, the proud father, pointed through the nursery window to a tiny pink bundle wailing its heart out. The baby was two weeks early, but was a picture of good health. She and Mommy would go home the next day.

That would be Penelope Tam Fortney Day.

If pride swelled Arch's chest any more, his buttons would pop off his shirt and fly down the hospital corridor.

Back in the room, Barbie was watching television. She looked weak, but who wouldn't after giving birth naturally in the middle of a kitchen floor. I felt weak from just witnessing the ordeal. The strangest thought had been swimming through my mind since I entered my house the evening before.

Thank goodness I scrubbed the floor that morning.

"She's beautiful," I said and gave Barbie a hug. "You did a good job."

Petey had gone to the other side of the bed, and Barbie pushed a strand of hair behind my daughter's ear. "You did a good job, too. Thank you."

I released an audible sob from somewhere deep in my heart. Arch put his hands on my shoulders and squeezed gently. We probably looked like neon lights glowing with pride.

"Has Rick told you what we're naming our little girl?" Barbie asked Petey.

She shook her head.

"We're taking part of your name as a reminder that you were there the minute she popped into the world. We're naming her Tammy. That's long for Tam."

"That is sooo cool." Petey jumped up and down. She grabbed her dad's hand and pulled him to the door. "Come on, let's so see Tammy again."

As they disappeared, she rambled on. "She's named after me, isn't that so cool?"

Barbie smiled up at me. "She's a brave girl. I don't know what I would have done without her." She closed her eyes and rested.

Petey had been my daughter for a little less than two years, and I didn't know what I'd do without her either. Or her baby sister. Or her father. For some reason, I'd been doomed to live in a fast-paced, crazy world that constantly threatened to blast me into outer space. My family was the weight that kept me grounded.

And, the next day, I would need them even more for my fight for the right for a traffic light. Clever. *Fight for the right for a traffic light.* Maybe that would be my slogan.

Chapter 3

Monday morning arrived, and you would have thought I would soon be reporting in as Mr. Rogers' neighborhood assistant. I was truly excited. I giggled and danced around the kitchen scrambling eggs, popping bread into the toaster, and singing my usual welcome to the morn to my little family.

"Rise and shine," I yelled down the hallway.

"I'll rise, but I won't shine." Petey entered the room and took her place at the table.

"Whatever, my little drama queen." I set her breakfast in front of her. "Just so you get a move on so I can get to my new job of counting cars."

Arch brought LoJ into the kitchen and set her in her carrier onto the counter. I dabbed a spit bubble from her mouth. "There's Mommy's precious widdle baby," I cooed.

My husband gave me a tender kiss on the check. "You okay, sweetheart? You're acting a little more chipper than usual." He looked truly concerned. "You're not suffering from postpartum depression, are you?"

"Heck, no. I'm just really into this doing something for the community thing. Counting vehicles, compiling statistics, and reporting to the city council has my engines all revved up."

"Well, good. I'm happy for you." As he sat at the table, he mumbled, "I think."

I served him breakfast. "Oh, come on. Carrie Sue and Linc are prepared to handle the garage for the next week. You and the girls won't be affected at all."

He glanced at the clock on the wall. "We're up an hour and a half earlier than usual. That's a little bit of an effect."

"I need to be out there on the corner of Oak and Haverford from seven in the morning until seven tonight. It's just for one week. You don't really mind, do you?" I planted a kiss on top of his head.

"I don't mind," Petey piped up. "I get to help Dad with LoJ. He needs me, you know."

"Of course I do. I can't think of a better way to spend the earlier part of an evening than with two of my three favorite girls."

"That's the spirit. And, I'll be home to spend the later part of the evening with you." I gathered my coffee thermos and LoJ, kissed Petey and Arch and headed out the door.

"What are we having for dinner?" he asked.

"My crystal ball says what ever kind of pizza you pick up on your way home." I shut the door.

In no time at all, I had dropped LoJ off at Mom's and set up my open-air office. My bright orange lawn chair, complete with an umbrella to provide shade, fit neatly behind my TV tray. It was a fold-up metal one from the early sixties and had been stashed in Mom's storage room since the late sixties. It wobbled a little, but served its purpose.

I had all the important things: thermos of coffee, sandwiches, and cold drinks in my trusty Igloo, clipboard, and sunglasses. Could I ask for anything more?

Yes. A bathroom. I'd barely set up and nature called.

Across the street, Alice Clooney removed a padlock and chain, which secured the rockers outside her old filling station turned antique store. Her husband, Gus, ran the Standard station until ten years ago when he had a heart attack while having sex in a closet.

Unfortunately, he was with a maid from the Stop and Flop Motel, and it was a utility closet. He died among the mops and buckets. Alice had Gus cremated and spread his ashes on the lawn of the motel. Since he spent so much time there, she felt it was very appropriate. I remember Pop saying to Mom that Gus should have been spread at the other two motels way out on Highway 440, too. She never found that funny, but Pop did.

Alice had been stuck with her mother-in-law's antique furniture. She always hated it, but Gus insisted they keep it, never allowing Alice to buy new things for her house. A week after Gus passed on to the big utility closet in the sky, she took every stick of furniture they owned, moved it into the filling station, and hung out her "open for business sign." *The Old Bat's Antiques* shop was born and had thrived ever since.

And, hopefully, it had a bathroom Alice would not mind sharing with an unofficial traffic counter.

After dodging speeding cars, all of which owned working horns,

I made it across the road and into Alice's shop.

"If you don't mind, I need to use your restroom."

"Oh, good morning, Bertie." She smiled sweetly. "I'm sorry, but my restroom is reserved for customers only."

"For crying out loud, Alice. It's me, your friendly tow truck driver. I need to go and now," I begged.

She pointed to a sign behind the counter and then read it aloud, "No Fee. No Pee." Her grin looked like a sneer.

"You own the place. You can bend the rules."

"It seems to me we had this same conversation about five years ago, only in reverse."

"I don't understand."

"You towed my car over to Joe's House of Parts. I ask you to accept half the outrageous fee you charged." Alice leaned onto the counter.

"You know that was different. I worked for my father back then. I wasn't allowed to make deals. Everything had to go through him, and if I remember correctly he was unavailable. So, what do you say? Can I use your bathroom?"

"Let's see, what was it you said to me that night as you took my twenty dollars? Sorry. No can do."

My going to the bathroom had suddenly become an emergency. One that did not afford me the luxury of playing dodge car, getting into my vehicle, and driving to my garage. I pulled a ten dollar bill from my jeans' pocket and looked around for something inexpensive to buy. On a table next to the front door, I spied a huge brass sleigh bell.

"How much is this?" I asked.

"Five dollars." Alice didn't even look up from her newspaper.

"I'll take it. Will that get me a pass to the potty?"

Alice punched the cash register and took my money. I hurried to the back room.

When I returned, she handed me my bell and my change.

"Will I be able to come back this afternoon with this purchase?"

She wrote on the back of a business card, *Good for one visit.* I snatched it out of her hand, grabbed my bell and left. It wasn't until I got back to the other side of the road and took my seat that I realized I was huffing and puffing, more from anger than over exertion. *The Old Bat's Antiques* was an appropriate name for Alice's shop.

During the first two hours of my counting endeavor, I found it hard to keep up. Vehicles of all makes, colors, and sizes whizzed past. Several at a time. Horns honking.

"Hey, Bertie. Whatcha doing?" a couple of Sweet Meadow's residents called to me. Of course, they were flying by at fifty to sixty miles per hour. I didn't have time to do more than throw my arm up and wave.

I made little tick marks on my notebook to represent each vehicle. Around ten o'clock, I pulled a bag of chips from the stash under my chair and sat the opened package on the corner of my TV tray. I snacked as I did my count.

Just before the afternoon rush started, I ventured back across the street to Alice's facilities. Before she let me go into the back room, she collected my free-pass card. As I hurried through the antiques, I decided I needed to start a list of people who irked me. As a fun pastime, I could pretend to exact revenge on the people who made my list. For example, for Alice Clooney, I'd wish termites in her antiques.

After I'd found relief in the bathroom and made my way back to the front of the store, I felt a little less hostile. I wouldn't put her on my list.

"Want to see something funny, Bertie?" Alice pointed toward a television on a shelf behind her. She had a movie camera plugged into the front of it. I leaned over the counter in order to see the screen better.

It was a home movie of me sitting across the street in my lawn chair, shaded by my umbrella. I appeared to have a routine going. With my left hand, I popped a chip into my mouth and wiped the grease on my jeans. With my right hand, I made the marks on the paper, raised my hand over my head, and waved at someone passing by.

I popped, wiped, marked, waved, over and over and over again. By the looks of it, I could have been having a spell of some sort.

"Isn't that the funniest thing you've ever seen?" Alice laughed so hard she had tears in her eyes. I did, too, but not from the hilarity of the movie.

"Okay, Alice, you can erase that now. Very funny."

She sobered only long enough to say, "Oh, no. I'm sending this into that television show where you can win a lot of money for funny home videos. You may be my ticket out of this town. I want to travel." She went back to braying like a donkey.

"You submit that anywhere, and you'll travel all right. To the moon, Alice." I turned on my heel and stormed out the door. I made it halfway across the street.

"Bertie," Alice yelled at the top of her voice.

I didn't turn around. I ran to the curb in front of my station.

"Bertie," she crowed again.

I spun around to look back across the street. "Can you wait until I get out of harm's way, please?" I held my hands out and shrugged. "What?"

She held up a small object that looked a lot like the sleigh bell I'd bought earlier in the day.

"I'm going to lay this aside for you. You can pay me tomorrow when you come over to use my restroom. Be sure to bring a five-dollar bill so I don't have to make change."

"You are so going on my list," I yelled.

It would be a cold day on the Equator before I set a foot back in the Old Bat's place.

"I will never again go into your place even if it means I have to pee in these bushes." I pointed to the exact spot I'd used the night Mavis, Millie, and I cut down the tree. "It wouldn't be the first time, either."

I'm not sure if I felt a presence behind me or if I heard a snicker. I turned and found Tim Tuten standing there smiling.

Humiliation moved into my body and brought its cousin mortification with it.

"What now?" I asked him.

"Nothing. I just stopped by to see how your statistic gathering is going."

"Everything's fine. If you'll excuse me, I have work to do." I shoved past him and sat in my lawn chair. "The afternoon commute is picking up."

"Okay." Tim handed me a business card. "Would you give this to your husband and ask him to give me a call? A few of my friends are thinking about forming a bowling league, and I thought he might be interested in getting out of the house one night a week."

Great. Just what I needed in my life. Arch's new best friend to be Tim Tuten. Besides, what made him think Arch wanted to get away from home? It was a struggle, but I kept my lips from pouting.

"Sure. Whatever." The sleigh bell I bought from Alice lay on the edge of my makeshift desk. I picked it up. "Will you do me a favor?" I thrust the bell at Tim. "Wear this around your neck so I hear you coming next time."

Tuesday was a much better day. I made arrangements to have Carrie Sue take my place for fifteen minutes in the morning and in the afternoon while I took my business anywhere other than to Alice's.

During the day, I didn't do as much waving as the day before. There were two reasons for that. First, I didn't want to give Alice any more video footage. Second, my arm hurt so bad I couldn't lift it if I wanted.

I'd been back from my afternoon break a short time when Millie and Mavis pulled their car to stop right in front of me, blocking the traffic.

Mavis turned off the engine, and Millie rolled down her window. "What are you doing, Bertie?"

Panic rose inside me. "Mavis, don't stop there. You're going to get hit." I hurried to the curb. "Go around the block and pull up in here." There was plenty of room to park in the empty lot.

Before she could start the car, the impatient driver behind her pulled into the next lane into the path of an oncoming car. Mavis managed to speed out of the way of the accident.

Unfortunately, my temporary desk didn't escape. The back end of one of the cars climbed over the curb and into my TV tray sending it, my cold drink, and clipboard into the dirt.

I continued to count cars and mark them down on my now dirty notebook with the nub of a pencil. I was going to succeed at this task even if I had to bite off the end of my finger and write in blood.

Chief Kramer arrived to clear up the accident. All vehicles involved pulled into the lot and voices chattered all around me. I refused to be deterred.

Only one car had to be towed. When everyone had left except for Frick and Frack, I gathered my pitiful belongings, put them in my car and stacked my broken desk in a pile at the curb. Millie and Mavis were whispering and pointing at the ground and walking off paces as if measuring something. Whatever those two were up to was no concern of mine.

From that moment on, I was washing my hands of both of them. As I walked over to tell them so, I saw a new dent in the front of their car.

"Where did this come from?" I asked.

Millie stepped forward and ran her hand over it. "That's where Mavis hit Miff Hayden."

"Oh, good Lord." I clutched my fist to my chest. "Did you

hurt him?"

"Naw, just dented him a little."

Neither seemed upset about the fact they'd run over an old man.

"You didn't just hit him and run did you?" By now, I was screaming.

"Of course not. We stopped and tried to straighten him out with the sledge hammer we have in the back of the car, but it did more damage."

"Well, I would expect it would. Where is he? What did you do with him?"

"You mean Miff? He's gone up to that big peanut farm."

"You two lunatics killed Miff Hayden, and you're walking free. How? Why?"

"We didn't kill Miff. Bertie, I swear, I think you've been out here in the sun too long." She opened the car door and forced me to sit down and put my head between my legs. She thought I was going to pass out. I was afraid I wouldn't.

"Listen," Mavis said. "I didn't get stopped soon enough, and I bumped into Mr. Hayden's pickup. He said he didn't want to call the police, but if he had something heavy he could straighten it out. We gave him our sledge hammer, and he banged on the dent, but he knocked a hole in it. Anyway, we're going to pay to fix it. He was on his way out to that big peanut farm, and he's going to bring us back some green peanuts for us to boil."

"I like boiled peanuts," I said. I think I was in shock. I made my way to my car, got in and drove to Mom and Pop's. I never thought I'd live to see the day I'd run to my parents for stable conversation, but today I really needed it.

The next day, clouds threatened to rain on me while I watched my parade. The dampness made the fall air even chillier. I pulled the hood of my University of Georgia sweatshirt over my head and held my hot cup of coffee close to my lips. Steam rose, warming my face and bringing with it the aroma of the strong brew laced with hazelnut cream.

I love the smells and sights of autumn. Already the leaves were turning and each morning the ground took longer to warm up from the night's chilly dew. The gray skies only added to the mystique of the season. Actually, I think I really love it because Christmas is not far behind.

I made it through the morning spurt of heavy traffic, and Carrie relieved me for my mid-morning bathroom break. Shortly after lunch, Mavis and Millie arrived. My first thought was I really didn't want to contend with them, but when the two old women opened the trunk of their car, which I'd started referring to as a potentially deadly missile, I had to see what they'd do next.

If someone offered me a million dollars to guess what that might be, I would still barely have two nickels to rub together.

From their trunk, they both strained to lift a propane cylinder and lugged it a short distance from my chair. They then pulled out the base of what appeared to be a turkey fryer. After they hooked up the hose from the gas tank, they struck a match and lit the burner. I stared into the blue flame and inhaled an inviting aroma. Millie and Mavis carried a gigantic pot and set it onto the fryer base. The yummy smell grew stronger.

"May I ask what you two are doing?" Truly curious, I ventured closer to the fire.

Millie raised the lid of the steaming vat. "We're going to sell peanuts. They been boiling all morning, and they're ready."

Mavis put a sandwich board over her head and let the straps rest on her shoulder. The front sign read: *M and M's Hot Boiled Peanuts.* The back: *Nutz R Us. Get them while their hot.* With the way my life goes, you would think it impossible to amaze me. But, these two women continued to astound me on a regular basis. Of course I thought a more appropriate back sign would have been: *Us R Nutz.*

Miff Hayden brought a couple of bushels of green peanuts from the farm. They decided to boil them up in salt water and bring them to my corner to sell. While Mavis paced the sidewalk in front of me, hawking their wares, Millie dipped hot boiled peanuts into small plastic freezer bags and sold them to the people who pulled into the lot.

They were doing a booming business and, with all the activity in the lot, it was hard to keep track of traffic and my tick marks. Twice during the afternoon, when a car stopped to ask Mavis where they could buy her peanuts, the vehicle behind them had to slam on breaks to keep from rear ending the aforementioned stopped car. The screeching of the tires would cause me to dive from my chair for cover, and I would inevitably miss counting a few cars.

Normally, the corner witnessed one accident per week, but with so many distractions, there would probably be a few more before the end of my self-imposed assignment. This would be bittersweet. Sweet because it would up my percentage of accidents per passing traffic, making my argument to city council even stronger. Bitter because Tim Tuten's bucket-of-bunk allegation that I benefited from the accidents would possibly hold water.

That thought had barely squiggled through my tired brain when a three-car chain reaction happened. The vehicles only had a scratch or two on their bumpers. No wreckers were needed. No one was hurt except for me. I tore a hole in my jeans and skinned my knee while trying to make a hasty retreat to get out of the way in case they jumped the curb. They didn't, but I felt it was important not to sit idly by to see if they would be coming straight at me with thousands of pounds of metal.

By the time Carl Kelly arrived, Mavis and Millie had sold all their peanuts and were emptying the water from the pot into the bushes. He did the accident report for the fender bender and confronted the two women.

"Do you ladies have a street vendor's permit?" he asked.

Millie shook her head. "No, didn't know we needed one."

"Well, you do. I'm not going to write you up this time, but get one before you do this again."

"Where do we get one?" Mavis asked.

"At the county courthouse over in Shafer."

"Okay, we'll go there first thing in the morning." They got into their car and left.

"Are you aware that neither of those two have a valid driver's license?" Surely I had some obligation to make that fact known to the authorities.

Deputy Carl Kelly, one of Sweet Meadow's finest, put his hands over his ears and did a great impersonation of Sergeant Shultz. "I hear nothing. I see nothing."

I found that only mildly disconcerting. Mavis' driving was improving, but if Carl stopped her from practicing, she would never get her license, and I would have to haul her and Millie's carcasses around like a taxi driver. I didn't want to do that, especially when they had to go to the courthouse to get a permit.

On the other hand, having dealt with the permit office, it might be interesting to see the dynamic duo tackle the system as they tried to get permission to sell peanuts on a street corner. Unfortunately, I had to count cars in preparation for my own battle with our city council.

I snickered all the way to Mom's house. I'd love to be a fly on the wall tomorrow morning at Shafer County Courthouse.

Thursday morning, right off the bat, I decided this day would be uneventful. I didn't think my nerves or my heart could stand anymore mayhem like the past three days.

Totally optimistic, I carried LoJ into Mom's house.

"Your mom needs you in the kitchen. I'll put this sweet little pumpkin down for you." Pop took my daughter and cooed all the way to her playpen.

I found Mom sitting at the table, scribbling on a piece of paper. "Good morning. Pop said you need me."

She looked up. "Bobby and Estelle called last night. They're coming home for a few days. They'll be here late this afternoon."

My older brother and his wife lived several hours away and

came to visit a few times a year, usually on holidays.

"How long are they staying?" I poured myself a cup of coffee.

"Until Sunday. Before they get here, I need to go grocery shopping. I don't think I should leave LoJ here with your dad alone. He forgets where he puts things."

"No problem. You won't be gone but about an hour and a half. Bring her and her playpen to me. It'll do her good to be out in the open air for awhile."

"Are you sure?" Mom asked.

"She'll be fine."

By noon, I'd seen no sign of Mavis and Millie. Good or bad thing? I couldn't be sure.

Mom arrived shortly after noon. Unfortunately, she'd neglected to bring LoJ's playpen. From the trunk of my car, I pulled a carrier that strapped onto my person and nestled the baby against my chest. I could hold her and still have my hands free for my count.

Apparently content, LoJ slept peacefully. Cars were going by two at a time, but spaced nicely, making it easy to keep track.

A pickup passed by. Like many trucks in our area, it had a winch attached to the front which was used to pull buddies out of holes during an event called mud bogging. The cable had come loose, and the metal hook bounced under the vehicle causing sparks to fly.

I shouted and rushed to the curb. Waving both hands, I motioned for the driver to come back. In my enthusiasm to make the man aware he might possibly ruin the latch he was dragging, I woke up LoJ. She began to wail, more from fright than anything else.

While the truck made a U-turn in the middle of the highway, I bounced my baby and tried to coo her back to sleep. The pickup made its maneuver, pulling into the path of a black Lexus. They crashed to a stop ten feet from me.

Tim Tuten climbed from behind the wheel of the Lexus. His face flashed like a neon sign. Red. Blue. Purple. LoJ cried harder. I wanted to join her.

Tim bypassed the driver of the truck and headed straight for me.

"You are crazy. Aren't you?" he screamed at me.

"Me? What'd I do?"

"I saw you flag that unsuspecting driver down. What is so important that he had to make a U-turn?"

"His winch is broken." I continued to bounce and shush LoJ.

"So is yours." Tim leaned his face to within inches of mine. "You should be locked up until it is fixed."

"You self-absorbed, overbearing . . ." I couldn't think of an appropriate word. I didn't know enough about him to insult his occupation or his heritage. All I knew was he was a Baptist. That wouldn't work. I was a Baptist, too.

"Looking for the right words? How about concerned citizen?" Tim backed out of my face. "Or maybe a man who now has a crunched fender?"

"I'm sorry about that, but it certainly isn't my fault." I didn't mean to scream, but I had to talk loud to be heard over LoJ.

Deputy Kelly arrived. "Bertie, now what have you done?"

I rolled my eyes at him and reached up and dusted the powdered sugar off his uniform. "Did we interfere with your afternoon stop at ET's Donut Shop?"

He knocked my hand away. "Actually, I was picking up coffee for the Chief, and now it'll be cold by the time I get back to the office."

Carl pulled his clipboard from inside his car and took license and insurance cards from the accident victims. "Do we need a tow truck or can you two drive your vehicles out of the road?"

"I'll put my car on my back and carry it away before I let this maniac hook up to it." Tim Tuten pointed in my direction.

"And you'd have icicles on your ears in Hades before I'd tow you away."

The truck and car were pulled into the lot. Carl gave the pickup driver a ticket for making an illegal U-turn. He took it and drove away, winch hook still dragging.

He was just starting with Tim's information when the Chief called over his two-way. Carl stepped away to be able to hear what his boss was saying. Tim and I verbally flew into each other again. We said awful things. Things I usually reserved for my brothers who really deserved my wrath. I didn't know why the man rankled me so, but by his actions, the feeling was mutual.

Carl came back to us. "Okay, you two. I'm needed back at the office right away."

"Well, have a good day." I started to sit back down in my lawn chair.

"No, you two, get in the car." He opened the passenger's door.

"Why are you taking us in?" I almost added *Copper,* but thought better of it.

"Because my squad car is in a body shop having tree scratches removed from the roof. I have the Chief's car, and he needs it PDQ. My report isn't finished, and I'm not leaving you two here when you appear to be on the verge of killing each other. Now, get in. We'll finish the report at my office."

"I don't want to go to jail. Been there. Done that." Whining was never my best attribute.

"If you don't get in that car now, I'll handcuff you and haul you in for disorderly conduct." Carl shook his finger in my face.

I hate when he does that. I climbed in the front seat. Thankfully, LoJ had stopped crying and was sleeping. Tim piled in the back and slammed the door.

You would think that being dragged off to jail with Tim Tuten would be the worst part of the deal. Alas, that would not be the case. I stared out the window of the police car, my stomach twisting into knots.

The worst part would be when I had to call Arch to come to the jail to bail me out, along with his baby daughter.

Chapter 4

Chief Kramer met us in front of the police station. He took the keys and his coffee from Carl and sped away. Tim and I and LoJ followed the deputy into the building. I looked around to see if Jim Ed Swain and his trusty camera were waiting inside. I could imagine what the morning headlines would be—Tow Truck Driver Arrested with Baby in Tow.

Luckily, Jim Ed wasn't there, so I filed around the counter and went directly past the jail cell. Did not pass go. Did not collect two-hundred dollars.

It didn't take long for Carl to fill out the rest of the paperwork. Tim and I had quit arguing. Over what? I wasn't really sure. I still had no idea why this man detested me.

LoJ began to cry again. Probably because she was tired of being lashed to my chest. Since I was struggling, Tim helped me get out of the harness.

"Thanks," I said and offered a smile.

He didn't smile back, but while I dug in the diaper bag for a bottle, Tim Tuten, the most annoying man in the world, took my daughter from me and cradled her in his arm. As he gently rocked her, he spoke softly. To say the least, I was surprised, but touched.

"Okay, we're through here, but the Chief isn't back with the car." Carl stapled a stack of papers together. "You'll either have to wait until I get the car back, or you'll have to call someone to come and get you."

"Do you have a third choice, like maybe walk across hot coals?" Exhaustion made me sarcastic.

First I called my house. Arch didn't answer so I called Pop. Luckily, he answered instead of Mom.

"Can you come down to the police station and get me and LoJ?" I whispered.

"Sure, sweetheart," he whispered, too.

"And, Pop . . . I don't want Mom to know where I am. Okay?"

"She's taking a nap. She's not feeling well."

"Really, what's wrong?"

"She went by to get LoJ on the way home from the grocery store. Alice filled her in on the details about you and the baby being loaded into the police car and hauled away. Your mom's been in bed ever since. I'll be right there."

I closed my cell phone and stared at the floor. Poor Mom. Even as ornery as my brothers had always been, she'd never had to get them out of jail. Her sweet, loving daughter, on the other hand, had been bailed out twice in less than a week. I might be reduced to tears. I'd have to buy her something extra nice for her birthday this year.

When LoJ became fussy, I took her from Tim and cradled her next to me. Her baby scents erased some of the smells of the slammer. I hoped we'd break out soon.

The door opened behind me. I turned expecting to see my father, but instead my brother Bobby ran toward me, with his arms extended. He loved me and wanted to comfort me. I was so touched . . . in the head.

Bobby zoomed right past me. He grabbed Tim Tuten and clutched him to his chest. In the meantime, my chest was crestfallen. How dare my loony brother embrace the enemy?

"Rudy Tuten. How long has it been?" Bobby pounded Tim soundly on his back sending him forward a step.

"More years than I care to count," Tim said.

"Wait a minute. You're Rudy Tuten? That's not the name you told me. What's going on?" I sputtered.

This was the same boy who had once been Bobby's best friend in grammar school. Why had he changed his name? When did he grow into his long nose and floppy ears? Anger and confusion battled inside me.

"I stopped going by Rudy when I moved to a new town. I was tired of being called Rootin' Tootin'."

"Jeeze, I called you that all the time. I had no idea it really bothered you enough to make you change your name."

"Of course it bothered me. I was twelve-years old, insecure, had the beginning of acne . . ."

"And big ears and a nose, don't forget them," I added.

"Yes, big ears and a big nose and the biggest crush on my best friend's sister. She was a cute little girl with long reddish-brown hair and mahogany brown eyes who made me weak in the knees every time I saw her."

I had no idea he thought of me like that. How sweet. A tiny

tingle climbed my spine.

"Why didn't you tell me?" I asked.

"It's hard for a young man to proclaim adoration for the same girl who went to the trouble to collect thirty empty toilet paper rolls and passed them out to a group of kids in the lunch room."

"Oh, I remember that." Bobby chuckled. "When you and I," he pointed to Tim/Rudy, "entered the cafeteria, they all placed the tubes to their mouths and yelled 'rootin' tootin'." My brother doubled over with laughter.

"Exactly. That kind of thing will destroy a child." Tim sighed.

Regret crawling through my body made me shiver. "I'm sorry. It was just a childish prank. I've outgrown things like that."

"If I remember right, you've recently called me a doo-doo head on several occasions," Tim said.

"Join the club," Carl Kelly interjected. "I've been on the receiving end of her witless comments more times than I care to count."

I stuck my tongue out at him. He looked at Bobby. "Would you mind taking Mr. Tuten and your sister back to their cars? We need to clear this place up for the next group of prisoners."

"You never arrested us. And, we all know this is the most excitement the station has seen since . . ." Since when? I couldn't think of a time.

Carl smirked. "Since the last time I hauled you in?"

I groaned.

Bobby took LoJ from my arms and gave his sleeping niece a kiss on her head. "Come on, sweetie, let's get your mother out of here before they decide to have her committed to the nut farm for observation."

I stood perfectly still, trying to get over my desire to jump on his back and pummel him. Since he was carrying my child, I couldn't chance making him drop her.

Bobby turned to see if I was behind him. "Get a move on, Jail Bertie, I have to get you home before Mom has a stroke or something."

After we all climbed into Bobby's car, I started thinking about what Tim Tuten said about me embarrassing him, and I wondered if that was why he was giving me such a fit about the red light at Oak and Haverford. He didn't strike me as the type who would carry a grudge over a juvenile joke played many years ago. Yet, I couldn't think of any other explanation.

"Tim, I'd like to ask you something?" I was in the back seat, so I leaned forward. "Have you been dogging my steps because I was mean to you when we were kids?"

He turned slightly. Sadness darkened his eyes. Something very hurtful had happened in Tim's life. Instinctively, I knew it had nothing to do with me. But what? Why was he making it about me?

"Two years ago, I lost my wife and baby girl in a car accident. It was at a busy corner just like the one at Oak and Haverford. There should have been a red light installed a long time ago, but the city didn't see the need. One afternoon on her way back from the grocery store, a car pulled into her path, and Beth and Mandy were killed instantly.

"I left Atlanta and moved back here because I wanted the slower pace. I go past that intersection every morning, and I've witnessed far too many accidents there to ignore it any longer. That morning, when I saw you parked on the side of the road, the idea came out of nowhere. You could get the city to put a traffic light in there. You're a business owner, a life-long resident of Sweet Meadow, and if I remembered right, and I did, you can be pretty verbal when the need arises."

"She does have a mouth on her, doesn't she?" My loving brother gave us his two-cent's worth.

Bobby's words didn't faze me, but Tim's did. I could still hear Arch's first wife screaming for her baby from inside the twisted metal of her car. She died a few hours later. It had been my first fatal accident with the tow truck, but the horrendous memories were as sharp as ever.

The thought of something so unspeakable happening to Arch and the girls made me nauseous. I swallowed hard and allowed Tim's pain-laced voice to nudge me into his corner. "I'm sorry about your loss. That must be hard to see so many accidents on your way to work. I guess it keeps it all fresh in your mind."

"It does, but I think that if I can be of help in getting a light installed on that corner, then I can say I've done something to help save lives."

"But you aren't the one doing anything. You're forcing me to do the work. Why?"

"I went to the council when I first realized how dangerous that place was, but they blew me off. Something about not having the money to spend because it would cut into their Christmas party fund. Apparently, that party is held in high regard, because they wouldn't even discuss it."

I understood his frustration. "I've hit that same stumbling block. That's why I'm out there doing my own personal survey so I can present the statistics to the council and hopefully convince them to do the right thing."

"If anyone can do it, Bertie can." Bobby pulled into the vacant lot where our cars were waiting to be recovered.

Did my brother just say something nice about me? That would be a first.

"I agree," Tim said.

He opened the door and helped me and LoJ out. "I'll be at the meeting Monday night when you present your findings. I've been telling everyone what you are doing. You can expect a crowd to be there to support you." Tim ran his finger down my baby's check. "Bye, sweet thing." Melancholy laced his voice.

My heart ached for him and his loss. As he walked away, I hugged LoJ a little tighter. A prayer whispered past my lips. I was so thankful for my girls and the wonderful husband who must be wondering what happened to me.

"I'm going on home, Bobby. I'm glad you're here for a few days. I'll see you tomorrow."

"You bet, Jail Bertie. I'll tell Mom you didn't get any tattoos while you were in the pokey." He laughed with his usual jovial hilarity.

"Oh, one more thing." I hurried back to him. With my balled fist, I hit him in the stomach. Needles of pain radiated all the way up to my funny bone, but to hear him gasp for breath made it worth it.

"What was that for?" he asked, rubbing his tummy.

"Don't call me Jail Bertie ever again."

When I drove past his car, he was still latching his seatbelt. He rolled down the window, and I stopped. "I'm going to have posters made up and put all over town. 'Wanted Dead or Alive—Jail Bertie. If seen, shoot on sight.'" He drove away.

At home, Arch sat on the porch step. He gave me a light kiss and took the baby from me.

"Hello, my sweet baby girl," he cooed to his daughter. "Did you have fun on your field trip with Mommy to the bad old jail? I'll bet you did. Did they handcuff you, too?"

"Okay, very funny. How did you find out already?"

"I certainly didn't hear it from a Jail Bertie." He laughed.

"When I get my hands on him, I'm going to kill Bobby Byrd."

"Then you'll go to jail for a long time. Like it that much?"

"There is nothing to like about that place. Carl Kelly is there for one thing." I realized Arch was yanking my chain. I couldn't let him get the best of me. "On the other hand, the strip search was kind of exciting."

I ran up the steps and into the house. Arch caught up with me. We hugged with LoJ squeezed gently between us. As crazy as my life is, I wouldn't change one thing about it. Especially this part, when Arch's lips touch mine and all feels right with the world.

Petey and LoJ were sound asleep. I added all the tick marks on my clipboard and properly noted them in my survey tally. Arch was watching the eleven o'clock news. Since Sweet Meadow was too small to have its own television station, our news came from Atlanta.

Normally, I didn't pay much attention to the broadcast because things moved faster and sometimes scarier in the big city. Our town couldn't compare to the crimes and government folderol that went on in our state's capitol. But, once in a while, since we are in their viewing area, they tell about something going on in Sweet Meadow. Like the time the semi full of onions overturned on 440. Phew! Squashed onion aroma permeated the air for days. Everyone who worked that accident smelled like a walking hotdog.

Tonight, the news lady brought our fair community to life in a big way.

"We take you now to Sweet Meadow." Kim Maynard, anchor for an Atlanta station tossed it to another reporter who was standing in front of our town's bank.

"Yes, Kim, I'm standing in front of the bank where a robbery took place just before closing this afternoon." Lisa Kearns waved her hand at the building like she was showing off a refrigerator on *The Price Is Right*. "Police tell us two men apparently in drag robbed the only bank here in Sweet Meadow. Earlier I talked with Chief of Police Kramer."

A taped interview started to roll. It was still daylight, and Chief Kramer held a donut in one hand and coffee in the other. Evidently that was where he'd scurried off to when I was being hauled into the jail. I gave a silent *thank you* that the news crew had been across town at the time and not filming at the police station.

I jumped over the arm of the sofa and nearly knocked Arch onto the floor.

"Look," he said and pointed at the screen.

A security tape rolled, and Chief Kramer described the robbery. "Two men dressed as women entered the bank late this afternoon, handed the teller a note demanding all the money be put into their straw purses. The note said they had guns and knew how to use them. One of the suspects made the comment that this wasn't his first robbery, so we are looking into that possibility."

As I watched the tape, a sick feeling rolled around in my stomach.

"Do you know who that looks like?" Arch asked in a high, squeaky voice.

For a moment, I couldn't answer because my jaws were locked in an open position.

They played the tape again, and he and I leaned forward to get a better look. It was fuzzy, but I had a sinking feeling we knew the robbers personally.

"It looks like Millie and Mavis." I shook my head. My mind wouldn't fully absorb the possibility of the dynamic duo commit- ting such an act. Forget the fact that Mavis had been arrested once as an accessory to the same thing. This could not be the two octo- genarians who somehow had become my charges.

The news anchor recapped the story and finished with, "They reportedly made their get-away in an old Cadillac. If you have in- formation about the two suspects, call Chief Kramer."

I took a throw pillow from the sofa and placed it over my face as hard as I could.

"I don't think it's possible to suffocate yourself," my loving hus- band said. "I guess I better get over there and talk to those dingbats and find out for sure if that was them."

He was right—I wasn't having any luck snuffing out my life with a small pillow. I threw it aside and stood. "I'll go. After all, I'm responsible for teaming Frances and Jessica James."

When I arrived at Millie's house, I found the two old women dressed in flannelette pajamas, knocking back Khalua and cream. They claimed the milk made them sleep better. I didn't bother to point out they probably passed out instead of just going to sleep. They looked so cute. Mavis had her hair curled with bobby-pins. Her fluffy slippered feet were propped on the coffee table. Millie sat in her La-Z-Boy. The room smelled of booze and Ben-Gay.

Looking at the elderly women, it was hard to believe only a few hours earlier they'd robbed a bank.

"What are you doing out so late?" Millie asked.

"I just thought I'd pay you a visit and see how things have been going." I stood in the middle of the room so I could easily see both of them. "Did you get your vending license yet? How's the driving lessons going? Did you rob a bank this afternoon?"

Mavis' gaze snapped to Millie. She pointed at her partner in crime.

"I told you those two looked like us, didn't I?" Millie said.

Mavis began to laugh. "You sure did, and you also said that Bertie would turn us in for the reward money."

They both broke up. "I knew she would have to get her nose into it; I just didn't know she'd fly over here this late at night." Millie slapped her knee. "She's always been like that."

"Hey, do you two not see me here in the room with you?" I stomped my foot for emphasis. It didn't faze them. They continued to cackle and snort.

Suddenly, Mavis jumped up and shuffled her furry feet out of the room. "I gotta go to the bathroom," she called over her shoulder. "Don't say another word until I get back. I don't want to miss anything."

I sat on the sofa and cradled my face in my hands. Until Mavis returned, Millie and I never uttered a word.

"Okay, where were we?" Fuzzy-feet asked.

"Bertie was asking if we'd robbed a bank. Did we?" Millie leaned back in her recliner and eased her glass to lips.

Please say no. Please say no. Please say no, I repeated over and over again in my brain.

"I can't believe you think we are capable of robbing a bank," Millie said.

"Well, in all fairness to Bertie, I was accused of that before. Remember?" Mavis reached across the end table and patted Millie's boney hand. "What I can't believe is that she thinks either of us would be caught in public in the dresses those two wore. What a small opinion you must have of us."

"Let me get this straight. You are more disappointed about that than the fact I thought you actually robbed the bank?"

They both nodded.

I prayed insanity wasn't contagious, because those two had a raging case of it. "You two are beyond crazy. You are barely capable of living in a society. Of course that may not even be an option after this latest stunt."

Millie rose and went to the kitchen. Quickly she returned with a glass of Khalua and cream for me. "Here, drink this. You need to chill out. Mavis and I did not rob that bank. Didn't you notice that one fellow kept scratching his privates? I don't have any privates to scratch. And I think it bears repeating, I would not be caught dead in a dress like that." She tapped my glass. "Now, be a good girl and drink up."

I drank it all in one gulp. When they offered me another one, I declined and had instant coffee instead. Before I left, I asked the M&M's one more time. "You swear to me you had nothing to do with the bank robbery this afternoon."

They raised their hands and vowed they hadn't.

On the drive home, I decided it might not hurt to talk to Deputy Kelly in the morning, just in case. I parked in my driveway and noticed the front door of the house standing wide open. With a broom in his hand, Arch stepped onto the porch.

"What are you doing?" By this time I was at the bottom of the steps.

"We have a mouse. I tried to scoot him out, but he didn't like the idea."

"Great." I don't abide rodents well. "Where is he now?"

"In the kitchen. I scooted him outside, but he ran back in before I could close the door."

Carefully, I went inside. My gaze scanned every inch of the floor for the little critter. "It's hot in here," I said.

"The doors have been open for a while. I'll turn the air conditioner on a little until it cools off." Arch walked to the window unit on the far side of the kitchen, his broom readied for combat should the need arise.

I stood in the doorway between the kitchen and living room. After he adjusted the temperature, the cool air quickly swept across the entire room with the force of an Artic blast. It felt good against my skin damp with perspiration brought on by a case of nerves the size of Dallas. I'd worked up quite a sweat dealing with Millie and Mavis and the possibility they might have to spend the rest of their lives behind bars. At home, I found we had been invaded by a mouse. Thankfully, the strong breeze of the A/C cooled me off quickly.

"I'll stop by the hardware store tomorrow and pick up a trap." Arch put the broom away.

"The mouse won't hurt the girls, will it?"

"No, it's probably been here for a while. I was reading and had the light off in the kitchen. I heard his little toenails on the floor. When I looked, the light from the living room reflected in his eyes. His little beady eyes, I might add. I hoped I wouldn't have to kill it, but apparently he wasn't going to just pack up and move out."

"You're my hero. You'll get him, O Great Hunter."

As Arch headed down the hallway, I took a final look into the dark kitchen. When I didn't see any tiny eyes glaring at me, I flipped off the living room lamp and ran to catch up with my husband.

On my way to work the next morning, I saw Carl Kelly coming out of ET's Donut Shop. I whipped into the parking lot and skidded to a stop, throwing gravel at his feet.

"Bertie, you're a hazard," he said and wiped the top of each shoe on the backs of his pants legs.

"I need to talk to you about something," I hollered through my car window.

"What's up?"

"Do you have any leads on yesterday's bank robbers?"

"A few, but I can't talk about them."

"Can you tell me if you recognized them from the video I saw on the news last night?"

"Did you?" he asked, his voice laced with caution.

"Well, they did remind me of Millie and Mavis. Did you see a resemblance?" I held my breath.

"Bertie, Bertie, Bertie. Your screwy way of thinking never ceases to amaze me. You are accusing two sweet, albeit eccentric, old ladies of robbing a bank. You should be ashamed of yourself."

I felt lower than the scum that used to gather at the bottom of my brothers' aquarium. Carl was right. I should have more faith in Millie and Mavis.

"I'm sorry. I know better. I'm glad you have a more level head than me, and you didn't hurt their feelings by accusing the poor old things of this terrible act."

"That's why I wear the badge, and you drive a tow truck." He winked at me.

I nodded in agreement.

"Besides, you know neither one of those ladies would be caught dead in those ugly dresses." Deputy Carl Kelly had the nerve to turn and start to leave.

"Hey, you skunk. You thought the same thing and you accused

them of it, didn't you? Otherwise, you wouldn't have just said the same words they said to me."

As he retreated to his vehicle, I continued to babble. "You have a lot of nerve telling me I should be ashamed of myself. You should be feeling pretty guilty right about now to have even let that thought enter your mind."

Carl slammed his car door.

"Hey, I'm talking to you," I shouted.

He drove away.

He wasn't as smart as he thought he was because as he walked back to his car, I'd seen smudges up the back of his nicely creased, dark pants from where he shined his shoes. If I'd been more child-ish I would have snickered for the rest of the day thinking of others laughing over his dirty pants legs. However, I wasn't quite that childish, so I just smirked for half of the day.

At my survey station, I noticed the traffic was really heavy. I'm not sure why unless people were starting early to escape Sweet Meadow for the weekend. Why they would want to do that, I wasn't sure.

We had a public pool with fake palm trees to simulate the trop-ics. The new bartender at the Dew Drop Inn had a master's degree in drinks with umbrellas in them. Never mind they all tasted like orange juice and rum. The last bartender could only serve beer in long-necked bottles and wine from a box. So the orange juice-rum thingies were very well received by the locals.

We have the Stop and Flop Motel with specialty rooms to fit

every taste. I don't know that from personal experience, but I've heard rumors. One story, floating around for years, claimed the honeymoon suite had a huge bathtub in the shape of a clear, champagne glass which rose six foot off the ground. The occupants had to use a ladder to climb into the bubbling water.

The tub was destroyed many years ago in a freak incident. One that has been the topic of many whispers and hysterical laughing fits. It seems Cora White followed her good-for-nothing husband, Webb, to the motel. After he entered the honeymoon suite where Mid Cole awaited him in the bubble bath, his wife pulled an axe from the fire box near the office.

She chopped off the door handle and entered the room just as Webb was sinking into the bubbles. Cora raced to the ladder, dropped it to the floor, then whacked the stem of the champagne glass tub. Amidst the protests of the bathers, she continued to hack away until it broke and the massive clear Plexiglas vessel crashed to the floor leaving the two naked adulterers sprawled on the floor.

It's rumored the owner of the motel arrived at the door at the finale of the show. Cora walked past him, handing him the axe on the way out. "Send Webb the bill," she said. By nightfall, Cora had left Sweet Meadow and was never heard from again. As I said, it's only rumored, but Webb does walk with a limp that could conceivably have been caused by a nasty fall.

But I digress.

With the traffic being so heavy, it was hard to keep an accurate count, but I did my best. By late afternoon, the Peanut Ladies had not shown up. I guess they hadn't gotten their vending license yet.

With only thirty minutes left, it looked like it would be an accident-free day. I was happy no one would be faced with that sorrow, but it would lower my accident-per-passing-car ratio.

Alice came out of her shop to secure the rocking chairs with a chain and padlock. She offered a quick wave, which I snubbed. *The Old Bat.* She reached inside the door and held up a huge sleigh bell like she forced me to buy before I could use her restroom.

"Here, I want you to have this as a peace token. And, by the way, I erased that video I took of you." She reared back and threw the bell with more force than Nolan Ryan on a good day. It was low and on the inside—inside of an open car window that is.

The bell appeared to have hit the driver of a Toyota, startled her, causing her to swerve into the next lane. Of course, you know what happened next: screeching tires, crunching metal, yada, yada, yada. When the dust settled, no one was hurt, no one needed to be towed away, but I got to add another statistic.

At home that night, Arch had begun his strategy to regain owner-ship of our home. He baited a regular house-mouse trap with cheese and placed it under the kitchen sink. The two of us manned our post on the sofa and waited to catch our prey.

Within a few minutes, the trap snapped. Arch and I hurried to collect our prize. All we found was a sprung trap minus the cheese. Our furry little friend had stolen the bait and gotten away Scot free.

"They had another type of trap at the hardware store. I'll swing by there in the morning." Arch pitched the little trap into the trash.

For a few moments, he stood silently.

I rubbed his back. "Don't worry, honey, you'll get him next time."

Chapter 5

Saturday morning, the girls and I stopped by my parents'. Although we'd all be having dinner together on Sunday before Bobby and Estelle left to go home, I wanted to spend a few extra minutes with them. LoJ was the center of attention. They all cooed over her. Estelle asked if the girls could stay with her while I went grocery shopping. Petey was excited to spend time with Uncle Bobby, who was below her maturity level.

I agreed and left for the first day I had for shopping alone in the supermarket in quite some time. For a change, I'd have time to read labels and peruse the shelves for new and exciting products. Usually, I was between naps and feedings (LoJ's, not mine) and on a real time crunch. Who would have thought a trip to the supermarket could be so exhilarating?

Down the produce aisle, among the fruit and nuts, I ran into Millie and Mavis.

"Hey, Bertie, solved any bank-robbery crimes lately?" Millie asked.

"Very funny. Have you gotten your vending license yet?"

"We wanted to talk to you about that." Mavis shoved her buggy into a display of oranges. Luckily, she didn't start an avalanche.

"Talk to me about what?"

"They won't give us a license until we meet a few requirements, but we don't understand what they want. Millie and I thought maybe you could go with us on Monday to the courthouse and help us get it all straight," Mavis said.

"Can you do that?" Millie shoved the buggy aside, again shaking the oranges.

I wanted to get away from them before the obvious happened. "Sure, I'd be happy to. Gotta run. See you later." As fast as possible, I scurried away from the vegetables, fruit, and fruitcakes. I would circle back later and pick out my produce.

The second aisle held canned fruit, veggies, and assorted juices. And Booger Bailey's wife.

I accidentally made eye contact and was forced to speak. "Good morning, Mrs. Bailey."

"My, my, my. Bertie Fortney. I was just thinking about you."

That couldn't be good.

"I really, really need someone to pick up the twins after school on Monday. I immediately thought of you."

"Doesn't everyone?"

One of Mrs. Bailey's twins talks incessantly and the other says nothing at all. I hate hauling them around.

"I'm so sorry, but I really have a full day on Monday. I couldn't possibly—"

"Booger has to do community service then because of the altercation he had with you and I have no one else to turn to," she whined.

"I had nothing to do with the crime Booger is being punished for. I've explained to you many times I was sent into your house by the police department. He was holding the chief hostage. Somehow I managed to disarm Booger and then he was arrested. End of story. I didn't cause him to get into trouble." The incident had occurred six months ago. Mrs. Bailey needed to let it go.

"I understand, but that doesn't help me with my problem on Monday. Art and Bart will be waiting in front of the school at 3:15." As she trotted away with her cart wheel flopping, she said, "Remember, Art gets hyper if you're late."

I tossed a few cans of veggies into my basket and literally ran past the next aisle so I wouldn't meet Mrs. Bailey again. That meant I missed out on the pastas and rice. At this rate, my poor family would starve to death in the coming week.

At the end of the next row, I stole a peek to see if there were any more landmines laid for me. I didn't see anyone I knew, so I went to the meat counter. I needed to grab some protein, which I hoped would keep my family going.

The ground beef looked pretty lean, pork tenderloins were the perfect shade of pink, and the lamb chops called my name. I'd never cooked lamb before, but Mom always did at Easter. I thought I'd give it a try.

Spending a little alone time there among the raw meat, I experienced a Zen-like state. Jeeze, I needed a life.

Feeling very proud of myself, I spun my buggy around and, with a thud, ran right into another landmine.

"Hey, Bertie, how's it going?" Ethel Winchell was barely tall enough to look over the handle of her basket. Her blue hair stood up in the back and waved at the front. Cute.

"I'm fine. How about you?"

"Well, my bursitis is acting up. I don't suppose you could give me a ride to my doctor's appointment on Monday, could you?"

I opened my mouth to respond, but she added, "Of course you can't. That was thoughtless of me. Well, I'll be on my way." Ethel pushed past me. She winced and emitted a low groan.

"That must be very painful. Of course I'll take you. What time?" My shoulders slumped.

"Ten o'clock." Ethel moved on with a little more briskness than she'd exhibited a few moments before. Did I have a cartoon bubble over my head that read: *Will drive you anywhere. Just ask.*

I hurriedly made my way up and down the aisles, grabbing a few items off the shelves. I couldn't get through the checkout fast enough. While I was placing my groceries into the car, I heard someone calling my name.

Abe DeJorgi, the store manager, ran out of the store. After throwing the last bag into the car, I jumped into the front seat and slammed the door. Abe tapped on the window.

I rolled it down a few inches. "My dance card is full, Abe. I can't meet you, or take you anywhere on Monday."

"That's good to know, Mrs. Fortney. I'll remember that. Here." He handed me my wallet. "You left this at the counter. Sorry we can't get together on Monday, but if you have another free day, let me know."

He left, and I buried my flaming face in my hands. In less than thirty minutes, I'd scheduled three fares for my tow truck/taxi and inadvertently propositioned the manager of the Piggly Wiggly. I vowed I'd never again go shopping without my girls at my side.

Arch bought a different kind of trap to capture his furry nemesis. He baited it with cheese and placed it under the sink. While we waited for it to do its job, he explained that the mouse would enter the opening at the bottom front of the galvanized box. Once in there, a door would flip his little tail into a holding bin.

Arch proudly announced it was guaranteed and could catch up to ten mice.

"If we catch ten mice, I'm moving," I announced.

"Don't worry. I'm sure it's just *one* little fellow."

Our butts had barely connected with the sofa cushions when a loud snap sounded, followed by toe nails scratching against galvanized metal. Just as Arch opened the cabinet door, the trap fell over knocking the lid free, and Mighty Mouse made a rapid dash for freedom. Slicker than okra slime, my brave husband flipped his wrist and sent the rodent out of the cabinet and onto my foot.

In case anyone should ever ask you, mice have very sharp nails and can do considerable damage when placed on human skin and allowed to spin their little wheels in a vicious attempt to escape. But escape he did, leaving his would-be captors shaking and, in my case, injured.

I cleaned my wounds with alcohol and wondered if I should seek medical attention. Since the scratches had already faded and no blood appeared, I voted against a trip to the hospital for rabies treatment. Of course, that would not have surprised anyone. Least of all me.

Arch and I headed for bed.

"Well, it's back to the old drawing board," he announced.

"Go for it." I dug through dresser drawers and pulled out anything I could use for protection. A ski mask, leather gloves, and a pair of Arch's thick hiking socks. Tomorrow night, I'd be ready. One cannot be too careful when combating a mouse with a strong will to survive.

We all gathered around Mom's table to enjoy Sunday dinner. Each of us took turns bringing everyone up to date on our lives. I related my past week of city road surveying. Bobby told everyone about meeting up with his old pal Tim Tuten. Of course, he reminded us that happened when he was bailing his sister and six-week old niece out of jail. That's going to be the topic of conversation around our table for many years to come.

Arch's topic of the day was his quest to capture our mouse. He told in detail about his failed attempts.

"I have the perfect thing." Estelle jumped to her feet. After disappearing into the hallway for a short time, she returned with a tube of mace.

"Take this. Wait until you hear it, sneak up on it, and blast the little critter."

"I don't think we should do that. This mouse could conceivably take it away and spray us," I said.

Everyone laughed, but I was dead serious. I feared this particular rodent.

"Don't worry, sweetheart." Arch wrapped his arm around me and pulled me close.

I chewed on my bottom lip. "Okay, I won't." *Not much, I won't.*

At home that night, once we'd gotten Petey and LoJ tucked into bed and out of harm's way, we began our mouse mission.

Arch and I pretended to be drinking coffee and watching television in the living room. He held the mace canister at his side like a gun, ready to draw at a moment's notice. True to form, we heard the tiny scratching as the mouse tip-toed across the old linoleum on the kitchen floor. Arch and I also tip-toed to the door separating the two rooms. Sure enough. There he was, tittering about, looking for food. He ignored us completely. Probably because he'd seen us in action and felt we posed no threat. We were just there for his amusement.

Little did he know we were about to put an infallible plan into action. Slowly Arch raised his weapon and aimed. A nanosecond before he shot a jet of mace into the kitchen, the air-conditioner kicked on, sending a powerful blast Arch's and my way. On its journey, it brought every bit of mace mist he had just squirted and deposited it in our unsuspecting faces. The mouse ran unscathed back under the sink.

I believe I heard little mouse laughter, but it was hard to tell because my husband and I were gasping for air. Somehow we made our way outside which was hard to do with our eyes flooded with gas-induced tears. We coughed and gagged for several minutes. Finally, we could go back inside, but we left the door open for another hour so the air would go out and not to the back of the house where our dear, unsuspecting children lay sleeping.

I say unsuspecting because, thankfully, they had no idea how stupid their parents are. Yet.

"I don't think we should tell anyone about this," Arch said.

"I couldn't agree more." We toasted with cold coffee. "I was just wondering, when we do our tax return, can we claim Mighty Mouse as a dependent?"

"That's funny." Arch smiled at me. "I'm going to try to list all the traps under home security."

"I'm not sure you can do that since our home still isn't secured."

It was a beautiful fall day in Sweet Meadow. The sun shone warmly through the kitchen windows. The inviting aroma of bacon frying filled the air and helped mask the remains of mace.

I did a timeline of things I had to do during the day. The first order on my list included fixing breakfast, packing lunches for Petey and Arch, gathering all the baby stuff LoJ would need while at Mom's. *Check.*

As my little family marched single-file out the door, Mighty Mouse skittered past us. We all screeched to a halt. He stopped at the edge of the porch. Through beady eyes, he glared and flicked his whiskers. With a flip of his tail, he bolted off the stoop and disappeared across the yard.

"Well, I guess our house guest has moved and left no forwarding address." I laughed.

"I don't blame him after you sprayed him with that horrible

smelling mouse spray." Petey pinched her nose.

"How did you know that?" her father asked.

"I was on my way to the bathroom, and I saw you two at the kitchen door. Before I could speak, you sprayed that poor thing and then ran out the door coughing and hacking. It stunk so bad, when I got out of the bathroom I locked myself in my room and didn't come out until this morning. That sure was stinky stuff."

"It was mace, sweetheart. Your Aunt Estelle thought it would help us stun the mouse and then we could just release it into the wild. Sorry you had to smell it, too. It was stinky, wasn't it?" Arch rubbed his eye which was still bloodshot from the night before. As scratchy as mine felt, they must look the same.

Arch and Petey drove off to school. LoJ was dropped at Mom's. Checked with my two drivers, Linc Johnson and Carrie Sue Macmillan. Lined up work orders for auto repairs and dispatched any tows waiting. *Check.*

I dropped Ethel Winchell at her doctor's office and told her I'd be back in a couple of hours to pick her up. Millie and Mavis were ready and waiting on their front porch. Soon we were at the permit office.

"We're baaack," Millie shouted.

"So I see." A young woman came to the counter. "Is this the backup you threatened me with the other day?"

Oh, no. My brain waves flashed a neon sign: *Danger Ahead.*

"I'm just here to help them understand what they need to do to obtain their vending license. They want to sell boiled peanuts along the roadside like hundreds of other people do throughout the South."

"Sure thing. I can take care of that." The woman reached under the counter and pulled out a form. "You can step right over there and fill it out."

Flanked on each side by Sweet Meadow's dynamic duo, I moved to a small plank of wood attached to the far wall.

"Okay, name of business?" I read.

"Peanut Ladies," Millie answered.

"What happened to the name *Nutz R Us*?"

"We didn't think that was appropriate. Peanut Ladies suits us better." Mille seemed quite proud of her thought. Personally, I know *Nutz R Us* fits them perfectly.

"Business owner's name. Will that be one or both of you?"

"Uh, no," Millie whispered. "Put it in your name."

"Mine? Why mine?"

"They say we have to give them a driver's license and insurance card on the vehicle we will be using. Otherwise they can't give us a permit to haul our wares to a street corner in order to bend," Mavis said.

"*Vend*," Millie corrected.

"Do I understand this correctly? Since neither of you have a license to drive or insurance for your beat up Caddy, you expect me to open this business for you, with my legal papers and my good name."

"That's it." Mavis pointed to the form. "Just write all that out right there. They'll give us our permit, and we'll be on our way."

"Over my dead body!"

"Now, Bertie, we hoped it wouldn't come to that." Millie laughed out loud.

"Don't threaten me, old woman." I stared nails at her.

"I was just kidding. Every night when I say my prayers, I always ask God to give you a sense of humor, because you are definitely devoid of one."

Mavis hooked her arm through mine and pulled me aside. "Look, you will be helping two elderly woman keep their hands and minds occupied. We'll make extra money and be able to put it back into something useful for the community. You'll be a part of making Sweet Meadow a better place."

Millie joined our little discussion. "Mavis is doing really good with her driving lessons. You should see her parallel park in front of the Chow Pal Diner."

Mavis beamed.

"A professional couldn't do it better. She'll take her test next week and then get insurance. We'll come back when that happens and take it out of your name, if it will make you feel better."

"What would make me feel better would be you two sitting on your front porch, fully clothed, rocking to your heart's content."

"As lovely as that sounds, sweetheart," Millie put her arm around my waist and led me back to the unfinished form for a vending permit, "it ain't happening." She tapped the paper with her boney finger. "Just sign your Roberta Eunice Byrd-Fortney, and we'll be on our way to Nutsville."

"I'm already there, and you two are the head nuts." With much trepidation, I signed the form, and just like that I was the owner of a peanut business.

After taking Millie and Mavis home, I picked up Ethel from the doctor's office and deposited her at her front door. I checked off two of my taxi fares. As soon as I finished the last one, I'd go back to the office and work on my argument to present to the council in a few short hours.

I grabbed a burger and ate it on my way to pick up Art and Bart, Booger Bailey's twins.

Art has a propensity to talk non-stop from the moment he gets into my vehicle until he slams the door on his way out. Bart, on the other hand, doesn't talk much at all. They were waiting for me like good little fellows. With them aboard, I pulled away from the curb.

"I haven't seen you in a long time," Art said.

"Yeah, it has been a—"

"I got elected captain of our dodge ball team," the little darling interrupted. "Barney *Macaroni* thought he was gonna be the captain, but I showed the coach I was made of better stuff. When old Macaroni hurled that heavy ball at me, I just head-butted it right back at him. Hit him square in the nose."

"Oh, my goodness, did you hurt him?" I knew Barney Marconi. He took after his mother in size--tall, thin, with delicate features. A dodge ball to his face could do permanent damage.

"Blood squirted from his nose just like the time Mom hit Dad in the face with a frying pan." Art jostled Bart with an elbow to his side. "Remember that?"

"No," Bart said in his prolific way with words.

"Sure you do. Dad said that Randy Carson's mom had boobs like Dolly Parton and the next thing Dad saw was stars. Remember?"

Bart shrugged and turned to look out the side window.

"Yeah, boy, Dad got blood everywhere," Art continued with his story.

I had to stop him before he told all the family's personal

business.

"I don't think your parents would appreciate your telling that story," I reprimanded.

"I don't know about that," Art said. "Dad tells it all the time, and he says Mom got down on her hands and knees to beg his forgiveness."

"I remember now." Bart spoke more than one word. I couldn't believe my ears.

"Mom was on her hands and knees all right, but she told Dad that if he came out from under that bed, she'd hit him again." I'd waited a long time to hear Bart string a few words together, and I got to tell you, it was worth the wait.

I laughed all the way to Franklin Street. One of those lose-your-breath-tears-in-your-eyes-nose-running kind of laughter that we all fall into sometime in our life.

As the two boys got out, Art turned back. "Are you going to be okay? You look like you might have busted a main spring or something."

I swiped the back of my hand across my nose and tried to speak, but nothing came out. I just waved good-bye and drove away. I had to get my composure before I appeared before the council that night. It wouldn't do for me to break up laughing while trying to convince those straight-laced people to put up a traffic light to save people's lives.

That wouldn't go over well at all. But for now I could laugh all the way home and maybe I'd get it out of my system.

The Sweet Meadow city council consisted of four regular members and a chairman. Cy Linder led the monthly meetings with an iron hand. At the exact stroke of seven, he banged his gavel, calling everyone to order.

The council hall was packed. In the past, I attended a few meetings for various reasons, but never had I seen so many in attendance.

"It's nice to have all these people here to support me in my cause," I whispered to Arch who sat to my right, bouncing LoJ in his lap.

On my left, Tim Tuten leaned closer to me. "They're all here to keep the council from allowing an erotic café to open in the city limits." A low chuckle came from Tuten.

"Oh. Of course," I said. I fanned my heated face with my notes. With my thoughts being so wrapped around gathering statistics, starting my own peanut business, and evicting a defiant rodent, I'd forgotten the decision in the matter of the naughty establishment had been held over from the last meeting.

A group of out-of-towners wanted to open an erotic café on Highway 440 just inside the city limits. For the past month, it had been a hot topic of contention. By the number of citizens in attendance, everyone in town had an opinion on the matter.

The ladies from the Garden Club along with their husbands, those who still had husbands, that is, filled the front two rows of the large meeting hall. All the women had on garments which covered their legs and were buttoned with choking tightness at their throats. I fingered the V opening on my neckline. Did that make me a loose woman who would be in favor of a restaurant with nude waitresses? Of course not, but just in case, I clutched the front of my blouse closed.

Cy asked for the proposal for the café to be read, then opened the floor for discussion. Olympic synchronized swimmers could not have moved with more precision than the first two rows of the congregation. They stood in unison, formed a line, locked elbows, and marched to stare down the men at the council table.

Clara Moore, President of the Garden Club, spoke first. "We will not allow such an establishment to darken the streets of Sweet Meadow. The idea of nude women serving food to men acting like young boys with raging hormones is unthinkable."

I wish it were unthinkable, but from the moment Tim reminded me about the café, I could think of little else. Would the owners bring in their own employees or would females from our fair town apply for positions . . . I mean jobs?

I tried to dispel horrid images of women I knew serving burly truck drivers in the nude. The women would be nude, not the truck drivers.

"I think that would be very unsanitary," Millie said. "I could never eat in place where the waitresses don't wear hairnets."

The audience rumbled with laughter.

"Order." Cy pounded his hammer. "Ladies, I appreciate your interest in this matter, but as the head of the city, we on the council think any new business could be a plus to Sweet Meadow."

Tilly Linder shot out of the perfectly-formed line and leaned in to glare into her husband's bugged eyes. "As the chairman of this group of nincompoops, have you considered how bad your head will hurt when I hit you with your own gavel?" He rolled his high-backed leather chair out of her reach.

"Well, I see your point, too, Tilly," Cy said with a frog in his throat.

I joined the snickers going around the room, but swallowed hard when Arch stood up.

"I have a comment," he said.

"The floor recognizes Arch Fortney." Cy pointed his gavel at my husband.

"Have you ladies considered how much revenue a place like that could bring to our town? People who come to eat at the café will also buy gas, visit our shops. It could be very profitable for everyone."

First, I banged my head on the back of the seat in front of me, and then I raised my hand.

"Yes, Bertie, do you have something to add?" Cy asked.

I stood. "I'd like to borrow your gavel when Tilly finishes with it." I glared up at Arch. "Are you telling me you're in favor of a strip joint under the guise of an eating establishment being built in the same town where your two girls will be growing to adulthood?" Shocked, I couldn't believe this person was the man I married and allowed to father my child. "I don't even know you," I shouted above the uproar which divided the room into women and . . . "Men. You're all alike." I stomped my foot and turned my back to Arch only to come face to face with Rootin' Tootin'.

I was trapped. Like a rat.

"I didn't say I was for the café. I was merely pointing out the plus side to permitting new businesses to come to Sweet Meadow,"

Arch shouted above the ruckus. He turned me to face him. "I'm a high school principal and a science teacher, but I have a degree in Economics. I'm trained to look at things like this from a monetary standpoint. It would bring patrons to the gas stations, drug stores, convenient stores."

"Don't forget the free clinic," Millie added.

While everyone's attention was on her, I sat down and tried to slide out of sight. Arch pulled me back up. With his arm around me, he whispered in my ear. "Just so you know, if I had a vote, it would be *no*."

My heart melted and erased any thought of duplicity in our marriage. I knew Arch Fortney for the true man he was. Even if the café came to town, it wouldn't interest him any more than having a gavel pounded upside his head. That was true love.

"Let's put the matter of the erotic café to a vote." Cy regained order.

The first four members voted *no*. Before he could cast his, the last councilman, eighty-two year old Bob Bord had to be awakened.

"How do you vote, Bob?" Cy asked.

"About what?"

"About allowing an erotic café to be built in our city limits. You have to stay awake, you old buzzard." He looked at the stenographer. "Strike that last comment."

"What's an erotic café?" Bob sat up straight.

"It's an establishment where the waitresses are nude when they are serving your food," Cy explained.

Bob shuddered. "I vote unequivocally *no*."

That really surprised me. Mr. Bord struck me as the kind of

man who would jump at the chance to see women naked. The knowledge that I was wrong warmed my heart and renewed some more of my shaky trust in men.

"There is no way I want to walk into the Chow Pal Diner and see Mildred Locke in her birthday suit," Councilman Bord spoke clearly into his microphone.

Guess I was right to start with. Bob Bord would jump at the chance to see women naked. He was just particular about which women.

Mildred magically materialized from the group. Being tall and lanky, she easily reached across the table and placed her ample hands around Bob's throat. "How dare you say that about me, you old poot?" Mildred gave his fragile head a few shakes. It took several Garden Clubbers to pull her away.

As she huffed out of the hall, Bob rubbed his throat. "You woke me up for this? Just leave me alone."

Everyone laughed except for the business men who had wanted to build the café. They stomped their way out of the meeting grumbling loudly about backwoods hillbillies who didn't know anything about enterprise.

How dare they say such a thing? I jumped to me feet. "I know what the Enterprise is, it's a spaceship," I yelled.

Cy banged his gavel several times.

Tim and Arch pulled me back into my seat. "You're going to get us kicked out of here before you can present your findings for the stop light," Tim said.

"I know you're excited." Arch squeezed my hand. "Just calm down until it's your turn."

"Okay, unhand me, and I will." I jerked free from them. "Are we next?"

"One more item, then you." Tim pointed to a printed agenda that had been on his seat when we first entered the hall.

Chairman Linder shuffled through a few papers. "Next we are to make a ruling on whether or not Karo Stevens can build an outhouse next to his home in downtown Sweet Meadow." Cy motioned for him to step forward.

"Okay, Mr. Stevens, our attorney has advised the council that we must hear your argument before we can deny your permit to build the above mentioned privy. What do you have to say about it?"

"I say I have been a resident of Sweet Meadow all my life. Born and reared right in the house where I live now. From the day I was born until 1952, I used an outhouse located a few yards from our back door. It was recently brought to my attention that I am old. I want to feel young again. The one thing that comes to mind when I remember my youth is traipsing out to the outhouse to take care of necessities." Mr. Stevens waited for Cy's reply.

"Listen, Mr. Stevens, it sounds to me like you are having a mid-life crisis. Can't you just do what most men do and have an affair?"

Mr. Stevens was a friend of Pop's. He had to be at least seventy-nine years old and had been widowed for about fifteen years. He used to date Millie Keats until she caught him stealing her underwear. I scooted to the edge of my chair. I didn't want to miss any of this.

"You know, Linder, I've always heard you were a moron, but until this moment I never knew how true that was." The older man broke into a wheezing and coughing spell. He recovered quickly.

"I'm way past mid-life. As I see it, I'm past old age and living on borrowed time. I've lived alone since my dear, sweet wife went to the great vegetable garden in the sky." Mr. Stevens added a sniff I suspected was for dramatization because I'd never heard him say anything remotely kind in regard to his wife.

"In the last days of my life, all I want to do is drink my prune juice, trot out to the little shack out back where I can answer nature's call, and read Playboy and National Geographic." He turned to face the audience. "They take me places I'll never get to go in real life." He winked.

While most of the people around me laughed aloud, some men chimed in with "Amen."

I started to point out that sounded like something Arch's dad would have said, but Cy pounded his gavel loudly, and the room quieted.

"Okay, Mr. Stevens, we've heard what you have to say. We have decided you can build this privy you so badly want, if it is plumbed to city specification and connected to the city sewer system. If you agree to that, then we will take a final vote." Cy spoke and the councilmen nodded in agreement. Well, everyone but Bob Bord. The only nodding he did was off.

"Wake up, Bob," the council said in unison.

When the last vote was cast in favor of Karo Stevens, I began to feel very confident that the wise, elderly gentlemen had Sweet Meadow and her citizens' best interest at heart. Surely they would look just as favorably on my cause and pass it with the benevolence it deserved.

Chapter 6

"N°ext, we will hear from Roberta Fortney," Cy Linder announced.

As I made my way to the front of the hall, Bob Bord cupped his hand around his one good ear, which wasn't all that good anyway, and asked, "Who is she? She looks familiar."

"You know her. Thomas Byrd's daughter. She married Pete Fortney's son," Cy told him.

Bob strained to look at me. "Why, Bertie Byrd, as I live and breathe. You sure have grown up . . . and out."

"Hey, I just had a baby." I bristled like a wart hog confronted by a hound dog. "I admit I need to drop a few pounds, which I can and will do, but you are old and pretty apt to stay that way." In the most grownup fashion anyone has ever seen, I stuck out my tongue at the old goat. Admittedly, this is not the way to win friends and influence votes, but that wasn't a very nice thing Old Bob said and in front of a large number of townsfolk to boot.

Bang. Bang. Cy's gavel hitting the table roused me from my self-absorption.

"Bertie, just tell us what you have to say."

I pressed my temple hoping for relief of the headache slowly working its way up the side of my face. I think it had sprouted from the pain in my butt old man Linder's pounding gavel had produced.

"Okay, but could you please refrain from banging that thing," I pleaded, pointing at the wooden hammer clutched in his hand.

He laid it aside.

"Thank you." I spread my notes on the front of the council's table. "I'm here today to ask that you fine gentlemen allow the department of safety to put a traffic light at the corner of Oak and Haverford. It has been a dangerous corner for years, but with the completion of the paint factory in Shafer, the traffic going to and from that area has more than doubled in the last two years."

"What'd she say?" Bob asked.

"She wants a stop light," Cy said.

"Will that stop her from hitting the buffet?"

Behind me, the crowd erupted in laughter. Not wanting to appear as a person who couldn't take a little kidding, I forced a smile and bobbled my head a few times.

Bang. Bang.

"Sweet Meadow desperately needs that light at Oak and Haverford. I've been gathering data, and I'd like for ya'll to look at my facts."

"What do your *fats* have to do with a light?" Bob growled.

My patience was growing thin. "Mr. Bord, please stick with the subject at hand. And, in case, you're not sure what that is . . . ." I handed him a printout of my findings on the stop light situation. "Take a look at this. I'm sure you'll see my request is well founded."

I gave all the men a copy and stood silently while they read the report.

"Bertie, do you want us to believe you sat on the street corner for five days and counted every car that went by?" Mr. Linder asked.

"I had no choice but to do it that way because the council wouldn't appropriate the money for a traffic counter."

"No, of course we couldn't. That would cut into our Christmas Party Fund." Old Bob's announcement was quickly backed by the other members on the dais.

"Well, as you can see, I did it without cutting into your money for Irving's Chinese Takee Outee or whoever caters your holiday affair." Sarcasm has always been my strong suit.

"And we appreciate that." Bob Bord coughed and wheezed for a moment. "I love Irving's PuPu platters."

Another round of agreement sounded from the council.

"Strike those last remarks from the record," Cy instructed the stenographer.

Sharp pains stabbed behind my eyes, as well as a strong desire to strangle each and every one of Sweet Meadows' lawmakers.

"Mr. Chairman, are any of your men capable of focusing on my request?" You could have heard old man Bord's teeth drop, if he had any. Silence stole the air around me. Dizziness swirled my vision. Quickly, I took a deep breath and recovered.

"I've gone to a lot of trouble to compile statistics. I now put those findings before you and ask that you approve a stop light for the corner of Oak and Haverford. It is not for me I ask this. It is for all the citizens of Sweet Meadow. That corner is a hazard and it must be rectified."

"Listen at you. Little Bertie Byrd. All grown up," Bob said.

Were any of these nincompoops listening to me? Apparently not. Every time I tried to drive home my point, one of the council members flattened my enthusiasm with an imaginary steamroller. Well, I would not be dissuaded.

"I demand that you listen, discuss, and then put the matter to a vote." The back of my throat vibrated making the word *vote* quiver past my tongue. It sounded like I'd swallowed a whistle.

"Hey, Bertie, you hurt my ears." Bob placed his hands on both sides of his head. "I was fire chief for forty years and no siren ever caused me that much pain. Can you deepen your voice a little so it's not so shrill? You know, maybe talk like a man."

I grabbed Cy's gavel and shook it at Bob.

"You old goat. Can you be quiet long enough for the council to vote on this matter? Lean back, close your eyes, and nap like you normally do until we are ready for you," I yelled at the old man and then turned to the stenographer. "Strike that last remark."

"Okay, calm down, Bertie." Cy regained control of the meeting. "Do you have an estimate of how much a stop light and installation would cost the city?"

I pulled a piece of paper from a folder and gave it to Cy. "I got this from the Department of Safety. I think it has everything you need to know."

After looking at it, he passed it to the others. When it was handed to Bob, he didn't take it because he was asleep. At least, while he napped, he wasn't verbally attacking me.

"What else do you need to make a decision, Mr. Chairman?" I pointed at the audience. "Several people are here to verify how much we need a traffic signal at that corner. Would you like to hear from them?"

"No, we have enough information to make a decision." Cy leaned forward and looked down the line at the first councilman. "Are you ready, Wilford?"

Wilford pressed a button in front of him. The *no* vote registered beside his name on an electronic board hanging behind the men. The next two men voted no also. Cy did the same. We all looked to Bob Bord. He was asleep, his head drooping to the side, drool spilling from the corner of his mouth.

"Bob?" Cy shook the man who promptly slithered out of his chair onto the floor. Feet first, old Bob shot from under the council table. His size eleven, gun-boat shoes slammed into me, knocking me face down on his chest. We were nose to nose, old Bob and I. From my up-close-and-personal position, I knew the truth.

"He's dead," I screamed.

As fast as possible, I scrambled off him. From then on everything was a blur intertwined with screams, gasps, and a lot of *oh nos* until Booger Bailey pointed his finger at me and cried, "Bertie killed Bob Bord."

The day before the funeral, Tim Tuten stopped by my garage. "Everywhere I go, someone says something about you killing Old Bob." Tim actually seemed surprised. "What is wrong with the people of Sweet Meadow?" he asked.

"My theory is the gene pool here is stagnant." I giggled when I said it, but he didn't.

"I'm serious. Don't the things they say disturb you?"

"You mean things like *Bertie has always Bord people to death?* Or, that *old Bob was Bord stiff with Bertie's prattle?*" I chugged down the last of my cold coffee.

"Yeah, don't you just want to shake their livers loose?" Tim certainly took mockery to heart.

"Are you kidding? If that kind of teasing could hurt me, I'd have been dead years ago. I have two brothers. Thick skin is part of the game." I would never admit to anyone, especially Rootin' Tuten that it bothered me on several levels. I learned long ago to just let it roll off my back like rain off a sloped roof.

"What are you doing here?" I asked Tim.

"I've made a few more notes to help strengthen the fight for the stop light."

With all the killing-old-Bob stuff going on, I'd forgotten that on the next Monday night, I'd have to present my argument again. This time the council would be a vote short. Not that I thought it would matter. The four still living had all voted *no,* and I didn't foresee them changing their minds. We would need a miracle for that to happen.

I looked at the memo Tim handed me.

"Not having a stop light will leave the city vulnerable for lawsuits," I read. "What does that mean?"

"Now that it has been brought to their attention exactly how dangerous the intersection is, if someone gets seriously hurt there, they can sue on the grounds of negligence on the city's part. They were warned and did nothing about it."

"That makes sense."

Tim's cell phone sounded. After his quick call, he put it back in his pocket. "I have to go. Would it be okay if I rode with you and your dad to the funeral in the morning?"

"Sure. Meet us here at nine-forty-five."

He'd almost made it out the door, but looked back. "Bertie?"

"Yes?"

"I hear you fell over Bord. Did you get wet?" Before I could throw my coffee cup at him, he slammed the door and chuckled his way to his car.

"Very funny, Rootin' Tuten."

What a beautiful funeral Bob Bord had. The church was loaded with all his family, friends, and, by the way some mourners glared at me, his killer. No one said anything like that to me, but their BB brains caused their eyes to blink in Morse code fashion. Each dit and dot shouted *you killed Bob Bord*. I believe that was the first time I spent an hour in a crowded place and didn't make eye contact with anyone.

As the funeral procession traveled along the familiar streets of Sweet Meadow, I sat slumped in the back seat of Pop's Caddy and tried to close out his and Tim's mundane conversation. His life since he moved back from Atlanta. The weather. Poor old Bob.

Once we turned onto Oak Street, I sat a little straighter to catch of glimpse of my garage. My business had been booming, and I hoped my illustrious drivers, Carrie Sue and Linc, weren't overburdened without me there.

Before we made it to my garage, we had to pass the now infamous corner of Oak and Haverford. We were six or seven cars
behind the hearse, when I heard the dreadful sound of metal crunching and squealing tires. As a matter of fact, Pop was responsible
for some of the latter, but he managed to stop inches from the car
in front of us.

I got out and wiggled my way to the front of the traffic jam.
On the uneven shoulder of the street, my tight skirt and heels made
walking a real challenge. Carl Kelly, who had been escorting the
procession had already turned around and returned to the scene of
the accident. Several gaping spectators had left their vehicles to see
what happened.

I quickly wished I hadn't been so nosey.

A car had pulled into the oncoming traffic and slammed into the
left rear quarter of the hearse. The crash had knocked the rear cargo
door open and Mr. Michaels from Lasting Peace Funeral home had
lost his . . . well, his cargo.

"You should have seen it," Coach Henderson kept repeating.
"Bob shot out of that meat wagon like it was a cannon, and then he
spun around two times."

Good Lord. Right smack dab in the middle of Oak and Haverford sat Bob Bord's casket. We all looked at it like we thought the
lid might pop open, and Bob would jump out.

"Come on, guys, help me get this back into the hearse." Carl
Kelly grabbed a handle and five others jumped to his assistance.
They slid the coffin in, but the door wouldn't close completely.

"We need someone to sit in there and hold the door. We only

have a few more miles to go. How about you, Mr. Bailey?"

Booger chuckled and rubbed his substantial stomach. "There's no way I could fit in there."

Several more were asked, and they all declined for various reasons, but I knew they were afraid to ride with a dead man.

"What is wrong with you guys?" I shouted at the herd of cowards. "Mr. Bord wouldn't have hurt you when he was alive. He certain can't hurt you now."

Carl backed up my statement.

"She's right, you bunch of sissies," he said.

"I think Bertie should do it," a very young male voice called from the crowd. Art Bailey. "Isn't she the one who killed Mr. Bord in the first place?"

"Any chance you can keep that kid quiet?" I asked Booger.

"You know better than that, Bertie."

Unfortunately I did.

"I think it's a good idea." Carl locked his hand around my upper arm and pulled me toward the back of the *meat wagon*.

I shook loose. "Oh no, you don't. Why should I have to do it?" I sputtered frantically. Spittle landed on his arm. I meant to wipe it off, but jabbed him with my fingernail.

"Ouch," Carl captured my hand. "That's assault on an officer."

"You wouldn't dare arrest me for that."

"Don't bet on it. I'll tell you what, hold this door until we get to the cemetery, and I won't press charges."

"You overgrown lump of ego. How dare you blackmail me like that? I ought to make a citizen arrest right here."

My indignation forced me to take a step forward. Carl moved

toward me threateningly. A vision of my baby daughter and her sister visiting me behind bars flashed through my mind. Then there was Arch's reaction to me adding to my growing rap sheet. I scampered toward the hearse.

Getting in proved to be a challenge. My skirt didn't allow for any movement like stepping on the back bumper or even bending at the knees. I tried hiking the hem up, but to do that, I would have chanced being arrested for indecent exposure.

Finally, Carl said, "Here let me help." He turned me to face him, lifted me, and then deposited my backside next to Bob.

"Scoot back," he demanded, but I couldn't move.

"Put your feet out straight." Carl lifted my legs even with my backside. With one hardy push on the bottom on my shoes, I slipped very neatly between the side of the car and good old Bob. Problem was, I was too far away from the door to hold it. Carl grabbed my feet and hauled me back outside. He turned me around, wrapped his arms around my upper body, and placed me, feet first, back into my narrow slot. Now I faced the front with my back to the door and no way to turn to hold the door closed.

"Wait here," Carl said.

"Sure thing, Bucko. I couldn't run if I wanted to." By now the crowd was finding all this humorous.

"I have eyes in the back of my head. I see all and know all. Those of you who find his funny . . . I hope you also find it just as hilarious when I raise my towing rates for all of you."

The laughter quieted to a buzz.

Carl returned with a piece of rope. He attached it to the door and handed the other end over my shoulder. "Pull tight on the rope.

We'll be at the cemetery very soon."

The procession was underway again. Calmness settled over me and warmed my soul. Somewhere in my intuitive brain a thought worked its way free and settled in my heart.

Councilman Bob Bord had cast his vote on the stop light for Oak and Haverford issue. He saw the need and voted *yes*.

With my free hand, I rubbed the casket. "Thanks, Bob. Would you do me a favor? Tell Pete, the old goat, that I send my love." A tear formed in my eye. "Oh, yeah, and make sure he knows I didn't really kill you, okay?"

My very best friend in the whole wide world is Mary Lou. She and her husband Rex have a son, Rex the Second. He's a year older than LoJ and has the face of a . . . well, let's just say he looks like his dad. I love the way Mary Lou's mind works. She's one of a kind.

Changing from my funeral clothes, I slipped into my pink jumpsuit. Carrie Sue and Linc needed me back at the garage. We were overloaded with cars needing repairs. As I scurried to the front door of my home, the blinking light on my answering machine caught my eye.

I pressed the *retrieve* button.

"Bertie, I need to talk to you as soon as possible. Fire," Mary Lou screamed and the message ended.

I quickly dialed her number. My heart pounded hard.

"Bertie!" she shouted into the phone. "Guess what?"

"What's on fire?"

She paused.

"Is the baby okay?" I gasped.

"Oh, sure. You're talking about the message I left you."

"Well, yeah." Sometimes the woman made me crazy.

"I just wanted to be sure you called me as soon as possible."

"But you yelled *'fire'*," I said.

"Would you have hurried to call me back if I'd yelled *'bean'?"*

She had a point. "Have you ever heard the story about the boy who cried wolf?"

"No, how does it go?" Mary Lou asked.

"Never mind. What's going on?"

"I needed to know how to get a bean out of Rex's ear." She sounded awfully calm for a mother with a baby in that condition.

"Jeeze, Mary Lou, how did the baby manage to do that?"

"Oh, no. It wasn't Second's ear. It was his father. Rex asked me if a pinto bean had gas inside it before it was cooked. Like an idiot I told him to listen and see if he could hear it rumbling around in one. Next thing I knew he had one stuck in his ear."

Nothing Rex did surprised me. "Did he get it out?"

"We just got back from the emergency room. I think the bean was pressing on his brain. On the way there, we had to stop for a funeral to drive by. All of a sudden he started yelling 'Bertie's in the back of that hearse.' He was really shook up. They had to sedate him at the ER."

I don't know why I didn't tell my dear friend that Rex had been right. Maybe because it would have taken away some of her illusions that Rex was nuts. Who was I to deprive her of that? Instead, I told her I was glad he was okay, and I hung up.

As I got out of the car at my shop, my parents waved to me from their front porch swing.

"LoJ's sleeping," Pop yelled.

Mom shushed him so my baby girl would, in fact, stay asleep. Pop rocked an imaginary infant and then completed the mime with folded hands to the side of his head.

I gave them two thumbs up. Inside the office, I found myself in the middle of a battle royal.

"You are such a jerk," Carrie Sue screamed at poor, trembling Linc. "I can't work with you, let alone marry you." She flitted past me.

Without turning around, I reached back and grabbed her by the seat of her pink pants. She'd built up a full head of steam, so stopping her wasn't easy. I held tight. She spun me around and jerked to a sudden stop, and I slammed into her back.

"What do you think you are doing, Bertie?" Carrie Sue tried to look at me over her shoulder.

"It feels like I'm stopping a charging bull."

"Let go of my pants, you crazy woman."

I did, and she turned to face me. "Listen to me, missy. You can quit Linc if you are so inclined, but you can't quit me."

Her shoulders sagged. "Darn, you're right, but I'm not sure how I can be around this place and not use a ratchet to remove the bolts in Frankenstein's neck." She shook her fist at Linc.

"You aren't woman enough to remove anything from my body," Linc announced, stupidly, I might add.

Carrie Sue's eyes danced in a macabre sort of way. She could be pure evil when the need arose. "When I get through with you, the only thing you'll have left in your pants to offer another woman will be your wallet, you long, tall snake in the grass." She lunged toward him, and I caught her around the waist, mid-lunge and down to the floor we went.

"Let go of me, Bertie." Carrie Sue floundered around on the floor, and I rolled out of the way of her flailing arms.

She tried to get up. "I'm going to deflower that lanky lizard."

In one last attempt to stop her, I grabbed her foot. Down she went, striking her head on the concrete floor, making a sound like a watermelon being thumped. Evidently she was ripe because blood squirted out.

I raced to her. She was out cold. I glanced up at Linc. The blood had drained from his face.

"Call 911. Hurry." I pointed to the phone. While he did as instructed, I grabbed clean shop towels and wet at few in the bathroom. As I applied pressure to the gaping wound, Carrie Sue regained consciousness. She touched her wound, covering her hand with blood.

She looked at it. "Did I really cut off Linc's . . .?"

"Good heavens, no. You fell and hit your head. Lay still. The rescue will be here soon."

Linc knelt by her. "They're on their way, sweet thing. I am so sorry we argued, and Bertie nearly killed you."

I could have disputed that last fact, but why? Why? Why? Why? No one would have cared or even listened to my side. The ambulance arrived and transported Carrie Sue to the emergency room. I sent Linc along with her since, in his present mental state, he'd be of no use to me.

I cleaned up the mess. Pop arrived to see what was going on. He decided to finish the repairs Linc had been doing when the ruckus started. I covered wrecker calls.

I took a five-gallon gas can to a young man who only had enough money to pay for one gallon and no money for the service call. Too tall for me to turn upside down and try to shake change from his pocket, the boy promised he would bring the rest of the money to the garage. I poured approximately one gallon of gas into his car. It started, and he drove off into the sunset.

Before I got back to the shop, Pop dispatched me to another call. A pang of melancholy clogged my throat. It reminded me of the good old days, when I worked for Pop. He stayed behind and worked on cars, and I'd run the tow truck from one end of town to the other.

Things had certainly changed. I now owned the business, and Pop usually hung around the house helping Mom take care of my beautiful baby girl. What a difference a couple of years made.

The call was simple. Man in ditch. Pulled man out of ditch.

Pop dispatched me one more time. "A car ran over an ice chest on the bridge over Connor's Creek. Traffic's blocked both ways. Hurry."

"Sure thing, Pop." I used to be very cynical about people not having their vehicle under enough control to swerve and miss an item or to stop short of hitting it. As I said, I *used* to be cynical, but that all changed the day I drove over a mattress in the middle of the road and ended up with my tow truck erupting into flames. Since that time, I've not criticized anyone for their misfortune or classified them as just plain stupid.

Miles of traffic lined the roadway leading to the Connor's Creek Bridge. I managed to nose the tow truck on the road shoulder all the way to the disabled vehicle. I would have to call on ever fiber of my body to keep from ridiculing Gussie Journigan for her stunt of the day. Apparently, a hard, orange plastic water container had fallen from a phone truck. It had bounced like a basketball, according to Gussie, directly at her. Just as it reached the front of the car, it disappeared out of sight, lodged between the road and the axle of her car, stopping the Honda instantly.

"Good thing I had my *seater* belt on," Gussie explained, "or that hunk of bionic plastic would have caused me to fly right out the windshield. That would have messed up my new hairdo." She fluffed her hair, then wet her finger and ran it over her eyebrows, one at a time.

"You think?" I asked. Little did she know, but she had a bruise in the shape of an arch emblazoned on her forehead where she'd hit the steering wheel. When it reached its full colors, it would look like a rainbow.

I knelt to look under the front of the car, which was raised about a foot and a half off the ground. The front axle rested on a tall Igloo water dispenser. Amazing. The hard plastic container kept the front wheels from touching the ground, keeping the car from moving.

"Okay, Gussie." I brushed dirt from my knee. "I'm going to hook the winch to your car and pull it off its perch. Stand back."

A short time later, her car dropped to the ground, but the water cooler shot out from under the vehicle like it was fired from a cannon. A loud crash of water-cooler-meets-Deputy-Kelly's-windshield ripped through the air followed by a collective gasp from the onlookers. I slammed the truck into park and raced in the direction of the squad car. I almost cleared the Honda, which I'd just freed from its roost, when I realized it was in motion, rolling down a slight grade, picking up speed. And what was it racing toward? Why, my tow truck, of course.

Luckily, I was on the driver's side, and the window was rolled down. I dove headfirst into the Honda seat and jammed the brake with my hand. It stopped. I shoved the shift into park and collapsed. Before I could catch my breath, someone was hauling me out of the car by the seat of my pants. I didn't really need to look around to see who it was. It would be none other than Deputy Kelly.

"How's it going, Carl?" I asked.

"Bertie, you're a bunch of carnival sideshows rolled into one. You know that?" He didn't look as blue in the face as I imagined he would be.

"You feeling okay, Deputy?" I tried to read his eyes, which were hidden behind mirrored sunglasses, but to no avail. "You're not going to hurt me, are you?"

He flashed his pearly whites at me, and I'll be ding-danged if he didn't start laughing.

"I've missed you out here on these calls, Lady Tow Truck Driver. Until this minute I didn't realize how much."

"Well, don't get used to it. I can't believe how much I haven't missed the heart-stopping drama that goes on at the scene of an accident." Gussie drove away, and I took the paperwork from Carl, who continued to laugh his butt off all the way back to his car.

The water cooler had shattered a small section of the driver's side of the windshield and landed on the side of the bridge. Carl would be able to see out the front glass to drive back to the station. I climbed into my truck and waited for him to get the squad car turned around so I could follow him off the bridge.

He gunned his engine and backed the car around to be headed in the right direction—putting the rear axle onto the cooler and stopping him dead in his tracks. It only took him a moment to realize that, with his front-wheel drive, he could drive himself off of the bionic item which had taken on a life of its own. When the rear of the car bounced to the ground, tall Carl's head hit the roof.

It was my turn to laugh.

My eyes were flooded with so many tears, I could barely see Carl get out of the car, pick up the orange cooler, and pitch it into Connor's Creek. But I could definitely hear him swearing. I drove by him.

"I've missed you, too," I shouted out the window.

At the garage, Carrie Sue and Linc were waiting for me. With all the blood she lost, I expected her to have her head shaved and gauze covering her from the neck up.

"Only needed two stitches." She lifted the end of a Band-Aid to show me the black sutures.

"Great." My stomach rolled. I looked away. "How long did the doctor say you will have to be out of work?"

Linc put his arm around Carrie Sue, and they both stared at me like I had feet sticking out of my ears.

"What is it? Do you have a concussion? Am I going to be arrested for battery or some such thing like that?" Maybe to most that would sound farfetched, but in my world anything was possible.

"No, nothing like that." Carrie Sue wrapped her arms around Linc's mid-section. Because he was so much taller than her, she pressed her cheek against what would be his pectoral muscles, if he had any. She giggled like a school girl on her first date.

My stomach rolled again. "What's going on? Did they x-ray your head and find your brain missing? Is that it? You can tell me, I won't judge."

"No, Mrs. Bertie." Linc smiled like a squirrel that had just hidden away the last of his nuts for the winter. "Carrie Sue and I have set the date for our wedding."

They'd only been engaged a short time, but hadn't appeared in any hurry to tie the knot. After the skirmish they had a few short hours before, I had to wonder if marriage would be a good thing for my two drivers.

"That's wonderful, I guess." I tried to appear happy.

Carrie Sue lunged at me. Fearing retaliation for causing her to hit her head, I raised my arms to protect my face. Instead, she hugged me.

"I want you to be my coordinator and help me with all the details for my wedding. I can picture it now." Carrie Sue formed an imaginary camera lens and swooped around the room. "I want everything to be opossum pink and Connor Creek green."

"I never heard of those two colors," I said.

"Oh, you know that pink at the end of an opossum's cute little nose," she explained.

"I've not been that up-close and personal with upside-down marsupials, but I'll take your word for it. And Connor Creek green would be what?"

"That pinkish green that lies on top of the water out back of Mama's house." She closed her eyes and sighed as if in ecstasy or having a bout with gas. Not sure which.

Whatever it was, I couldn't stand by and watch it. "Do you mean pond-scum green?"

Carrie Sue opened her eyes. "Yes, if you must refer to it as that, but I prefer Connor Creek green. Now, will you help me put on the best wedding Sweet Meadow has ever seen?"

Why not? I was only a wife, a mother of two, and running a business. How much of my time could a small wedding take?

"Sure, I'd be honored. What's the date?"

Linc stepped forward. "We decided on November 7th. That's four weeks from next Saturday."

"How many people?" I asked.

"Probably two-hundred and fifty," Carrie Sue screeched.

Uh oh, my question now would be how much time could a wedding extravaganza take? "Do you even know two-hundred and fifty people?"

"Of course, all of my family and dearest friends. Oh, and you, too, of course," she added.

Should I ask what category that left me in? Naw, I'd rather be surprised.

Chapter 7

The special meeting of the council, which had been scheduled because the last one was interrupted due to death, was called to order on Monday evening. I was to make my second plea to the council for the stop light, but my entourage didn't go with me. Mom had a Garden Club meeting to attend. LoJ had a fever. Arch assured me he could take care of her. So, Tim Tuten and I braved the task alone.

I gave the council the same argument I used the week before. Just as Tim had told me, I pointed out the possibility of major lawsuits because of negligence. All the men listened, but I knew they already had their minds made up. I had one more bone to throw out for them to chew on.

With a hitch in my throat, I explained what I sincerely believed. "Last week, Bob Bord didn't get a chance to cast his vote, but I believe he wanted his decision known and that happened in quite a display of drama. When he flew out of that hearse into the center of Oak and Haverford, Bob Bord was saying 'look how dangerous this is. We need a stop light right here.'"

A band of passion squeezed my heart.

"Oh, bull feathers," Cy Linder bellowed. "All Bob was doing was making his exit with flair. He couldn't care less about a stop light."

"Now, Cy, the little lady may have a point. After that accident on the way to the cemetery, I could see the need," Wilford said.

"Yeah, I think so, too," another councilman chimed in.

"Okay, let's put it to a vote." Cy banged his gavel.

The first three voted *yes* and Cy voted *no*.

"The motion passes and will be submitted to the safety department first thing in the morning." Cy Linder congratulated me. "Good job, Bertie."

Feeling pretty proud of myself, I took a seat next to Tim.

"That concludes all the items on our agenda. We now need to discuss filling the opening on the council left by Bob Bord. His term wasn't due to be up until next year. First, do we have anyone who would like to volunteer for the position?" He looked out over the group of about a hundred people.

Tim Tuten jumped to his feet. *Wow!!* Was he going to take on the job of councilman?

"I'd like to nominate Roberta Fortney. She is a life-long citizen of Sweet Meadow, she knows almost everyone, and look at the great job she did fighting for a cause which will benefit the whole town."

I heard Tim's words, loud and clear. He didn't stutter or stammer. However, my brain couldn't absorb their meaning. Oh, yes it could.

I sprang from the seat. "Mr. Chairman, Mr. Tuten is running on a caffeine high and knows not of what he speaketh. I do not wish to—"

"Wait a minute." Booger Bailey's demand quieted the group.

"If Bertie is qualified to be on the council, so am I. I put my hat in the ring." He took off a dirty baseball cap and pitched it onto the floor in front of the table.

"I agree," I said.

"Thanks, Bertie." Cy smiled widely. "Since we have two people seeking the open position, we will have to run a mini-campaign for the best man, or woman, in this case, to win."

"No, no, no. I didn't agree to that. I agreed Booger should have the position. Take my name out of the running."

"Can't do that. It's already been recorded by the stenographer."

"Well, unrecord it. Strike that last comment," I directed the woman who was frantically pounding on her steno machine.

She shrugged and look to Cy.

"You'll do a great job, Bertie." Tim latched onto my elbow and pulled me back into my seat.

"I don't want to do any kind of job in this capacity, great or otherwise."

"Come on, let's at least talk about it. There needs to be fresh, young blood working on behalf of the city. Besides, would you want Booger Bailey making decisions you and your family would have to live with?"

Ouch that hit a nerve. "No, I wouldn't want that. Okay, if you're sure I can do this."

"I'm positive. You can hold your own in any argument for a good cause. Actually, you can hold your own in an argument for any reason, but let's put that attribute to good use."

"Okay . . . I guess I can do it."

Tim stood. "Mr. Chairman, Roberta Fortney accepts the

nomination."

"You need to keep up with us, sonny. That's already been established. Now, here is what we're going to do. Both of the candidates have four weeks to go out into the community and let the fine citizens know what the candidate will do to make our town a better place. At the November 9 meeting, we will have a vote from those in attendance for the best person to replace dear, departed Bob Bord."

Cy's gavel reverberated through the hall. We were dismissed.

Arch appeared to be very proud of my decision to run for the position as a member of the council. He promised to encourage all the teachers at his school to show up and vote for me. Better yet, he said he'd relieve me of as many home duties as possible. After all, he'd been a single dad from the time Petey was very young until he and I married.

I know he meant it to be helpful, but it does sort of jab your heart to know you can be so easily replaced.

"Don't look so sad." He kissed the end of my nose. "I could never replace you, even if I wanted to. I think this is something you'll be very good at, and I just want to make life as easy as possible for you."

I nuzzled his neck. The scent of his lingering aftershave comforted me in the same way the aroma of Nana Byrd's freshly-baked cinnamon rolls did when I was a child. The two smells warmed their way into my heart and my soul. I knew exactly what love felt like.

"Thank you, sweetheart," I whispered to my dear husband. "I'll make you proud."

"You already do."

For the next few days, Tim flittered around like a worker bee. He gathered info about things which appeared to be important to Sweet Meadow and the surrounding communities. Four nights in a row, he showed up on my doorstep to brief me on his findings. Arch took over my household duties, and once the dishes were done and the girls in bed, he'd join me and my campaign manager.

"I've set up a meeting with the Friends of the Library," Tim explained. "They want the council to raise the library's funds at the next budget meeting. They say there is no way to keep a fresh rotation of new books with the piddly amount the library currently gets. The head of the group showed me invoices for books, and when compared to what the city gives them, it's easy to see the only way the library remains open is because of donations from private citizens and the money raised by the annual book sale sponsored by the Friends of the Library. They would like to use the money they raise for computers and media equipment, but as it stands, they have to put it back into buying books."

"I understand that completely. Students need sources to re-search their reports and to learn how to use computers. Sure, they get to do that during their hour in class, but they need a place to go to experiment with what they've learned," Arch added.

"It sounds like you've already talked to them and got their

feedback. All they have to do is ask the council."

"They need someone on their side to present it to the council. If you get them on your side, you'll be voted in, and then you can work for them to get the money approved. So, I've set up a meeting tomorrow night for you to tell them you understand and that, if elected, you'll do everything you can to help them," Tim announced.

Arch squeezed my hand. "You'll do just fine. Read over Tim's notes, commit them to memory, and you'll wow them with your knowledge."

If only I had a third of Arch's and Tim's confidence in me, *then* I'd do just fine.

After we climbed out of the car in the library parking lot, Tim handed me a stack of business cards. "Here, I went by the garage and picked these up. Pass them out to everyone so they know your name and that you are a business owner."

"Okay, but most of these people already know."

"Well, just in case."

Inside the library conference room, a group of about forty people, mostly women, waited for me. I dropped my purse behind the podium. I was right. I knew almost everyone there. Millie, Mavis, Ethel Winchell, Helen Weidemeyer. As I passed out a business card to each person in attendance, I introduced myself to the ones I didn't know.

"Hi, I'm Bertie Fortney, and I'd like to be your next councilwoman." A rather down-and-out older gentleman took my card and while he looked at it, I glanced down at his feet and saw several plastic bags from the Piggly Wiggly. They appeared to hold his worldly possessions. I thanked him for coming and moved on. A wave of sadness for the less fortunate gave way to gratitude for what I did have. I said a silent prayer.

In the front row, a well-dressed business man shook my hand and accepted my card with gusto. "Thanks," he said. "It'll be great to have a woman on the council. That's what it's needed for years. The feminine touch."

"Thank you. I'll see what I can do about that."

At first I was nervous about talking in front of so many, but a few minutes into it, I relaxed and told them about me, my love for Sweet Meadow, and how much I'd like to make it a better place for my girls to grow up. I then told them I'd like to hear what they had to say.

Mr. Well-Dressed raised his hand first. "I'm not a member of the Friends of the Library. What books are they buying that the library's budget doesn't allow for?"

Ethel Winchell rose. "We need more books on crafts like knitting and crocheting."

"I think we need more volumes of books that tell us how to heal ourselves," Helen added.

"And large print. Definitely large print," Millie said. "I can't read those teeny, tiny letters in those romances. Don't they know old people like to read about true love and happily ever after stuff?"

"Okay, so if the budget was raised for the library to buy all the books it needs, then what would the Friends of the Library spend the money on?" the man asked.

I could answer that question. First I glanced at the notes Tim had given me. "At this time, there is only one computer accessible for public use. The FOTL would use their funds to buy more computers and the students could use them after school for research." I glanced at my notes again. "Also, it's been said the group would like to invest their monies for scholarships for students interested in library science." Hey, that sounded pretty good. Like I knew what the heck I was talking about. Everyone was looking at me. Smiling. Nodding.

I basked in my glory for a moment, allowing my gaze to scan the audience. Suddenly, I found myself staring at the bag man I'd met before starting my speech. He wasn't paying me any attention. He was staring somewhere in the vicinity of Mavis and Millie. All the while, he picked his teeth with my business card. Probably because I was looking so intently in his direction, Millie and Mavis looked at him, too. He removed the card from his teeth and blew a kiss in the direction of the women.

Oh, good heavens. Before I could rid my mind of the image, Millie threw a kiss back to him. *Ewww.*

From the front row, I heard a sound. Low at first, but it got progressively louder. Mr. Well-Dressed had his eyes closed, his arms crossed, and his middle finger and thumb tips touching. Deep in what appeared to be transcendental meditation, the man hummed in a droning, annoying tone. Was he praying he was through having to listen to my voice, or was he asking for help for me and my endeavor? Jeeze, who knew?

"I'd like to thank you all for coming tonight, and I assure you that if I am privileged enough to be added to the council, I'll do everything I can to get the budget adjusted to help the library," I said loudly to be heard over the hummer. Everyone clapped.

Several congratulated me on a good job and when the crowd dwindled away I came face to face with the little man who had picked his teeth with my business card. Much to my chagrin, he handed it to me.

"Here, little lady. I need to give this back to you. I don't live here in Sweet Meadow, so I won't be around for the voting. But thank you for being so kind."

What a dilemma? Do I refuse to take the card and hurt his feelings, or do I take the damp thing and chance getting some type of horrible disease? I took it and quickly laid it on the table beside me. With as much finesse as possible, I wiped my hand on my skirt and made a mental note to change before I held either of my girls.

"I'm sorry you'll be leaving Sweet Meadow. I hope your stay has been pleasant."

"Oh, it has, but if I stay too long in one place the law starts leaning on me."

"Well, we're pretty friendly here. Chief of Police Kramer is as meek as a kitty." Why was I building up our town to this man? It was apparent he wasn't interested in a lasting home, yet there I stood, almost begging him to stay. Maybe I was just tired. It had been a long day.

"You know something?" The man picked my card up and glanced at it. "Is your name Bertie?"

I nodded.

"Well, Bertie, I might just decide to hang around here for a while. You seem awfully nice, and there are a couple of cute women in this town. Maybe I could get hooked up with one of them."

Oh, good night. You always have to take that extra step, don't you, Bertie? You know, the one that takes you over the edge of the cliff. Now what do I say?

"Well, I wish you the best. Have a good life." I raced past him so fast I'm surprised he didn't spin around like a cartoon character. I needed to warn Mavis and Millie to stay away from him.

At the back of the hall, a small group awaited me. Each congratulated me on my decision to run for the council and then proceeded to tell me exactly what cause they wanted me to help them fight for. Their needs ranged from getting a permit to build a mother-in-law cabin on property zoned for only a single-family dwelling, to getting permission to shoot their neighbor's pig.

I cleared the blockade and practically ran into the parking lot. Mavis drove past me in her dilapidated red Caddy. Trying to flag her down, I waved frantically and shouted for her to stop. She was alone. Where was Millie?

Mavis did stop several yards from me. Millie and the homeless man from the meeting climbed into the car.

"Wait." I sprinted to them. Millie rolled down the window.

"What do you think you are doing? You can't get in a car with a total stranger." I yanked the back door open. "Get out of there." I stamped my foot and hooked my thumb to show the man the way.

Millie got out of the front seat. "He's not a stranger. This is our friend, Tom Barrs. Tom, this is Bertie Fortney, Mavis' niece, by marriage I might add, lest you think Bertie gets her rudeness from my friend's side of the family."

Relieved the two old women were not senile enough to get into the car with someone they didn't know soothed the sting of Millie's insult. "You scared me to death. I thought you were being abducted or something. I got the idea Mr. Barrs was just passing through town. Did you used to live in Sweet Meadow?"

"No, this is my first visit, but with the friendliness overflowing in the place, I should have been here a long time ago." The man wiggled his eyebrows at Millie, who emitted a nervous giggle.

By this time, Mavis had gotten out and joined us.

"I'm confused. How long have you known this man?" I asked.

"About fifteen minutes. After his discussion with you, he approached us and said you had told him he should hang around and give Sweet Meadow a chance because Chief Kramer was so lax in his job Tom wouldn't get arrested for vagrancy." Millie laid her hand on Tom's dirty shirt sleeve.

Mavis stepped forward. "You know that's not true, dear. Why would you tell him that?"

"I don't think I said that. At least not in those words. It still doesn't explain why you let him get in your car. He could be a serial killer." My blood pressure was on the rise. The three people before me were all seventy or eighty years of age, yet I was the one teetering on the verge of a stroke.

"He wouldn't hurt a fly. He asked if we knew where he could spend the night." Mavis had such an unsuspecting aura around her. Unsuspecting or clueless?

"We talked to him for a few minutes. Got to know a little about him and decided he could stay with us for a while. Just until he can get some money transferred from his bank account in Aruba," she added.

Clueless. Definitely clueless.

"Well, you can't take him home with you." I directed my next comment to Tom Barrs. "I don't mean to be rude, but I don't believe you have a bank account in Aruba. I can't let you go anywhere with these ladies. They are both missing a wheel in their hamster cages and cannot make rational decisions."

Carl Kelly stopped his squad car behind M&M's vehicle.

"Something wrong?" He joined us.

"This gentleman needs a place to stay tonight, and Millie and Mavis had him loaded in their back seat and were taking him home like he was a stray cat." I sharpened my tone to indicate to Carl exactly how serious the situation could have been. "His name is Tom Barrs."

Carl escorted Mr. Barrs away from the Caddy. A few minutes later, he placed him in the back of the squad car and came back to let us know what was going on. "He's a transient. No money. No ID. I'm going to take him over to the shelter and get him a meal and a bed for the night."

He glared at Millie and Mavis. "You two know better than to pick up strangers. You could have been killed. I know you are driving around without a license, and I've chosen to ignore it, but if you do anything that stupid again, I'll take your car keys away from you. Are we clear on that?"

"Yes," the women harmonized.

"I can't believe the first eligible bachelor we've had our hands on in years was snatched right out of our clutches." Millie looked up at me. "Bertie, you are the biggest killjoy I know. Thanks a bunch, Miss Buttinsky."

"That man was a real hottie." Mavis got into the car and slammed her door.

"He also has talent. He can touch his nose with his tongue. You don't see that every day," Millie huffed. She got into the car, too. After scraping a lamppost and bumping over the curve, they drove on down the street.

"I know you take care of fools and children, Lord." I lifted my gaze skyward. "But could you please add those two in there somewhere?"

A crack of thunder boomed through the sky.

"I don't blame you. I have a hard time taking care of them myself. Thanks anyway."

On my drive home, I passed Karo Stevens' house. My wrecker was in his backyard so I stopped to see if Linc needed any help.

After getting approval from the council to erect an outdoor toilet in his backyard, Mr. Stevens had quickly put up the old-time outhouse complete with exhaust stack and quarter moon shape in the door. Inside the cubicle, modern fixtures met the requirements of the sanitation department. Unfortunately, the privy, now lying on its side, had met with some sort of accident.

"What happened here?" I asked and helped my driver secure the chain around the toppled outhouse. A mercury light brightened the otherwise dark area of Karo's backyard.

"Those damn kids knocked it over. Ten minutes earlier and I was sitting right there." He pointed to the new commode, standing there in all its glory with light glistening off its porcelain finish.

It was a sight to behold. When I'm in my eighties, I wonder what material possession will be that important to me. Off the top of my head I couldn't think of a single thing.

After the toilet was righted, I drove on home. From the driveway I could see Arch through the kitchen window. He sat at the table, where he was probably reading the paper. With that beautiful picture, I had the answer to my question about what would be important to me in my later years.

Arch Fortney, the cheddar cheese on my apple pie of life, was what I wanted beside me when I was eighty, ninety, and beyond. I didn't know if that would come true, but I knew now he was inside our home, waiting for me. And, I couldn't wait to get to him.

Over a hundred years ago, a woman by the name of Leila Martone willed her two-story antebellum home to the Sweet Meadow Garden Club of which she was a founding member. Since that time the club used the house for monthly meetings, rented it out for wedding receptions, and used its ample yard for flower shows.

The Garden Club ballroom would make a perfect place for Carrie Sue and Linc to have their reception. I hadn't been inside since the night of my high school prom fifteen years earlier. Had I been out of school fifteen years? It didn't seem possible.

My neighbor, Barbie, fruitcake extraordinaire, had come from a very well-to-do family and had been exposed to the most grandiose receptions and formal affairs anyone had ever seen. She hated that life and had gone to great lengths to convince her parents to let her marry her one true love, CPA Rick, and allow him to take her far away from all the glitz and glamour.

Thankfully for me, she had absorbed a fair amount of knowledge about throwing one hellava party. Single-handedly, she made my own wedding reception the grandest Sweet Meadow had ever seen. And that was truly a remarkable feat, since it was not held in the magnificent ballroom of the Garden Club, but in the local tavern, the Dew Drop Inn.

This would be Carrie Sue's second marriage, but her first real wedding. She and her ex had been married by the justice of the peace in a town near the border of Georgia and Tennessee. Although she had a few ideas of her own, she wanted to hear what Barbie thought constituted a memorable reception.

We only had four short weeks to put it all together. So, Barbie and I went to check out the ballroom to get ideas for the reception to be held immediately following a ceremony at Sweet Meadow First Baptist Church.

"This is beautiful." Barbie surveyed the inside of the ballroom. Three huge crystal chandeliers lit the area. "Can we get up there?" She pointed to wrought-iron balconies overlooking the hardwood dance floor.

"I assume we can. Sup Wells tried to fly off there the night of our prom. So there has to be a way." I cringed remembering the way Sissy Moran screamed when Sup landed on her. If she hadn't broken his fall, he surely would have killed himself. Of course, by the time Sissy's date beat the crap out of Sup, he'd have been better off dead.

"*Soup*? That's a strange name. What's it short for?" Barbie asked.

"He told everyone his name was Superman, but we all knew it was Superdent. He was born with a big indentation in his forehead. As he got older it went away, but the name was already recorded on his birth certificate."

"Sorry I asked." Barbie walked through a doorway, and I followed. We found a set of steps leading upstairs. "Do you suppose this is all original to the house? Did the Martone's have parties here?"

"I believe so. Nana Byrd researched and wrote an article for the Garden Club newsletter about the family who built this place. Apparently, the Martones made their fortune in the marble business. Leila loved flowers. Most of the camellias and azalea bushes surrounding the mansion were planted by her over a hundred years ago. Anyway, she started the Sweet Meadow Garden Club and then, when she passed away, she left the house to them."

Barbie and I tiptoed down the long hallway like we thought someone might be sleeping in the rooms. She opened the first door we came to. Sheets topped all the furniture of a bedroom.

"That's strange. Why is this room still set up? No one has lived here for over a century," I wondered aloud.

"This plaque says it was left the way it was the day Old Lady Martone croaked." Barbie strolled inside and peeked under a dust cover hiding a bed.

"Look how small this is. Surely she and her husband didn't sleep together in this tiny thing."

"I don't think she ever married. Nana Byrd was a young girl at the time of Leila's death. Before she died, Nana said she and her friends were afraid to go by here because the old woman would throw rocks at them if they looked at the house."

Barbie laughed. "Surely that was just a child's recollection. Ms. Martone had class. You can tell by the furniture and by the paintings. They're original DeVoe's from the eighteenth century. Very rare. Wonder why they are left unguarded?"

"We don't have any art thieves in Sweet Meadow. The closest we've ever come was the time some kids stole Grimace and the Hamburglar from the McDonald's over in Shafer. They set the statues on the principal's porch and rang the doorbell." I cackled. "Then they hid across the street and just about got caught because they were laughing so hard."

"Did the principal ever figure out it was you?" Barbie asked. She's a sharp cookie even if she acts like she's two eggs short of an omelet.

"No, thank goodness." I studied a portrait done in oils hanging on a wall near the door. "I wonder if this is Old Lady Martone. She certainly has a sour look. No wonder Nana Byrd and her friends were afraid of her. She is scary looking."

Obviously fascinated with the furnishings of Leila's bedroom, Barbie continued to look under the yellowed sheets.

I might have been just as interested if I hadn't been suddenly surrounded by an artic breeze which didn't appear to be coming from the air conditioning vent. It encircled me and caused chills to wiggle through every part of my body, including the base of my tongue where it's attached in my throat. I released a gurgling sound from that very spot.

Barbie spun to face me. Her perplexed gaze gave me cause for concern.

"Wazz wong?" I asked.

Her eyes widened. "Why are you sticking your tongue out like that?"

I touched my fingers to my mouth and found she was right. My tongue rigidly protruded out of my mouth. I had to help it roll back in. Just as quickly as it came, the strange sensation left leaving me sweating in the fall air.

I looked into a mirror. "That was weird." I flicked my tongue in and out, but it seemed no worse for wear.

Barbie went into the hallway. "Maybe Ms. Martone doesn't like you saying bad things about her."

When I looked around the room and realized I was alone, I high-tailed it out of there and quickly caught up with Barbie. "That's crazy," I told my nutty friend. "Probably just a reaction to all that dust in there." Just in case, I stayed glued to her side.

She peeked into several of the other rooms off the hallway. Evidently, they had once been bedrooms in the Martone mansion, but now served as storage rooms for the Garden Club. At the end of the hallway, you had the option to go right or left. In those small passageways, doors led to the balconies overlooking the ballroom. I went one way. Barbie went the other.

We each stepped out onto a different platform, surrounded by a wrought-iron banister and waved at each other.

"Hi, neighbor," Barbie shouted. "This is almost as much fun as sitting in my oak tree."

Yes, that's right. Barbie sits in a tree for hours at a time, watching our neighbors go by, and contemplating world peace. When I first met her, I found that strange, but lately, I found myself joining her on a regular basis. We sit on tractor seats attached to a huge branch. Once I took up the practice, I found it more relaxing than a bubble bath and a glass of wine.

"This is neat. Are you getting ideas for the reception?"

Barbie's expression darkened. She grabbed the railing. "Come here. Quick."

Chapter 8

Something was terribly wrong with Barbie. More than usual, that is. My heart pounded hard against my chest. Was she having a heart attack or stroke? She needed me to come to her. I ran from my balcony, down the hall, and onto the platform where she was standing.

"What's wrong?" I put my arm around her shoulder. A loud crack rang out and the platform dropped from beneath our feet. We clung to each other and screamed in unison. The front part of the six-foot-square platform had folded down against the wall. Luckily for Barbie and me, the back part stayed attached and we were standing on the bars of the banister, hanging approximately twenty-five feet in the air.

Barbie screamed again.

"Don't move. We might break it loose, and we'll fall the rest of the way down." How would we ever get out of this?

Barbie screamed again.

"Will you stop that? You're causing my nerve endings to burn. Just relax. Someone will rescue us." I hoped.

Finally she calmed.

"Let's just stay unruffled and talk quietly until someone comes to rescue us."

Barbie gently nodded.

"Okay, what did you call me over here for anyway?"

"I wanted to see if you thought the balcony was loose. It felt loose to me, but I wanted to be sure."

"Are you crazy?" I shouted in a voice that vibrated me, Barbie, and the planks of wood hanging precariously from the wall. "If you thought it was loose, why didn't you get off of it? Why did you call me to add weight to it?"

"I didn't realize you were that heavy. I know you've put on a few pounds since you had LoJ, but . . . ."

I had my hands at my side, pressed against what was once the floor of the balcony. I braved the situation enough to raise my palm in front of Barbie's face.

"Sweetheart, please don't say another word. I fear I will have to pitch you off here. Just be very, very quiet until someone comes." She did as told. After awhile, I began to need something to take my mind off the fact that I was hanging really high in the air and, if someone didn't come along soon, we would both probably plunge to our deaths. I didn't want to leave this earth with hard words between Barbie and me.

"Do you think I could lift you up to the doorway, and you could crawl out and go get help?"

"It's worth a try." She turned slightly.

The sound of wood cracking froze us. Even as a child playing Statue Maker I had never been so still. My heart may have even stopped beating. Poor Barbie's skin paled to translucent. I took her hand.

"Don't worry. We'll be fine. Someone will miss us and come looking for us."

With tears in her eyes, she looked at me. Her lips trembled. "I have to pee."

"No, you don't. You're just nervous and think you have to go." I forced what I hoped was a reassuring smile. "I don't think homely Leila Martone would appreciate your relieving yourself on her ball-room floor."

I didn't think the terror in Barbie's eyes could magnify, but it did.

"Wazz wong?" I asked.

As if it were the most natural thing in the world, my friend reached over and shoved my protruding tongue back into my mouth.

"I think you offended Ms. Martone again." Barbie shivered. "Maybe you should be quiet until we get down."

I nodded.

"Hello? Anybody there?" someone called from the foyer.

"Yes, we're in the ballroom. There's been an accident," Barbie hollered.

Mrs. Thornton, my eighth grade English teacher, looked up at us and gasped. "Stay right there. I'll get help."

She disappeared, but returned several minutes later with three firefighters. The men came up the same stairs Barbie and I had. They pulled us up to the second story floor. Once we were back downstairs in the ballroom, I gave Mrs. Thornton a hug.

"Thank you. How did you find us?" I asked.

"The sheer curtains in the master bedroom were flapping like the window might be open. It looks like it's going to rain, so I decided to check it out." She twisted a tissue through her fingers. "I'm glad I did. You could have been seriously hurt, dear. I'll go close that window now."

The president of the Garden Club arrived. "I'm glad you two weren't seriously hurt."

"We are, too." Barbie tried to herd me out of the house, but I stalled to see what Mrs. Thornton found upstairs.

"No, there wasn't a window opened anywhere," she reported. "That's strange. I know something was making that curtain flap."

Barbie and I exchanged knowing glances and escaped as rapidly as we could without showing how creeped out we were. Apparently, Ms. Martone still occupied the house. Neither Barbie nor I intended to tell anyone. It was a secret we would keep forever.

When I got home that night Arch gave me a big hug and kiss. I mention this because it was bigger than usual.

"I just called the garage, and Linc said you'd been gone all afternoon."

"Yeah, Barbie and I were hanging around the Garden Club, making plans for Linc and Carrie Sue's reception." I decided not to elaborate on the statement since Arch and Barbie's husband were constantly putting us in timeout from each other. Although we never meant to get into trouble, somehow we always did. I'd break that bit of news to him at a later date, if ever.

Arch seldom called the garage. "Is something wrong? Is that why you were trying to call me?"

"Not wrong. Your brother Bobby called to invite us to spend next weekend on a houseboat with him and Billy. It'll just be your brothers and their wives and the two of us. Your mom said she'd watch the girls. We'll meet them next Friday evening and sail around Lake Reavis until Sunday. Doesn't that sound like fun?"

"You want me to get on a boat with my two brothers? Are you crazy?" I dropped my purse onto the sofa and poured myself an ice-cold glass of tea. I drank several gulps. "Have you never heard the story of them backing a twelve-foot John boat with me in it under a low branch from which two snakes hung? They are sadistic and dangerous."

"Don't be silly. They've outgrown all that childish behavior. Bobby needed to know this afternoon so he could reserve the house-boat, so I told him yes. I'll call him back if you don't want to go, but I'd really like to."

Arch asked so little. "Okay, but those two are accidents waiting to happen. If they make your girls motherless, don't say I didn't try to warn you."

The phone rang. Arch answered it. "Yeah, I'll tell her. Not a problem."

I stirred the pot of chili Arch had simmering on the stove and took a taste.

"That was Tim." Arch joined me by the stove. "He's set up a meeting for you to speak at the Garden Club in two days."

I choked on the hot soup. I didn't want to go back to Leila's house so soon. I needed time to heal from the trauma of the near-death experience and the encounter with a spirit from the other side.

"You okay?" Arch asked. "Too much chili powder?"

"No, not at all. I just swallowed too quickly." It wasn't really a lie. I had sucked it down the wrong pipe.

I didn't have a good excuse for not going to the Garden Club, so I'd have to buck up and face the unavoidable. After all, Carrie Sue wanted her reception there, and now Tim Tuten had scheduled a time for my constituents to listen to me and ask any questions they might have. I just hoped he didn't expect me to stand on a balcony to make my speech.

On my way to work, I stopped by the corner of Oak and Haverford where Millie and Mavis had set up their peanut stand. A large umbrella provided shade over a card table, their lawn chairs, and a turkey fryer which kept the boiled peanuts hot. They had been there every day since I applied for their vending license.

I glanced into the back seat. Since LoJ slept peaceful, I rolled down my window so I could hear if she awoke and then eased out of the car.

"How's business?"

"We're just getting started this morning, but we've sold out every day by three o'clock." Mavis smiled up at me.

"Great." I glanced across the street to the Old Bat's Antique Store where Alice was unchaining her merchandise left outside. "Where do you go if you have to use the bathroom?"

Millie nodded toward Alice. "We use the Old Bat's."

"Does she make you buy something every time you have to go like she made me?"

Millie laughed out loud. "Not hardly. A few years ago I walked into her storage room looking for Alice. I caught her and Coach Henderson . . . how should I put it?"

I tried to find a way to stop Millie from saying aloud what my mind was picturing in full Technicolor. But I failed.

"Let's just say that if I were you, I wouldn't buy that cherry dinette table she has on sale."

"Nooo. Don't tell me that." The vision was all too real for me because Carrie Sue had shoved me into the boys' locker room when we were in junior high school. Fortunately, no students were in there, but Old Coach Henderson was just emerging from the shower in all his glory. My first glance at a naked man had almost scarred me for life. Now the mental picture flooded back with a vengeance.

"You're blackmailing her so you can use her bathroom?" I asked.

"Heavens no. Since that day, we've never spoken of it, but she's always very nice to me. I have a permanent fifty-percent discount on any merchandise in her store and the free use of her restroom."

"I tell you one thing—neither of us go back there unless we know exactly where Alice is." Mavis punched Mille with her elbow. "Ain't that right?"

"Absolutely. By the way, I hear you're talking to the Garden Club tomorrow night. Are you sure you want to run for the council? It'll be a time consuming job, and you already have your hands full with your precious girls, your wonderful husband, your business," Millie said.

"And us," Mavis added.

"I know, but I believe I can do a good job."

LoJ started to cry. "Speaking of my precious girls, that one needs feeding and changing. Gotta run. I hope to see you at my personal appearance tomorrow night."

"We wouldn't miss it for the world." Millie waved.

"See you there." Mavis did, too.

On the morning of my Garden Club meeting, my nerves seemed a little more rattled than usual. I'd gone over my speech several times the night before and once at the breakfast table for Arch and the girls. It all sounded natural and like I might know exactly what I was talking about. Yet, I felt out of sorts.

Since there wasn't much going on at the shop, I drove over to see how the peanut ladies were doing. A line of customers waited patiently while Millie dipped the steaming hot peanuts from the pot, drained them, and put them into plastic bags, one pint at a time. Mavis collected the money. A gust of autumn wind ruffled the paper money in the till.

After the rush cleared, I tapped the top of the metal box. "Do you think it is wise to keep that much money in there? Someone might rob you."

Millie pulled out about fifty ones. "We empty the box twice a day and hide the money in here." She placed the dollars in a bank bag hidden under the mat in the trunk of the car.

"Business must be good. What are you going to do with your profit?" I helped her close the deck lid.

"We've already been doing something with it. We are donating it to a worthy cause," Mavis said.

"That's nice to know. Glad I could be of help."

"Bertie, you could be of real help if you'd stay here and mind the store for us for about fifteen minutes. We need to run to the bank to open a business account, and we both have to sign the bank cards." All the while she talked, Millie climbed into the passenger seat and Mavis into her side of the car.

I'm not sure I had a choice. They were already driving away. "Sure, just hurry. I have to get back to the garage."

By the time they returned, I'd sold three bags of hot boiled peanuts and consumed quite a few myself.

Mavis took my hand. "Are you feeling okay, sweetheart? You look distracted."

"I'm fine, just a little nervous about standing in front of so many people tonight. I'm okay with a few, but Tim expects there to be at least one hundred people there tonight."

From their car, Millie pulled a blanket and spread it on the ground right there in the middle of the dirt lot.

"Sit down," she instructed.

"Why?"

"Just sit."

The ground was hard and very uncomfortable.

"Pull your feet close to your body and put your soles together. Now, put your arms out and lean forward, stretching as far as you can."

Is there anyone in this world who can explain to me why I do things two old women tell me? Especially these two women. M&M. Murder and Mayhem.

My back cracked so loudly even they heard it.

Mavis rushed to me. "Wow. That can't be good."

Pain equaling that of childbirth ripped from my tailbone to the base of my neck. Involuntary muscle spasms caused me to collapse onto my back. I demanded my body not force a scream past my tightened lips. Since it never listens to me, I screamed with all my might.

"Good Lord, child. Let me help you up." Millie grabbed one arm, Mavis the other and pulled me to a sitting position.

The pain subsided enough for me to breathe. "And why, pray tell, did I need to do that little exercise in how to induce excruciating pain with very little effort?"

"You must have done it wrong, Bertie." Millie helped me to my feet. "It was supposed to relieve your stress and make you forget about being nervous."

"Well, you certainly took my mind off that."

"Yeah, Millie and I got us a video on yogurt. We've been doing that every night."

Slowly and with both my hands supporting my aching back, I carefully got into my car. "Yogurt, huh? Thanks."

They really had made me forget about my stage fright because if the spasms in my back didn't stop soon, I wouldn't be able to make that appearance.

Dr. Johns gave me a waist support, pain pills, and muscle relaxers. Evidently, they also worked on stage fright because I certainly had lost my fear of facing a crowd. I also had no problem with whether it rained or whether it was daylight or dark. Even the fact that I couldn't feel my left leg from my knee down didn't seem to concern me.

As I entered the ballroom of the Garden Club, I had a feeling something wasn't right, other than the obvious balcony-hanging-down issue. Covering the door above the scene of the destruction Barbie and I had caused, hung a huge picture of Booger Bailey. He'd actually shaved for his pose.

The still-righted balcony was draped with a sign that read *Vote for Booger. His nose is clean.*

Catchy. Stupid, but catchy. Why were those up there if it was my night to address the Garden Club?

"Booger spoke here last night. I'll make a note to check for things like that before your next meeting," Tim whispered. "Maybe we need to get a banner with your face on it."

"I don't know about that."

Booger's face was so large and a horse fly had chosen to land right on his nostril opening, keeping me from concentrating on my speech. I'd look into the crowd and try my best to focus, but in-evitably my gaze would wander back to the picture and the insect perched inside his nose.

Halfway through my spiel about myself, I felt a light mist of water hit me on the right cheek. I tried to stay on track, see where the water was coming from, and to ignore Booger's horsefly. I'd look at the fly, get hit with water, look that way, and speak. My ac-tion certainly must have looked a little strange. Suddenly it dawned on me where the water was coming from. In a fake-out, I started to look at the fly and then quickly glanced at that demon spawn, Art Bailey. Sure enough, I looked at him just in time to see him squirt me with a water pistol.

I stepped down from the podium, held out my hand, and Art put his weapon into my palm.

"Thank you," I said and returned to the stage and laid the gun in front of me.

I opened the floor for questions. "Do you have any questions about my take on any topic?"

"Is it true you endangered your two daughters by discharging a lethal substance into your home?" That question came from a little blue-haired lady I'd seen around town, but didn't really know.

"I'm sorry, I don't know what you mean?"

"Well, did you or didn't you spray mace in the confines of your house with your girls inside said house?"

"Oh, you mean when my husband and I were trying to sedate a mouse who refused to be caught? That was an accident. We meant to do the mouse in, but the A/C kicked on and sent the mace back into our faces. Boy, did we feel silly." I fanned my face in mock embarrassment.

"Does the ASPCA condone disposing of rodents in such an in-humane way?" Another rowdy woman sprang to her feet. "Once you'd paralyzed the poor thing, what would you have done next? Bludgeoned it to death?" She didn't give me time to answer. She turned to the group which had the earmarks of an angry crowd and incited them further by yelling at the top of her lungs, "Is this the kind of person we want representing us in our government?"

"Lady, get a grip. It was a rat, you nit—"

Tim grabbed the microphone and pulled it away from me. "Peo-ple," he said. "Please take your seats. Mrs. Fortney is a concerned civil-minded citizen who is willing to give freely of her time to make our town the best it can be. How she disposes of a rat should not play into this at all. Please take your seats and try to confine your questions to those pertaining to Sweet Meadow."

I took the microphone back. "Thank you, Mr. Tuten. Ladies and gentlemen, I do feel I know a lot about our town, and I also feel I can do a lot to make it a great place to live. Do any of you have any other questions?"

"Is it true you were arrested for cutting down a tree and damaging a police car?"

"No."

"You didn't cut down a tree?'

"Yes."

"You didn't damage a police car?"

"Yes."

"Were you not hauled into the jail in that same police car?"

"Yes, but—"

"I rest my case."

"You need to rest more than your case. I was not arrested. As a matter of fact it was determined that I did something good. I tried to clear the view in hopes of cutting down on accidents at the corner of Oak and Haverford. I went to war with the council and was able to get them to put up a stop light at that corner."

The horsefly on Booger's poster was driving me crazier than the questions these old biddies were firing at me. If they didn't have any concerns for the future they wished to discuss, then I wanted to close it all down and go home. Suddenly I was feeling like an evil person trying to work my way into politics, when, in fact, I didn't want any part of it.

What I really wanted to do was to get that stupid fly out of Booger's nose.

All the unimportant and just plain stupid questions the people in the audience were asking annoyed me to no end. "Does anyone have a sensible question that has to do with the council or its workings?"

"I do." A tiny, feeble-looking man held up his hand. "In regard to the council," he started.

Finally someone with some sense. "Go ahead, please," I urged.

"Did you kill poor old Mr. Bord so you could get on the council?"

"Oh, for crying out loud. I didn't kill Bob. It was natural causes, or maybe he died from too many nonsensical questions coming from nincompoops who so lack intelligence they wouldn't know it if it bit them on their pompous asses.

"Now, if that's all any of you wanted to know, I'll take my leave." I picked up Art's water gun, aimed at Booger's poster, and shot that horsefly from its perch with one squirt. As I left the Garden Club ballroom, I took a final glance at Booger's nose which was now running like a leaky faucet.

"How'd it go?" Arch met me at the door with open arms and a big smile.

"Based on my life's scale from one to ten of miserable events, it was about an eight." I rubbed my cheek against the material of his shirt, inhaled his familiar scent, and wondered why I was considering taking on a job that took me away from all I held dear.

Arch shouldered the household chores and took care of the children just so I could pursue a position on the council. When had that become my dream? It felt disjointed. Yet, at almost every turn, someone was thanking me for stepping up to the bat for them with our city lawmakers. It sounded so impressive, like I was doing something important. Yet, when did the fulfilling sensation replace the trepidation presently torturing my soul.

"Hi, Mom." Petey entered the room carrying her baby sister. I scooped up LoJ and hugged Petey all in one swoop.

"My teacher says she's very proud of you for attempting to be the only woman on Sweet Meadow's council."

"Really? That's nice."

"What will you do on the council?"

"As a group, we will make rules and regulations to help the city run smoothly." Okay, this was my first attempt at even thinking about what exactly I would be doing, let alone explaining it. According to Petey's puzzled expression, I'd failed.

Arch herded us to the kitchen table where a plate of baked chicken and potato salad awaited me. I settled LoJ in her swing so she could be close to me while I ate. Arch and Petey had already eaten.

"Let me go wash my hands, and I'll try to explain what I'll be doing, if I'm elected." I hurried to the bathroom.

"Okay, let's try this again," I said after I finally took a seat at the table. "The council decides the proper way for things to be done to make Sweet Meadow a pleasant city. They have rules citizens must follow so they don't leave abandoned cars in their yards, or raise horses on a small piece of land. Stuff like that. Do you understand?"

"Can you get them to pass a law so Randy Carson can't throw a dodge ball right at someone's head?" Petey rubbed hers. "He does that all the time, and it hurts."

I pulled her to me and kissed the top of her blond head. "I'll see what I can do about that, but first I have to get elected. That means I'll be late coming home, like tonight. At least until after the election. Is that a problem for you?"

Petey's gaze snapped to her dad. "No, it's fine."

Arch smiled. "You can tell her, sweetheart. Go ahead."

"Next Thursday is the Mother-Daughter dinner at church, but Daddy says you have to make a campaign speech that night."

"Oh." My heart sank to my stomach. My mind spun trying to figure out if I could get out of the meeting.

"Daddy and I thought maybe Aunt Mavis and Mrs. Keats could go with me to the dinner. It wouldn't be the same as with you, but I'd get to go."

"Maybe I can get out of going to the other meeting and go with you." I wasn't sure how I could do that, but I certainly couldn't let Petey down.

"We've discussed this at length." Arch squeezed my hand. "Petey understands you are doing something important. She doesn't want you to miss your opportunity. I'm sure Millie and Mavis would be glad to go with her. Petey loves being with the dynamic duo. They'll walk to the church so you won't have to worry about her riding around with those two."

My husband and daughter were proud of the way they'd worked it all out, but I was sad I hadn't been a part of any of it. They didn't need me. My heart broke.

"Is that okay, Mom? Can I ask Aunt Mavis and Mrs. Keats?"

With the width of Petey's smile, I couldn't say no.

"Of course."

She started to leave the table, but I stopped her. "I'm sorry I can't go. Will you forgive me?"

"For what? I get to go to a dress-up dinner with two of the craziest ladies I know, and you get to go make a rule that means old Randy Carson will quit hitting me with that hard dodge ball. I'm going tell my teacher I'm proud of you, too." She hugged me and ran off to call M&M.

Arch leaned over and gave me a kiss. "Don't give it another thought. She's happy, and you're doing something important to you. I'm proud of you, too."

There it was again. Someone telling me how important getting on the council was to me, and yet I can't remember when it became so. My heart sang a different tune. Because of my commitment to run for that position, I was missing an opportunity to be with my daughter. Weighing apples to oranges, there was something wrong with the whole picture. My apples were hard and my oranges were sour.

Chapter 9

"M om," Petey hollered from the living room. "Aunt Mavis said she needs you at her house right away."

Throwing my dishtowel aside, I hurriedly took the receiver. "What's wrong?" I barked into the phone.

"Ah! No! Get away!" Mavis demanded. My hair stood on end. I could hear Millie screaming and sounds of a scuffle in the background. Panic raced through my heart.

Arch wrestled the phone from me. "Mavis! What's going on? Are you being attacked?" He held the receiver out and looked at me with worried eyes. "She hung up." Quickly he dialed 911. "Go get LoJ. We have to go."

"Oh, dear. Grab the baby's diaper bag," I told Petey.

By the time I gathered children and necessary baby items, Arch had alerted the emergency operator, and police were on their way. At a high rate of speed, we were, too.

Simultaneously, Carl Kelly, Chief Kramer, and the Fortney family arrived.

Carl and the chief told us to stay put, and they ran into the house. I gave them about five seconds before I charged through the door leaving a protesting Arch outside to protect our girls.

Frantically my gaze swept around the room, not sure what to take in or let my mind register first. The living room had been ransacked. Lamps turned over, papers and magazines strewed about.

Wrapped in a crocheted afghan and with an open magazine draped over her head, Mavis stood in front of the sofa. Appearing totally frazzled, fear glazed her eyes. She was screaming and pointing to the ceiling.

Kneeling on the floor in front of her and with his head buried under a thick sofa cushion, a man's rump stuck out. At least it was dressed like a man. His pants' legs were flapping around his shaking legs.

Where was Millie?

The two, big, burly police officers with guns drawn appeared to have been struck dumb. They stared at screaming Mavis, but didn't make a move.

"What's wrong?" I hollered to be heard above her squawking.

Before she could answer, a flock of bats buzzed at us. Carl and the chief quickly replaced their guns and struck out at the beasts as they dive-bombed the two men. I thought Mavis' idea of covering her head with a magazine was a good idea. I grabbed a copy of . . . *Playgirl?* What was that doing there? I opened to a picture of a naked man and placed it over my head and grabbed a backpack lying near the door.

I flung it about hoping to actually disable a few bats. With my eyes closed it was hard to tell. Suddenly, I realized the screaming in the room had escalated and that along with me, Carl was responsible for some of it.

I opened my eyes a fraction of a second before Millie emerged from behind the opened front door. She swiped Carl's revolver from its holster and fired a shot at the ceiling. One of the bats fell to the floor, flopped around, and died.

I jumped so hard, I may have sprained my body.

While Carl tussled with Millie for his gun, I opened the screen door, and Chief Kramer swatted the remaining bats outside. Shaking violently, I collapsed against the wall.

Carl sat Millie in an overstuffed chair. "Don't move."

I hurried to Mavis, who was still screaming bloody murder. "They're gone. Calm down. Take deep breaths."

Chief Kramer hefted the man who thought he was an ostrich to his feet. "Who are you?"

"Oh, Good Lord." Unfortunately, I recognized the man. Mr.-Pick-His-Teeth-With-My-Business-Card. I glared at Millie. "What is he doing here?"

She stood up, but when Carl stepped near her, she sat back down. "He is spending a quiet, enjoyable evening with Mavis and me."

"At least he was until those *bamn dats* showed up." Mavis cut her eyes to the right, but when she looked back at me, one of them stayed put. She pounded the side of her head until the eye went back into place. This bewildering phenomenon had been happening since the day I met her, and it still disturbed me.

"I told you not to let this man come to your house. You don't know him or anything about him." I felt like strangling Millie and Mavis.

"You're not the boss of us." Millie whined.

"If I were, I'd put you over my lap and spank your bottom."

"Oh, I like the sound of that." The homeless man smiled widely.

"That's it. Everyone stop right where you are." I'm not sure I've ever been completely glued together, but if I had, that was the exact moment my adhesive wore out. I came totally undone.

First, I took on Chief Kramer. "You are in charge of taking this man away from here and seeing to it he doesn't make his way back. You're dismissed."

He escorted the man out the door.

"Carl, are you going to arrest Millie on a weapon's charge?"

He looked at the old woman. "Since she discharged the gun in her own home, and no one was hurt, I don't guess I need to run her in."

"Good. Go help Kramer."

When Carl got to the porch, Arch carrying LoJ and with Petey walking close beside him, came into the house. "Jeeze, thanks for the help, Arch." Sarcasm dripped from Carl's tone.

"You told me to stay outside, Deputy Dawg." Arch can be sarcastic, too.

"That didn't keep Bertie out. It looks like you would have come to protect her."

Arch laughed. "Has Bertie ever struck you as a woman who needed to be protected?"

Carl rubbed his head where I once accidentally hit him with a heavy piece of wood. Well, it wasn't an accident that I hit him. I just thought he was someone else. Evidently, he still bore the scar of my error.

"I feel your pain, Arch. Good luck." Carl bounced off Millie's porch and disappeared into the night.

"Mom, we saw the bats fly out of here. How cool. Do you know they eat hundreds of mosquitoes every hour? Can I have one for a pet?" Petey bounded across the room to the dead mammal.

"Don't touch that." I jumped in front of her. "Stay right there." Sprinting to the door, I hollered for Carl to come back. I gathered the dead bat in a piece of newspaper. "Take this with you." I handed it to him. "Thanks."

He stared down at the package.

"Off you go. Thank you very much." I gave him a dismissive wave and spun to hunt out my next victim.

"You know something, Bertie?" Millie asked. "You've always said I had bats in my belfry. Guess you were right." Everyone except for LoJ and me cracked up laughing.

"No, you are just plain crazy. Why can't you understand how dangerous it is to let that man into your home?"

"But he's so cute," Mavis giggled.

"So was Ted Bundy, but you wouldn't want him in your home either." I exhaled a few hardy puffs of air, which evidently I needed. I sat on the arm of the sofa. "Do not let that man back into your house again. Understand?"

"Ah, nuts." Millie picked up some of the disarray. Mavis, Petey, and I pitched in. Arch rocked LoJ, who had slept through all the commotion, but now wailed loudly.

"By the way, which one of you hormone-driven wackos has a subscription to *Playgirl*?" I shook the magazine in the air.

"Mrs. Keats," Petey said.

"How do you know that?" My gaze pinned my daughter.

She politely took the magazine and pointed to the label on the front. "It says so right here. I could see it all the way across the room."

"Oh . . . well, okay." That certainly was awkward. Of course, my dear husband just found it amusing.

The next morning, while sitting in my office at the garage, I kept replaying the scene at Millie's in my mind. Bats flying around inside the house caused chaos galore, but the homeless man struck fear in my heart. I wish those two dingbats with bats in their house had enough sense to know how dangerous their situation could have been because their good hearts allowed a killer into their home.

Killer? Maybe that was too strong for a man who hid his head under a sofa cushion and left two defenseless—more or less—women to fend off a herd? . . . drove? . . . pack? . . . of bats. I really must look up bats in the encyclopedia as soon as I got home.

But first I had to do something about the homeless man.

"Carrie Sue?"

She peeked out from under the hood of a car she and Linc were working on.

"I've got an errand to run. I'm taking the truck. If you get a call, let me know, and I'll take care of it."

"Will do, Boss Lady." She can be so clever.

I'd only gone a few miles when Carrie Sue called. "Karo Stevens needs his outhouse set back up for the third time this week."

"Roger that." I had just passed his street, so I made a quick right turn at the next block. Evidently too quickly. The man behind me laid on his horn.

"Ah, blow your nose. You'll get more out of it," I mumbled. A glance into my rearview mirror showed me he was a friendly sort. He waved and waved. Poor guy. He appeared to have lost some of his fingers from his waving hand. Probably from an automobile accident because his first response was to blow his horn as opposed to doing the most sensible reaction—hit his brakes.

I found Karo in his backyard scratching his head. A couple of neighbors had joined him, and all of them were cursing the youth of today, and grumbling about ". . . wrecker fees are costing me more than the whole outhouse cost to start with."

"I have a suggestion, Mr. Stevens. Mind you, I'm just thinking off the top of my head here. The building is set on a concrete slab. Why not invest in a few anchors and permanently attach your potty room to the cement?"

"He did that, Miss Smarty Pants." One of the other elders investigating the situation felt the need to set me straight.

I could see that the bolts were attached to the outside of the toilet and easily removed to allow hooligans to play a game called 3-T's–Tip the Toilet. Since no one, short of Karo Stevens, had an outhouse anymore, that sport is dead.

"Maybe you need to anchor it from inside the building." My best solution was met with opposition.

"Those buggers will just go inside and remove them." Mr. Stevens had given that some thought.

"Then put a padlock on the door. It might be inconvenient if you're in a hurry, but it would beat having to call me or my driver out here three times a week."

He liked that idea so much that, after I finished my assigned task, he gave me a tip. "Place your money on *San Souci* in the fifth."

"Thanks Karo," I said. "By the way, is that like the syrup?"

"Ha ha. Like I haven't heard that a thousand times in the last century."

I didn't let my diversion keep me from my original mission. Since I wanted to talk to Carl, I was happy to see his squad car in the parking lot at the jail.

Since I usually pulled trouble behind me like a small boy with his Radio Flyer, Deputy Kelly didn't look too happy to see me.

"Now what, Bertie?"

"Oh, ye of little faith. Isn't it possible I just stopped by to see one of Sweet Meadow's finest?" I plopped my butt on the edge of his metal desk.

"With the same possibility that I would sit atop a flag pole in my underwear to raise money for Booger Bailey's campaign fund." The far away look in Carl's eyes made me wonder if this had been a real request he'd been contemplating.

Personally, the image in my head was too bizarre to give it any more thought.

"Okay, I'm here to get the skinny on that homeless man Laurel and Hardy insisted on taking home with them."

Carl had the nerve to look puzzled. "Laurel and Hardy?"

"Millie and Mavis. That was said tongue in cheek."

"Well, get your tongue out of your cheek and say what you

mean. I'm in a hurry. I have an appointment."

"ET will hold your donut for you. What do you know about the homeless man?" I crossed my arms and tapped my fingers on my elbow.

"The man is Tom Barrs. He was the CEO of his own business. Manufactured window blinds until ten years ago, when alcohol became more important to him than his family and business. His wife divorced him. Took what money she could, and moved to an island off South America."

"Would that be Aruba?" I asked.

Carl glanced at a fax printout with Tom's picture on it. "Yeah, that's right. How'd you know?"

"He told M&M he had money in a bank in Aruba."

"In a way, he does. He's been divorced for ten years now. The business totally folded, and Barrs has been in and out of shelters and jails ever since."

"Jail? Anything serious?"

"No, mostly public drunkenness. Nothing in the last three years though. He told me and the chief he's been clean during that time. He moves around, working from day pools, and living in homeless shelters."

"Broke and homeless doesn't make a person bad. Does it?" I slid off the desk.

Carl stuffed the fax into a file folder. "Actually, he's pretty intelligent. Well, he'd have to be to have started and run a successful business for twenty years. His friends were his downfall."

I raised a questioning brow. "What friends?"

"Demon Rum and Wacky Tabacky." Carl cocked a smile. "By

the way, Chief Kramer didn't appreciate your telling Mr. Barrs he should stay in our town because the sheriff was lax in his duties and would let a transient get away with more than other towns do."

Eek. I needed to leave before I ran into the Chief. "That wasn't exactly what I said, but the meaning was the same. Think I'll head out before I run into him."

"Wait, Bertie." Carl joined me on my walk outside. "Tom Barrs is painting Millie's house. Just thought I'd tell you before you went over there and pitched him into the street."

"You let . . . ?"

"I checked him out, and I feel he's a good man. He can earn money by helping Millie spruce up her home. Look at it this way, he'll keep those two women busy and out of your hair. If it makes you feel better, I'll keep an eye on him."

That would make me feel better, I think. "Okay, but the first sign of anything amiss, you promise to put a stop to it, right?"

"By amiss, do you mean like if I see him peeing in the bushes next to the porch?"

"Yes, exactly like that."

"Well, I'll certainly keep an eye out." Carl scurried away.

Maybe I'd better go by there and see how things were going.

All appeared quiet at Millie's. Very little painting had been done. Fresh, white paint covered a section of the right side of the house, about six feet wide and four feet high. Most of the morning must have been spent gathering supplies.

From the backyard, I heard a round of merriment rivaled only by children on a playground on the first day of spring. There I found two Abominable Snowwomen spraying water at a scantily dressed man who stood in an old galvanized tub. Covered from head to toe with white paint, Mavis dragged the hose while Millie used a nozzle to squirt a hard stream of water at Tom Barrs.

The trio giggled like kids. Tom's pants and shirt, also covered with paint, lay strewn on the ground. Rivers of white water cascaded from his hair, over his shoulders, and down his back and stomach. His boxer shorts, thread worn and dingy, clung to his skin like a pair of pantyhose, leaving little to nothing for the imagination.

Could a sight like that cause me to go blind?

Each time a blast of cold water hit his body, he gasped and shouted, "Wahoo!" He shook like a dog after a hard rain. Millie and Mavis roared with laughter.

Hidden by a huge azalea bush, I looked on with the same enthusiasm as watching a train wreck. Knowing it was going to turn ugly. Knowing I should stop it or at least close my eyes. Yet, wide-eyed, I waited for the disaster to happen.

"Come on, Tommy." Millie dropped the hose. "You do us now." She jumped up and down and clapped her hands.

"Yeah, do us." Mavis joined in.

"Okay." Tom stepped out of the tub. "Take off your clothes."

"Stop." I barreled out of the bushes. "Hold it right there. What do you three think you're doing?" I screeched.

"Whatever it is, I guarantee it's about to come to a stop." Millie stomped her foot like a naughty little girl being confronted by her mom.

"If you think you're taking your clothes off out in the open and letting this man spray you down like he's grooming a horse, you bet it's coming to a major halt. Right here. Right now." I tossed Tom his paint-stiff pants. "Put these on," I demanded. While he dressed, I faced down Millie. "What is going on here?'

"Lighten up, Bertie. We got into a paint fight, and we were just cleaning up."

"I think you should clean up in the house, don't you?"

"Not really, but if it wipes that dour look off your face, we will. Did you ever do anything spontaneous, Bertie? Just be silly and laugh your fool head off?" Mavis asked.

"Not since you two hooked up." With a nod, I indicated the two old women. "You have aged me a hundred years. You throw this character into the mix, and I'm sure I'm scheduled for a heart attack at any minute."

Millie took my hand and led me back to the azalea bush. "Deputy Kelly checked out Tommy. He's a very nice man. Not only is he a hottie, but he makes us laugh. Try it sometime, sweetie, you might like it."

I laugh. Well, sometimes. Or, at least I used to. Lately life seemed to be stepping on my toes leaving little time for frivolous moments. One look at the new light in Millie's eyes and I didn't have the heart to extinguish it.

"You are really moonstruck with Tom Barrs, aren't you?" My mouth curved to a smile.

Millie punched her fingers to the corners of my mouth. "That's the ticket. You should wear that all the time."

I grinned from ear to ear.

"In answer to your question," Millie glanced back to make sure we were still alone, "I really like that man. I even think my dearly departed John would approve of Tommy, don't you?"

Millie giggled. Seeing her so happy, I laughed with her. "I'm sure he would."

I pointed to the small section of fresh paint on the side of the house. "This is all he's painted so far?"

"Yeah. I don't think painting is Tom's strong suit. That's as high as he's going to be able to paint. You see," she leaned close so she could whisper, "he's afraid of heights. So, Mavis and I will have to paint from here up." She pointed to the spot above the newly painted area and then all the way up to the second floor.

A vision of either Millie or Mavis, or both, falling from a wobbly ladder, plunging twenty feet down to their death, shivered my timbers and quaked me to my boots. "You can't do that. It's too dangerous."

"But we told Tommy we would do the top so he wouldn't get in trouble with Deputy Kelly." Millie looked heart-crushed.

Dang. I couldn't stand seeing her happiness fade. Just looking up at the top of the house, I became dizzy. I certainly couldn't do it for him.

"Let Tom do as much as he can. I'll see if I can find someone to finish the upper half." I assessed the house one more time. I never noticed exactly how big it was. *Jeeze.*

"I know I can depend on you, Bertie. You're a real friend." Millie hugged me leaving a light white tint on the front of my coveralls. "Oops. Sorry." She dusted me off.

When she disappeared around the house, I appraised the paint-the-whole-house situation. As usual, I'd stepped into deep mud and had no way of getting out without losing my boots.

The giggling and squealing resumed from the backyard. "Come on, Tommy, do us now." Millie shouted.

Who was I to rain on their parade? Millie was right. I did need to smile more. All the way back to the garage, I did just that and even sang of few lines of "Zippity Do Da."

I spent the rest of the afternoon putting together a crew who could give freely of their time to paint Millie's house. Since Carrie Sue was on call Saturday, Linc said he'd be glad to help out. Elton from ET's Donut Shop could pitch in for a few hours. Donna Carson's husband, his brother, and if I played my cards right, Arch would be available, too.

A little thought niggled at the back of my mind. Millie had said they wanted to help Tom to keep him from getting in trouble with Carl Kelly. That tidbit hadn't digested completely with me. I needed more data for my brain to compute.

Carl answered on the second ring. "Police Department. Deputy Kelly speaking."

"Hi there," I said. "I went by Millie's to check out the house-painter. What credentials did Mr. Barrs have that made you assume he could paint a house?"

"He said he used to work with J & J House Painters in Atlanta."

"Did you check his references?"

"Sure did. I spoke with a man named Kenny. He said Tom

Barrs was reliable as long as he doesn't have a snoot full."

"Is that all he had to say?"

"He said Barrs doesn't get high any more. That was good news so I told him, if he painted Millie's house, I wouldn't arrest him for vagrancy."

"Well, there's just one slight problem with your conclusion."

"And what would that be?"

"Kenny didn't mean that Tommy, as Millie has taken to calling him, doesn't drink and therefore doesn't become high on alcohol. *Au contraire*, my Legal Beagle. He meant he doesn't do heights. You know, like climb high on a ladder as one must do to, in fact, put paint on the side of a house."

"If he doesn't go up a ladder, how does he paint the second floor?"

"Forget the second floor, how does he paint anything above six feet?"

"Ah, fudge. You mean to tell me he can only paint the bottom six feet of Millie's house?"

"Bingo! Millie and Mavis were going to take care of climbing up the ladder and doing the rest because they didn't want Tom to get in trouble with you. Of course, we all know that isn't the case, is it, Mr. Muscle Man? Because if one of those ladies fell and got hurt, you'd be in trouble with me."

"Bertie, you know that wasn't my intent. Why, I'd go over there and paint that place myself before I'd let Mavis or Millie get hurt."

"Good boy. Be there are eight o'clock Saturday morning with the rest of the painting crew. Wear old clothes." I hung up.

"You look like the cat that ate the canary." Carrie Sue entered the office from the work bays.

"No, just a deputy." I patted my chest. "And he'll probably give me indigestion before it's all over. How's it going out there?"

"I'm finished with the Lexus. Linc is just starting on the Mustang. Has Barbie come up with any plans for our wedding?"

"She's working on it. We took a close look at the Garden Club. Maybe a little too close."

"Yeah, I heard about that. My Uncle Ebo is going to repair the balcony you tore up."

"I didn't tear it up. It was rickety, and it fell. Barbie and I could have been seriously hurt if we hadn't been rescued by the fire department."

"So, I heard, you lucky duck."

Lucky was exactly how I felt, but not for the reason Carrie Sue alluded to. I was thrilled not to be a grease spot on the dance floor of the Garden Club. I would have made a bigger splat than Barbie, what with all the weight everyone kept saying I put on.

"Do I look fat to you?" I asked and then watched Carrie Sue's expression to see if it held disgust. Thankfully, I saw none.

"You're not the string bean you were in school, but let's face it. None of us are. You still have some of the fat you gathered when you had that sweet little LoJ, but you can get rid of that. I've been trying to stay in shape by running a mile every morning."

"Really, where do you run?"

"I get here an hour early, put on my running shoes, run from here to the new stop light at Oak and Haverford and back. I usually get back about ten minutes before you show up. I wanna look really good in my wedding dress."

"Have you found one yet?"

"Yeah, I think so. It's on hold at Acme Hardware and Bridal Shop in Lumpkin. I have to lose five pounds before it will fit."

"Why did you go so far away to get one? Even Atlanta would be closer than that. And did you say hardware store?"

"Yeah, you remember Betty Jo Smith, who moved away from here when we were in the eleventh grade?"

"Was she sent away to visit her aunt for about nine months?"

"That's her. Well, she's married now, and her husband owns a hardware store. She opened a bridal shop in one corner next to the deer and rabbit pellets."

Lord, let me go with the flow. I can't afford brain overload today.

"Great. What color is it? Pure white? Candlelight? Cream?"

"Pink."

"Of course, I should have known that." I smiled. "Barbie asked if you and I could meet with her over the weekend to hear her ideas. Can we work that out?"

"How about Saturday here at the garage?"

Just then the mailman arrived. "Hey, Bert." Howie never brought the mail in. That would show kindness on his part and it wasn't happening.

"What's up, Howie?"

"Need a signature." He handed me a certified receipt slip. While I signed it, he told Carrie Sue, "I always call her Bert."

"Yeah," I said. "Stop that."

Howie laughed. After handing me the piece of mail I signed for, he left, taking the rest of my mail with him. He put it into the mail box and then drove away.

"Jerk," Carrie Sue and I said at the same time.

"I'll go get it for you." She was headed to the door.
I opened the envelope and screamed.

Chapter 10

$\mathcal{C}$arrie Sue flew to my side before my scream had died.

"What is it? A death threat?" She snatched the paper from my hand.

I would ask her why she thought someone would threaten my life, but I was too busy hyperventilating. She, on the other hand, held her side to keep it from splitting from laughter.

"That's . . . not . . . funny," I said between gasps for breath.

"Oh, yeah, it is." She could barely speak.

Linc came into the office to see what the screaming was about. Carrie Sue was all too happy to tell him.

"The Garden Club sent Bertie a bill for $250.00 for repairs to the balcony she broke."

My brain ached. "How can those idiots think I'm responsible for that? I should sue them for almost causing me and Barbie to fall to our deaths. Those dogs are sniffing around the wrong fire hydrant if they think I'll pay this." I crumbled the request for payment into a ball and two-pointed it into the trash can.

Near closing time, Mavis and Millie stopped by. Only a few speckles of paint remained in their gray hair.

"Where are you two headed?" I asked.

"Since we couldn't help Tommy paint, we worked at our peanut stand for the rest of this afternoon." Millie deposited coins into the cold drink machine.

"We sold all our nuts." Mavis leaned on the counter. "I'm pooped."

"We were wondering if you found someone to paint the top part of my house." Millie took a big swig of Coke and burped like a line-backer.

"I got a whole crew of men who will finish that up on Saturday. Let Mr. Barrs do the bottom, and the rest will be taken care of. With as many painters as I've lined up, it should be done in one day."

They both came around the counter where I was sitting. "We're glad we get to go to the awards banquet with Petey. Sorry you can't be there, but we're happy to fill in for you." Millie's smile made me feel a little better about missing the affair.

"I can't tell you how much I appreciate both of you."

"Boy, those are words we don't usually hear from you." Mavis gave me a quick hug.

As they left, I watched them pull into traffic, forcing one car to burn rubber sliding to a stop.

Dear Lord, please take care of those two and anyone they come in contact with. Amen.

Saturday morning found the Fortney family in Millie's backyard. All the guys who promised to show up did. Bless their hearts. Even

Carl Kelly.

Millie and Mavis had their peanuts loaded into their car. Saturday was a big business day for them.

"Ya'll are really making a financial killing in your new venture, aren't you?" I closed the trunk for them.

"We're the big cheeses of nuts." I think a sunbeam bounced off Mavis' brilliant smile.

"Truer words were never spoken. By the way, you told me you were giving some of it to charity. Is that still the case?"

"Well, let's just say we are putting it toward a good cause." Millie slammed the car door in my face.

I tapped on the window, but she didn't roll it down. She just waved. Mavis backed out of the driveway and ran over a boxwood plant, which looked to have been hit several previous times.

My trouble radar was beeping at an alarming rate. Something mysterious loomed large on the horizon. Mavis and Millie were up to something. I just hoped I wouldn't be maimed or killed in their wake. Just in case, I upped the ante on my prayer for them.

Dear Lord, please take care of those two and anyone they come in contact with, especially me. Amen.

I left Arch with the other men in Millie's yard. Petey and LoJ were waiting patiently in the car for me to take them to Mary Lou's house. She'd graciously agreed to keep an eye on them, and Petey would be her assistant.

Anxious to get there, she whined from the passenger seat. "Can't you go any faster? Aunt Mary Lou's baby will be graduating from college before we get there."

"I'm doing the speed limit, my Drama Queen."

She looked out the side window. "I think a tortoise just passed us."

"You're cute. We need to decide what you're wearing to the Mother-Daughter Banquet on Thursday. We'll see what's in your closet tonight and decide if you need a new dress."

"I'm sure I have something I can wear. You are way too busy to go shopping, Mom."

Ouch. That hurt. Unfortunately, she was right. Today I had a meeting at the garage with Barbie and Carrie Sue to discuss her wedding plans. Sunday—church, most places closed. Monday and Tuesday Petey had to go to school, and in the evening I had to meet with Tim to discuss the upcoming debate with Booger on both nights. Wednesday after church, I would have to get my own clothes laid out for the debate the following day.

"I can almost hear those little wheels in your head. Please don't worry about it. Daddy says that once the election is over, things will slow down because then you only have to go to a meeting when the council meets. We'll survive until then."

"You're the best daughter anyone ever had." I rubbed the back of my hand across her cheek. "I love you."

"I'd love you more if you'd pick up the pace."

Stomping the gas pedal to the floor, the car lunged forward, throwing Petey back in her seat.

"I was just kidding," she shrieked.

I slowed. A few minutes later, as I backed out of Mary Lou's driveway, I waved to my precious girls. They didn't see me. My friend carried LoJ, and Petey raced inside to play with Mary Lou's son, Second.

Petey's comment about what I'd be doing after the election

splintered my thoughts. What exactly would I be doing if I was elected? Maybe I'd better ask my campaign manager that question. Tim would know. He knows everything.

Barbie and Carrie Sue waited for me at the garage. Pages of notes, primitive drawings, and clipped magazine pictures covered the counter.

"*Wow!* That looks impressive." I glanced over a snapshot of a church draped with white tulle and gigantic magnolia blossoms.

"These pictures are of my wedding." Barbie had every right to be proud.

"They're absolutely gorgeous."

"Can we do something like that in three shades of pink and bright green?" Evidently Carrie Sue hadn't changed her mind about the bright colors. Dang it.

"Oh, yeah. We can take yards of material in all the colors and braid them. It will be fantabulous," Barbie squealed. Carrie Sue bobbed up and down and clapped her hands. I moved closer to the trash can in case I hurled my breakfast.

"You know what else would be great?" The bride-to-be was on a roll. "Instead of those big white flowers, I'd love to have pink flamingos."

"Please tell me you don't mean real ones." I had to sit down before I fell down.

"Of course not. Plastic yard ones will do."

"Wait. I know. I know." Barbie took a note pad and scribbled on it. "We can cover them with pink caribou feathers."

Carrie Sue corrected our fine-feathered human goose. "I think you mean marabou feathers. Yes, that would be perfect."

I've been surrounded by wacky people all my life, and in most cases, I enjoyed it. They were role models for what I didn't want to be. But lately I wondered if maybe those around me were fine, and I was the one who was an apple short of a fruit salad. My mind did not work like theirs. I took the easiest, most logical route directly toward the end of my assigned task. Others, Carrie Sue and Barbie in this particular instance, reminded me of my brother, Bobby, who once played outfield in Little League.

There he was, chewing gum, kicking grass, and basically hanging out where the dandelions grow, waiting for the inning to be over so he could either get up to bat or have a cold drink. *Pow!* The ball was hit to him. He placed the back of his gloved hand to his forehead to shade his eyes from the sun. Without ever seeing it, the ball landed right in the center of Bobby's glove.

Three things happened. He was not beaned by the ball. The runner was out. And since that ended the game and our team won, Bobby was a hero.

I tried my best to get the officials to say it was a foul ball because Bobby didn't even know the ball was coming at him. Instead, Ump the Rump ejected me from the park for a week.

My point is, everyone else marches to a different drummer, and I keep trying to make things happen through normal channels, like keeping one's head in the ball game and using flowers instead of plastic flamingos at a wedding.

But, nooo. The people who touch my heart are touched in the

head. I may have a pillow crossed-stitched with that.

By the time I came out of my self-pitying trance, Carrie Sue and Barbie had most of the decorating plans made. We moved on to the food.

"I've asked Elton Taylor to cater the reception." Carrie Sue seemed proud of the fact.

Personally, I wondered if it would be wise. All I'd ever seen him make was donuts. Of course, his mother was an excellent cook, so maybe he had more up his sleeve than flour.

"Does he have a large repertoire of gourmet morsels to wow your family and friends, or will there be just a large tray of assorted donuts?"

Carrie Sue tilted her nose slightly. "Elton is the best cook in these parts."

"He does make a fine donut. I'll give him that." Truth be known, I probably owed my last ten overweight pounds to Elton's holeless donuts. "What will he be serving?"

"Chicken wings, deviled eggs, and Linc's personal favorite, Vienna sausages covered with chili."

"What? No chitlins and dumplings?" Oops. Hope I didn't give her any ideas.

"No, silly. I want different stuff, and my sister Annie had those at her reception," Carrie Sue said.

My whole body quivered for two reasons. First, because I didn't even know there was such a dish as chitlins and dumplings. I was just being a wise-acre. And second, because Annie married my old boyfriend, Lee Dew. But now that I think about it, I was thrilled he'd chosen to go out to get a loaf of bread and never come back to me. I hope he choked on all the redneck delicacies I'm sure they served at his and Annie's wedding. Not unlike the menu Carrie Sue and Elton had put together. The only difference with her wedding is that I'd have to eat what they served.

I scribbled Pepto-Bismol on my shopping list.

"Sounds like you have the food under control." Barbie directed her comment to Carrie Sue, but she gave me an expression that screamed *yuck*.

"Yes, yummy." I squeezed Barbie's arm to reassure her things would be okay, despite the greenish tint covering her face. I whispered, "It'll be fine."

"Glad to hear that. Carrie Sue, do you have the wedding party figured out?" Barbie asked.

"I thought we just discussed the party." Carrie Sue flashed a bewildered smile.

"I mean your bridesmaids and Linc's groomsmen."

"Annie will be my maid of honor and my other sister, Donna, will be my bridesmaid."

Ah, yes, the three Barrow sisters decked out in pink and green puffy dresses would be a sight to behold. Physically they clean up pretty good, but with their attitudes, especially Donna's, most people gave the women a wide path. They each wore an invisible layer of porcupine quills and, if anyone crossed them, they weren't afraid to spear that person and the horse they rode in on.

"What about groomsmen?" Barbie asked.

"Elton is the best man and Annie's husband, Lee, will be a groomsman."

Carrie Sue glanced my way. "Will that be a problem for you?"

"Why would that be a problem for Bertie?" Barbie asked.

"Bertie was engaged to Lee for several years before he married my sister."

"Oh, no, will that be a problem for you, Bertie?" Barbie's concern touched me.

"Of course not. I wouldn't trade my wonderful husband for two Lee Dew's. The best thing that ever happened to me was the day he left me and found a new life with Annie." I wanted to add a few comments about lice attracting lice and spawning nits, but then I realized I'd be talking about Carrie Sue's sister and her husband and their children. Yes, at the time Lee's leaving had hurt me, but Arch's love filled me with so much happiness, and he washed away all the sadness Lee had left.

"Lee is so far from my mind I barely recognize him when I see him on the street."

"I'm glad that's settled. Donna's kids will be in the wedding, too. Pam will be the flower girl, Jude the ring bearer, and Randy an usher." Carrie Sue counted them off on her fingers.

The darlings of Sweet Meadow. I long ago declared Donna's kids the most likely to be in jail by the time they were fifteen. Surely Donna could corral the little dears long enough to get through the wedding ceremony and maybe even keep Randy from picking any pockets while everyone's eyes were closed in prayer.

Worrying about those three was not part of my job description. As the wedding coordinator, I was to gather all the necessary materials to decorate the church and the Garden Club Ballroom. On the day of the wedding, I would be responsible for getting everyone down the aisle at the appropriate time. Since I learned I had to herd

Donna's three children, I added a cattle prod to my shopping list.

Carrie Sue, Barbie, and I finalized our plans to meet again Wednesday afternoon at my office. Then we would make hand-made invitations and decorate plastic lawn ornaments. In other words, we would feather the flamingos.

I gathered my shopping list. "Barbie, I'm not going to have any time during the week to go shopping for the things we'll need on Wednesday. Today is the only day I have. Do you have time to ride to Shafer with me to pick up our supplies?"

"I told Rick I'd be home by the time Tammy got up from her nap. As long as I'm home by then, I'd love to go with you."

"Great." I made another note on my list. "We're going to take off, Carrie Sue. I'll see you Monday morning."

"I appreciate you guys more than I can say." Carrie Sue hugged us both.

"No problem," I assured her.

"It's going to be just beautiful." Barbie snagged her purse, and we were off to Ingmar's Crafty Shack. The one and only party and craft supply house this side of Atlanta.

We pulled into the parking lot, but before I got out, Barbie stopped me. "Will you do me a favor?"

"If I can. What is it?"

"Don't leave me alone inside this place."

"Okay, but is there a special reason for that?"

"I'm afraid of Ingmar's husband. He looks at me cockeyed."

"Barbie, sweetheart, he is cockeyed. His left eye is crossed and has been since dinosaurs roamed the earth. He can't help that."

"Oh. Well, it's not just that. He winks at me all the time."

"He has a nervous tic in that same eye. He can't help it."

"He sticks his tongue out at me every time I go in there."

"Ingmar told me once he has a condition that causes his mouth to be dry all the time. He constantly licks his lips. He can't help it."

"The worst part is he always wants me to look at his fly."

"He means his fishing fly. He makes them in the back room of the craft shop, and Ingmar sells them. I'm sure that's all he meant. He can't help it if it sounded obscene."

"All right, if you think he's okay, so do I," Barbie said.

In less than an hour we had everything we needed to make personalized invitations. Ingmar had tulle in the colors Carrie Sue had specified and the feathers to cover the flamingo yard ornaments, which we would pick up at Wal-Mart on our way back to the garage to get Barbie's car.

"Oh, wait." Barbie charged down an aisle. "We need glue for the feathers."

While I unloaded the basket, Ingmar rang up our merchandise.

Suddenly, from somewhere in the back of the store, the unmistakable sound of flesh slapping flesh sang through the entire store.

Barbie returned to the register, plopped a container of glue down, and went on out to the car. I finished our transaction and joined her. Once inside the car, I had to ask, "What happened in there?"

"You were wrong, Bertie. That dirty old man asked if I wanted to see how his fly works. I took you at your word he was talking about a fish fly, and I said yes." Barbie slammed her body against the back of the seat. "Wrong. He unzipped his pants and before he could show me anything, I showed him I had a nervous tic in my right hand that reached out and slapped his face. I couldn't help it."

I took Barbie back to the garage for her to get her car and circled back to Millie's to see how the house painters were doing. The eclectic group had done a magnificent job of finishing the facelift of Millie's house. Arch would be finished with his part in another ten to fifteen minutes.

Millie and Mavis' Caddy sat half on the driveway and half on the grass. I went inside to see how their day had gone at their peanut stand. I didn't see them, but I heard shuffling in a backroom.

Snooping is so much fun. I eased my way down the hallway toward the grunts and groans I heard coming from Millie's bedroom. What were they doing in there? Tom Barrs was outside with the other men painting the house, so I didn't fear running into him and Millie doing the naked Mambo.

No, it had to be M&M. The door to Millie's room stood ajar. She placed a handful of money into an opening in the floor and then placed a plank over the hiding place. Together she and Mavis labored to shove a cedar chest back against the wall.

The piece of furniture scraping across the hardwood floor along with the elderly women's moans had kept them from noticing I stood in the doorway. "What are you two doing?"

The both yelped and clutched their hands to their hearts. "Bertie Fortney, you are going to send us to an early grave," Mavis said between gasps for breath.

"Dear, dear friend, I'm afraid that is no longer possible." Millie's color returned to her face. "And, after that scare I've aged another five years."

"Why are you hiding your money? From what I saw you have a bundle stashed under there."

"This is the money we've made selling peanuts." Millie latched onto my elbow and led me to her kitchen.

"They have a great facility called a bank. You put money in there until you need it. Ever heard of one?" I asked.

"Bertie, you are such a nerd. Of course we've heard of a bank, but we are using our money to fund a charitable cause. We don't want anyone to know we are doing it. Therefore, we can't leave a paper trail." Millie took a seat at the kitchen table.

"Besides, I have an aversion to banks after that unfortunate incident where I was accused of being an accessory to a bank robbery," Mavis added.

"Yeah, and then there was the episode a couple of weeks ago when you thought we robbed the local bank. After that we decided we better stay out of those places in case others thought we were the ones responsible for making an illegal withdrawal that day."

"Millie, I apologized for that, but it certainly isn't a reason to never use one again."

"Oh, we're only hiding our nut money."

"What if someone breaks in and robs you? You could be seriously hurt. I'd feel better if you put it in the bank. How about it?"

"The only person who knows it's there, beside Mavis and I, is you. You wouldn't rob us, would you, Bertie?"

"Mavis, you're a hoot a minute. You know I wouldn't do that, but someone else might. It needs to be deposited into a bank or at least a safe-deposit box. I'd feel better about it."

"Okay, we'll do that." Millie walked me to the back door. "Thanks for all your help with getting my house painted. The guys did a good job, didn't they?"

"Your place looks really nice. Now, remember, you promised to put that money in the bank. I want it done first thing Monday morning."

Both women smiled and nodded.

I'd walked out of their sight, but not out of earshot when I heard Mavis say, "You're not really going to deposit that money, are you?"

Millie never answered aloud, but I had a strong feeling she was shaking her head so hard her blue-gray curls were *boinging* like cork screws. Too tired for another confrontation, I ignored them.

Arch climbed behind the steering wheel, and I leaned back in the passenger seat and closed my eyes. In a few minutes, we picked up Petey and LoJ from Mary Lou's.

"Did you enjoy your visit with Mary Lou and Second?" Arch asked Petey.

"I sure did. Uncle Rex was telling us about when he was abducted by aliens."

Oh, good heavens. Mary Lou's husband believes all that space stuff he sees on television and reads in sci-fi books. I looked at Arch to see if Petey's revelation upset him. Other than a slight smile, it didn't appear to faze him.

"He told me about that, too. What did you think was the most interesting part about his story?" Arch definitely won my vote for the better parent.

I bit my tongue to keep from telling Petey that Uncle Rex was nuts and to ignore anything he ever said. Arch, on the other hand, made Petey think about every situation.

"I love the part when the aliens put his toes where his fingers should be and his fingers where his toes should be, and he had to scratch his head with his feet."

"Why did you find that so interesting?" Arch delved deeper into her thoughts.

"Because it was at that point I knew the man was nuts, and I should ignore him."

The sun had disappeared behind the horizon leaving us shrouded in evening dusk, but I was sure my brilliant smile glowed in the dark.

Arch reached over and squeezed my hand. "By the time LoJ and Petey grow into women, I'm going to be in a lot of trouble, aren't I?"

"It won't be as bad as being abducted by aliens," I reassured him.

From the back seat, Petey giggled. "Yeah, we'll leave your fingers and toes where they belong."

Chapter 11

The next day, after church, Petey and I rummaged through her closet in search of the perfect dress for her to wear to the Mother-Daughter Banquet coming up on Thursday night. We were soon smacked in the face with reality. It looked like we weren't going to find one long enough to cover her butt. She'd literally shot up and out of her clothes.

"I wish we had time to go shopping in Atlanta." I pulled the latest reject over Petey's head.

"I know you don't have time, Mom. You're working every day taking care of the towing business and garage. You're planning Carrie Sue's wedding and running for city council."

Petey dug all the way to the back of her closet and pulled out her Easter dress. It gave us our first glimmer of hope. The pale yellow, satin garment fell a little above her knees. Not short by fashion industry specs, but every time she raised her arm, her panties flashed boldly.

"It's a shame all the shops in Sweet Meadow close their doors at sundown." She tugged at her dress.

Studying the hem of the hopeful dress, I suggested the only

solution I could think of. "I can let it down a couple of inches and that would make it presentable, don't you think?"

"Yeah, that'll be fine. Or, you could keep me out of school and take me shopping tomorrow." Petey's devilish smile tugged at my heart.

"Good try, but you know I can't do that."

"Just kidding." She eased out of the dress and then, while I hung it up, she clasped her arms across her chest to hide her barely developing breasts. I tossed her nightgown to her.

When Arch and I married, Petey had legally become my daughter, but, in my heart, she'd been my little girl since very early in her father's and my relationship. She was racing toward being a teenager, yet I'd barely gotten to enjoy her childhood.

Sitting Indian style in the middle of her bed, Petey ran a brush though her long, blond hair. She looked like the pictures I'd seen of Nola, her mother. When he looked at his daughter, did Arch see it, too? Did he still miss his deceased wife on a daily basis? Or, had her memory faded enough to allow him to truly love me? Of course he loved me. I felt it in every part of my heart.

"Are you feeling sappy?" Petey asked.

That's exactly what I was feeling. Why? Guilt for not going with Petey to the Mother-Daughter banquet had really dampened my spirits.

I took the brush from her and ran it through her hair a few times. "Are you sure you're okay with going to the banquet with Millie and Mavis? I could try to get the debate rescheduled."

"Dad explained it all to me. If you are elected to the council, you will be doing a bunch to make the community better for me and

LoJ. Besides, other girls will have *serrated* mothers with them."

"*Surrogate* mothers," I corrected.

"Yeah, Dad said they are stand-ins for the real thing. I get to have two surrogate mothers. I'll feel so special."

"Oh, I've been so easily replaced by Sweet Meadow's terror duo." I pretended to remove a spear from my chest and then flopped onto her bed.

"I could never replace you, Mother Dearest." Petey slid under the cover and mumbled into her pillow. "And you call me a Drama Queen."

"Very funny." While I gave her a quick kiss on the forehead, she chuckled aloud.

She stilled and gazed pensively at me.

"Something wrong?" I asked.

"Do you think I'm too skinny?"

Was this a trick question, or did Petey have a deep-seated feeling about her appearance?

"I don't think you're too skinny, but I think the important question would be, do you?"

"It never occurred to me until Randy Carson said he likes women with meat on their bones and that I need to fatten up some."

I nearly bit off my tongue to keep from spouting obscenities. How dare that little twerp make my daughter feel inferior? I should have gone over to his house and pinched his head off. Of course, that would mean I'd have to go through his mother Donna the Hun. She would hurt me. Maybe I could think of a better way to handle this.

"Honey, you can't conform to what others think you should be. You have to go with what your heart tells you. Would you be happier with more meat on your bones, as you said?"

"Not really, but I want Randy to like me."

"No, you don't." Dang. I hadn't meant to say that. "I mean . . . maybe you shouldn't put a lot of faith into his opinion."

"In most things I don't, but I was just wondering about this one point. That's all."

"Randy's judgment may be a little off. You see, he doesn't have many positive role models in his life." I hugged her. "I think you are perfect just the way you are, and if he doesn't appreciate you, then he can go elsewhere.

"Besides you're too young to be worrying about boys. In another year or so, they will become important no matter how much your dad and I try to keep that from happening. Until then, how about concentrating on being young? The other stuff will come soon enough."

"I suppose," she said sleepily.

I turned off her light and had almost closed the door.

"Mom? Since he doesn't have good role models, do you think I could be one for him?"

"That's a very nice thought. What made you think of that?"

"Since I have two terrific role models, I think I can help him."

If pride was gold, I'd be a millionaire. Far above my expectation of being a good mother, Petey's words brought a rush of tears to my eyes. "Wow, that is so nice to hear. Thank you for saying that."

She hesitated a moment. "You're welcome. I can't wait to tell Mavis and Millie about them being my two good role models."

That loud crash which was probably heard around the world was my ego splattering onto the floor.

"I'm sure they'd be glad to know you think so highly of them."
My constricted throat garbled my words.

"Oh, Mom, one more thing."

At that moment I wasn't sure I could stand one more thing from
my daughter. But I think it's in my mommy contract that I ask.
"What's that?"

"I was just kidding. You and Dad are my heroes. Night."

I'm sure she must have giggled, but my heavy sigh drowned it
out. "Good night, sweetheart. You're my hero, too."

Monday morning brought rain. Linc and Carrie Sue kept the roads
hot pulling cars from ditches or hauling them away from crash
scenes. Yes, I said scenes, more than one. Common sense would
dictate that in a community as small as Sweet Meadow, accidents
would be minimal. On most days that held true.

However, on rainy days, the precipitation soaked into people's
brains and rendered them incapable of driving. What do they do,
try to swerve out of the path of flying water droplets? It would appear that way.

By noon, both of my drivers were soaked to the bone, tired, and
hungry. When the call came in that Karo Stevens needed his outhouse up-righted again, I went leaving Carrie Sue and Linc behind
to feed their faces and dry out.

I had barely arrived on the scene when Mr. Stevens shook a bag
in my face. "I just got back from the hardware store. I hope you're
happy. I spent a fortune."

It was hard to tell if he was angry, kidding, or just plain crazy. If I won the race to be on the council, maybe I could convince them to make off-balanced people wear signs around their necks. Ah, that wouldn't work. Everyone would have signs. Of course, I wouldn't because my job would be to herd and ride roughshod over those with signs.

"Why should I be happy?" I asked the crazy coot.

"The last time you were here to set this dang thing up, you told me to get anchors to bolt it to the concrete slab, but I never did. I knew when you showed up here you'd read me the riot act for not doing what you told me."

Wish everyone took my words to heart like that. Most people ignored anything and everything I said.

"Okay, Mr. Stevens, let me get it pulled upright, and you can secure it so it won't happen again."

"I also got this." After showing me two metal brackets he purchased, he held them up against the front of the outhouse which still lay on its side. "See, I'll attach these, and then I slide a two-by-four board into place and lock it. That way, those mean boys can't get inside to loosen the bolts of the L-brackets and tip my crapper."

He was getting on my last nerve. I wanted to scream, *don't care. Don't care. Don't care.* Even the rain pounding against my head did not drown out the drone of old man Stevens' voice.

"Let's just flip this puppy up and then you can do anything you want to with it." I secured the chain around the small building and gently pulled it back into place. Two exterior wall boards fell off.

"Those stupid kids. Now they've done it. I'll have to practically rebuild this thing." Karo shook his fist in the air, lost his balance, and fell against me. I righted Karo with almost the same effort it took to set up his outhouse.

"You're strong," he said and felt my muscle.

"Yeah, thanks." The rain continued to pelt my body. "I gotta run, Mr. Stevens."

"Let me pay you." He pulled what appeared to be a roll of one-dollar bills from his pocket. It would take old Karo ten minutes to count out the cost of my services.

"Listen," I clutched my hands around his, "I've made enough from you and your royal throne. This one is on the house." I jumped into my truck and took off.

At a red light in the middle of town, I looked in the window of Marge's Ladies Apparel shop. There hung a beautiful deep purple skirt and matching jacket. A lavender blouse completed the business outfit. How perfect that would be for a councilwoman. I whipped into a diagonal parking place and splashed my way into the store.

The suit fit me to a T. I found another one just like it in Petey's size. Wouldn't that be neat for her and me to have matching outfits? A thought like an electrical shock buzzed through my brain. At age twelve, would I have wanted to dress like my mother? I would have rather stuck a fork in my eye. Okay, bad idea. I looked around for something Petey really might like.

There on a mannequin I found it. A dress made of soft, matte satin called Petey's name. The short sleeves and V-neck bodice with sage green skirt embroidered with dark green and ivory flowers took it from a little girl's outfit to a sophisticated dress any young lady would be proud to wear. We would look good in our new outfits. I just wished we were going to the same places.

The rain continued through the afternoon. Howie, the mailman, made his delivery and dripped water all over my office floor.

"I need a signature on this one," he said.

I obliged. When I saw the return address my stomach quivered. Sweet Meadow's Garden Club. "Here." I shoved it back at Howie. "I don't want this."

"Too late. You sign for it, you own it. Have a good day." He left.

Reluctantly, I opened the envelope and sure enough, there it was. Another bill for the broken balcony. It wasn't going to go away on its own. After I looked up her phone number, I called the president of the Garden Club. Mr. Moore informed me I could find his wife, Clara, at the Garden Club's mansion.

Rain poured, but I needed to make the situation of the balcony repairs disappear. It was that or else kill Clara Moore. Either way, I'd have to brave the rain, which blew sideways and straight down all at the same time.

I found the front door of the Garden Club unlocked. From inside I heard hammering. Following the sound, I found Ebo Biner putting the wrought-iron railing around the newly erected balcony.

"How's it going, Ebo?" I called to him from the dance floor below the balcony.

"Oh, hey, Bertie. Not bad. Not bad at all. I'm just finishing up this little repair job, which could have been avoided if Clara would have come off the money for me to secure it before it fell. Now,

she's all up in arms because it costs so much to totally replace it."
Ebo gathered his tools and appraised his job. "That'll take care of it
for today. I'll paint it tomorrow, and it'll be ready for the big debate
on Thursday."

"So, Clara knew there was a problem with the balcony before
it collapsed?"

"Sure, she got me to do an estimate on it about six weeks ago.
You would think the money comes out of her pocket instead of the
trust fund old lady Martone left for the upkeep of this old house." He
descended the stairs and joined me near the front entrance. "Well,
gotta run. Emma will have dinner waiting for me."

"Be sure to tell her hello for me."

"I'll do it."

When he opened the front door, rain blew in and puddled on
the shiny wood floors. I supposed Clara would find a way to blame
me for that, too. Where was she? I didn't like being in the Martone
house alone.

"Clara?" I peeked down the hallway in the direction of the
kitchen.

"Yes?" She stuck her head through the doorway. "Oh, hi, Bertie.
Did you come to pay your bill for the repairs?"

"I came to talk to you about that. I don't owe for those repairs,
and I'm not paying them."

"Of course you are, dear, after all you and your friend the tree
sitter were on it when it fell."

"That's right, and we are in the process of deciding whether or
not to sue the Garden Club for negligence. There should have been
a sign across the entrance of that balcony telling us it was unsafe to

stand on. You've known for at least six weeks the structure was un-
sound." I pulled the invoice from my purse and handed it to Clara.
"I'd like this marked null and void. I want you to make it very plain
to the other members it was not my fault it fell, but it was your fault
that my friend and I were almost killed."

"I can't do that."

"And why, pray tell, can't you?"

"Because I embezzled money from the maintenance fund and
gambled it all away in Tunica, Mississippi."

"First of all, how has that become my problem and second, why
aren't you in jail?"

"Because no one but you knows, that's why. I trust that I can
depend on you to keep that bit of information under your hat."

"Keep it under my hat? Are you nuts? That would make me
an accessory to a crime. You are going to call Chief Kramer and
turn yourself in right now." I latched onto her elbow and pulled her
along. "Where's the phone?"

"We don't have one."

Just then a telephone rang from behind a door a few feet from
us. I yanked it open and found it to be a janitorial closet with mops,
buckets, brooms, and a phone. I snatched up the receiver.

"Hello!"

"Okay, Clara, listen, Bertie Fortney called to see where you
were. I told her you were there. It wasn't until a few minutes ago
that it dawned on me she probably wants to talk to you about that
bill for the repairs. Get out of there right away. Heaven only knows
what she'll do if she gets all worked up. You know she's crazy."
Metzger Moore thought he was issuing his warning to his wife.

Little did he know Crazy Bertie Fortney listened on the other end.

"Really?" I whispered hoping to deceive him a little longer.

"Yeah. I told you that would never work. She's not the kind to take this lying down. I know you were hoping to get her to pay so no one would find out the funds are all gone, but she's a sharp cookie. Crazy, but sharp. I never believed she'd just pay the bill and that would be the end of it."

"Mr. Moore. Guess who this is?"

"Well, I don't believe you're my wife, are you?" He emitted a nervous giggle.

"Guess again."

"That wonderful, intelligent, tow truck driver?"

"You're getting closer. It's crazy Bertie Fortney."

"Gotta go." The line went dead.

Clara raised her free arm over her head like she thought I might strike her. "I'm not going to hit you." I released her elbow, and she stumbled backward. "Not as long as you do what I say." I dialed the police department's number. I told Chief Kramer he was needed at the Martone Mansion.

"He'll be here in a few," I said to Clara. "You're going to tell him what you did."

"I can't do that, Bertie. They'll put me in jail. Ethel Winchell has been doing everything she can to get me kicked off the Garden Club board so she can have my job. If she finds out about the money, she'll make them prosecute me to the fullest extent of the law. I didn't mean for it to get out of hand. I just borrowed a few dollars and thought I could make a quick profit, and then I had to take more to try to win back and replace what I'd lost. My daughter needed money for an operation. You'd do the same thing if it was one of your daughters."

How sad. I had no idea. Of course I'd do what was necessary, but would I steal? A better question would be, if I stole, why wouldn't I use the money I stole for my daughter instead of chasing an illusive dream of instant wealth?

"I'm sorry about that, Clara, but you have to understand that I'd be as guilty as you if I didn't tell anyone."

"It's not like I'm not going to pay it back. I'm in the process of selling my grandmother's dishes she brought with her from Italy when she married my grandfather. I'll have all the money except for the two-hundred and fifty dollars that I billed you for the repairs. It was a stupid thing to do, but where our kids or grandkids are concerned, sometimes we have no choice. You understand, don't you?"

"I understand, but I still don't feel right about it. You promise you will be repaying the full amount?"

"The full amount except for the two-fifty I billed you. In all fairness you were the one on the balcony when it fell. Please help me out. Please, I'm begging you."

"Bertie, I'm here. Where are you?" Chief Kramer called from the ballroom.

"We're back here."

He found us hanging out in front of the broom closet.

"What's the problem?" he asked.

Oh, dear, what to do? I looked at Clara who had tears in her eyes and a begging gaze. I felt sorry for her. I glanced at Chief Kramer whose puzzled stare startled me. I was caught between a crook and a hard cop and very little time to make a decision.

"Bertie, why am I here?" Kramer asked.

"This woman is a crook."

Clara gasped.

"She is making me pay for the repairs to the balcony which fell when I stepped out onto it. I don't think it's fair, but she won't change her mind. I want you to witness this transaction so she can't extort more money out of me at a later date."

"You made me come out in this torrential downpour for this foolishness?"

"Well, it's not foolishness to me." I got my checkbook out of my purse and scribbled the full amount and gave it to Clara. "There. And don't ask for any more."

She squeezed my hand in silent thanks. I spun on my heel and went to the front door. The puddle of rain on the floor bothered me. I went to the bathroom off the foyer. After gathering a handful of paper towels, I dried the floor.

The chief and Clara's voice easily carried to where I was.

"Thanks for coming," Clara said.

"I'm not sure it was necessary, but glad I could help. By the way, I saw your son-in-law at the driving range yesterday. He said Becky came through her surgery just fine. Glad everything went okay."

"Me, too. I'm glad that's over for her."

"I've got to get back. Tell Metzger I'll see him at the debate Thursday night."

"Sure."

I mopped up the water from the beautiful floor and hoped it would win me points with old lady Martone. After all, I would be debating with Booger in her house in a couple of days, and I didn't need any spirits sending me bad vibes because I allowed her home to be marred.

I just finished, and Chief Kramer helped me to my feet.

"Thanks." I dropped the soppy paper towels into a trash can. "Uh, Chief . . ." I lowered my voice, "I know it's none of my business, but what was wrong with Clara's daughter? What type of surgery did she have?"

He blushed a bright crimson.

"I didn't mean to embarrass you. I guess it was probably some woman procedure, huh?"

"Yeah, let's just say if she is so inclined she can now get a job as the head girl at Hooters."

I closed my eyes and visualized my head exploding. *Pow!* Chief Kramer's laughter faded into the distance. Clara's daughter had a boob job, and I had just help finance it.

I strolled to my vehicle, buckets of water raining around me, and I didn't even care. I wanted it to cleanse my body of the icky residue of the past thirty minutes. Before I drove away, I glanced at the window directly above the entrance. The window was closed, but the lacy curtain of what I knew was Miss Martone's bedroom shimmied like someone was standing next to it laughing their butt off.

Suddenly, the absurdity of the whole situation struck me funny, too. I laughed out loud until the curtains stopped moving. Instantly, my laughter stopped, and I drove away.

Dismal weather or no, I covered a lot of territory during the day. Since rain prohibited Millie and Mavis from selling peanuts, I assumed they'd be home. I stopped by to check on them. In their driveway, I parked behind an unfamiliar Buick. Even though rain pounded on the roof of the porch, it did nothing to drown out the heated discussion going on inside the house.

I knocked, but when no one answered, I opened the door.

"You may have the hottest body in the Over Seventy Club, but that doesn't give you the right to snatch up all the eligible bachelors within fifty miles," Mavis screamed at Millie.

"I can't help it if they are naturally attracted to me. It's a curse I've had all my life," Millie countered.

"It's a curse you use to your advantage. You flaunt your stuff like a hooker in Forsythe Park." Mavis thrust her hands to her hips and did an exaggerated walk around the coffee table.

I walked into the room. "What are you two fighting about?" I startled them.

Mavis was the first to recover. She shook a gnarled, menacing finger in Millie's face. "This hussy tried to steal my boyfriend."

"No, I didn't. Mickey's tried to get me to go out with him for years. If I wanted him, I could have had him already."

"Mickey who?" Instantly a brain freeze hit me. "You don't mean old Coach Henderson, do you?"

"Old is in the eye of the beholder, Miss Priss." Mavis had been hanging around Millie too long. She'd caught a severe case of sharp tongue.

"Yeah," Millie joined in. "We aren't old. We're ripe with age. Ready to be plucked."

"The only thing you two are ready to be plucked for is the funny farm. Calm down and tell me what's going on."

"Mickey came calling on me, and Millie started flirting and strutting her stuff like a heifer on an auction block."

"I was just warmin' him up for you, and who are you calling a heifer?" She pushed her body against Mavis' front.

With her belly, she shoved Millie back. "You with the sagging udders."

I pushed the women part and stood between them. "Stop that, right now," I demanded. "We can work this out."

"I don't think so." Mavis backed away. "I'm going to have to move back in with you and Archie."

Oh, no, that couldn't happen. Not now. Not ever.

"As lovely as that would be, we don't have room for you. Your only option is to work this out, and I wholeheartedly believe it is possible." I motioned for them to take a seat.

"Now, Mavis, do you like old . . . I mean, Coach Henderson?"

"Yes."

"What about you, Millie? Like you said, you've had a chance with him for years and didn't move on it. Have you changed your mind about him?"

"Heavens, no. I'm in love with Tom Barrs."

"The homeless man?" Why did that shock me? In my universe it would be the next natural addition in my zoo of lunatics.

"He's not homeless any more. He lives with me," a man's voice came from behind me.

Since my nerves were so raw with tension, I don't remember turning around. I may have just levitated to look behind me. Old

Coach Henderson emerged from behind closet door number three.

"What are you doing in there?" My voice had the same tone as Linda Blair's while possessed.

"I took cover to keep from being torn apart by these two. I came by to see if Mavis would like to go to a movie with me tonight, and the next thing I knew these two squared off like lady wrestlers."

"Come on out," another male voice called from the back door. Tom Barrs came into the room from the kitchen. "I got the plastic pool filled with mud. You two can go at it out there."

Although I'm seldom amazed by anything, the next thing that happened took me aback. The four octogenarians began to make their way out the back door.

Once I regained my motor skills, I ran out into the back yard. The rain had slowed to sprinkles and drops. Randomly rippled muddy water gathered in a kiddy pool in which Millie used to grow lettuce during the summer months.

"Stop," I screamed seconds before Millie and Mavis stepped into the mud wrestling ring. "You can't do that. Get back in the house right now." Like children, they marched single file into the kitchen. I stopped Tom. "You, empty that mud out before you come in."

After he finished his job, Tom joined the rest of us. We all dried off. "I have a solution for this." I moved Coach Henderson next to Mavis and Tom Barrs next to Millie. "This is how this should be worked out. Now, you each have a male friend to spend time with. And Millie, you leave Mickey alone." I think I sprained my tongue calling old Coach Henderson by his first name. "Is that agreeable with all four of you?"

They smiled at each other and then giggled like children.

"Okay, you four. Don't make me have to come back and put you into time-out. Okay?"

"We'll play nice," Mavis said.

"Yeah, we will." Millie hooked her thumb at the kitchen table. "Let's go finish our game of strip poker." They all scrambled to the table.

My first instinct was to demand the men go home and the women go to a time-out corner until they came to their senses, but suddenly I wondered why I cared. If they wanted to see each other naked, far be it for me to stop them. What was my fear? That they'd get pregnant, ruin their reputations, and not be able to go to the prom?

The fact was I didn't feel like running interference any more today. I didn't want to think about what their next shenanigans would be, nor did I wish to remain and bare witness. Bare being the operative word.

I'd done all I could for one day. I left them to whatever floated their boats. In most places, full moons brought out strange behavior. In Sweet Meadow, rain appeared to be the catalyst for the weird and weirder.

Chapter 12

With my arms loaded, I entered my house. "Honey, I'm home," I yelled.

"Mom, look what I got." Petey ran to meet me. She waved a sheet of notebook paper in front of my face.

I threw the packages over the back of the sofa and sat LoJ's carrier on the recliner. "Let me see. What is it?"

"I got an *A* on my science test. Woohoo!!"

I swept her into my arms and swung her around. "That's terrific, sweetie. Like father, like daughter." I winked at Arch who stood in the kitchen doorway.

He gave me a peck on my cheek and ran his hand over my very damp hair. "Bad day?"

On my left shoulder sat an imaginary angel who encouraged me to not spread my tidings of crappy things which had taken place on the wettest day I'd seen in a long time. Why burden my dear husband? On my right shoulder sat the devilish voice of doom yelling, "Go for it."

"You be the judge if it was a bad day. I set up a tipped outhouse, helped finance Clara Moore's daughter's boob job, and kept

Millie and Mavis from mud wrestling to settle an argument over Old Coach Henderson. What do you think?"

"Well, let me tell you about mine," my dear husband said. "Mack Jones was doing a demo in his lab for his fourth period chemistry class. The chemicals exploded, and the whole building had to evacuate during the hardest part of our tropical depression, and we live nowhere near the tropics. As principal, I had to explain to the hundreds of whining kids why I couldn't just let them go home. The faculty herded them to the gym and cafeteria, but only after the fire was contained and all the students had been soaked to the bone.

"As the principal, I had to run from the point of origin, to the lunchroom, and then to the gym trying to keep order. The dictionary says order means '. . . *straightening out so as to eliminate confusion.*' The person who wrote that never tried to bring order to hundreds of teenagers who felt like prisoners and looked at the faculty as the guards. That, of course, would make me the warden. I expected a full-fledged riot to erupt at any moment. As it was, several fights broke out, and I had to break them up."

At that moment, I realized my strong, stable husband was shaking. I put my arms around him and held him. LoJ began to cry. Petey took her sister from her car seat and carried her to her bedroom.

I drew back to look at Arch. I saw a slight red and purple mark at the top of his cheekbone. When I reached to touch it, he moved away. "Did one of your students hit you?"

"Actually one of them hit me with a chair." He moved back into the kitchen where our dinner awaited in a take-out pizza box.

"Did you see a doctor?"

"Yeah, the superintendent insisted. Nothing is broken. Just a bruise."

"Sit down." I pulled a chair away from the table. "I'll finish the salad. Did the doctor say you should stay home tomorrow?"

"No, he said a mild painkiller should help, but I won't need to miss work. I have an assembly scheduled first thing in the morning, which I wouldn't miss for the world. The teenagers of Sweet Meadow are in for a few choice words."

"What happened to the kid who hit you?"

"There was too much going on to be sure who it was. I have an idea, but it doesn't matter. I would rather have them in school where I can personally work on them with messages of what's right and wrong."

"Do you think they will become model citizens just because you talk to them?"

"Good heavens, no. I know which boys were involved in the fight, and I have ways of getting their attention. They just need thinking time, and they can do that while they are trimming shrubbery, pulling weeds, and cleaning restrooms. I've already talked to most of their parents this afternoon. I gave them the choice of allowing me to issue my own brand of punishment, or I could suspend the kids and the parents could have the little darlings home with them for a few days. I'm proud to report I have their support. One-hundred percent."

"You go, Mr. Principal." I planted a light kiss in the vicinity of his boo-boo. Despite the pride I felt for the way Arch handled the toughest of situations, I felt uneasy about his safety. It never occurred to me that, as the head of the high school, he could be hurt, but the rapidly darkening bruise on his face glared at me. Not only could he be hurt, but he had been.

"You win," I said.

"Win what?"

"You had a *badder* day than I did."

"There's no such word as badder. Besides, I think one balanced out the other. Let's call it a tie." He smiled and then winced with pain.

"At least I won't have to take drugs before I go to bed." I set the salad on the table. "Petey, dinner's ready. Bring LoJ with you."

In short order, Petey bounced into the kitchen lugging her baby sister. I took her and placed her on a blanket on the floor where she could doze while the rest of us ate dinner. Picking up the plastic bag, which held the new dress I'd bought Petey, I untied the knot at the bottom.

"I bought you something. I hope you like it," I told her as I unveiled the dress.

If I had any doubt she would like the dress, it all disappeared when I saw her face. She glowed. She clutched her hands to her chest and sighed. Not in her usual drama queen style, but a truly heartfelt appraisal of the dress.

"I take it that means you like it."

"It's . . . beautiful."

Oh no, was she going to cry? Since I was already fighting tears, if she started, I'd lose it, too. She took the dress from me.

"Can I try in on now?" She swiped her tears with the back of her hand.

"Sure, I can reheat your pizza when you're ready to eat. Do you need any help?"

"I can get it." She took off down the hallway.

"I want to see you in it," I told her.

"Me, too," her dad said.

A few minutes later, a beautiful young lady emerged from her bedroom. The dress fit perfectly, and the smile brightening Petey's face said all there was to say.

"*Wow.*" Arch rose from his seat. "Where's my little girl? What did you do with Petey?"

"I look different, don't I?" She spun around.

"You look beautiful, and you just made me realize it won't be long before I'll have to beat the guys off with a stick." Arch choked.

"Oh, Daddy, I'm too young for all that." She winked at me.

What a smart young lady. Keep Daddy in the dark as long as possible. I winked back. Petey gave me a big hug.

"Thank you. I would have been happy to wear my Easter dress, but this is so much better. I really do understand why you won't be at the banquet, and I know I'll have a lot of fun with Mrs. Keats and Aunt Mavis, but I'll miss you."

"I'm sorry." My heart was torn in a hundred pieces. "I'll make it up to you, I promise."

"Just win the race so you can pass that law keeping Randy from hitting me so hard with a dodge ball. That's how you can pay me back."

"Great. You go change and come and eat. I'll get right on that Randy and the dodge ball issue."

She went to her room singing. "Go Mama. Go Mama. Go Mama."

"You are so good with her." Arch wrapped his arms around me. "She and I are the luckiest people in the world to have you and LoJ in our lives."

"Oh, no, I'm the lucky one. Every day I am surrounded by the wackiest people ever put on God's green earth. Coming home to my stable, loving family is all that keeps me from dancing to lunatic music. It's something I give thanks for on a daily basis."

After the day I had, I'd have to do a double dose of bedtime prayers and maybe spin around four times and spit through a V in my fingers to ward off the evil spirits. Since I didn't have the energy for it, I'd have to pass.

Wednesday afternoon, Barbie met me at my office. She, Carrie Sue, and I were going to work on the handmade invitations for the upcoming wedding. That only took about two hours, and we were soon knee deep in pink boas and long-legged, pink flamingos. As Carrie Sue cut the feathers from the boas, Barbie and I glued them onto the plastic lawn ornaments.

By the time we were through with them, we all had pink fuzz dancing in our hair. Barbie had one feather affixed to each of her eyebrows. "You look like a female Groucho Marx." I laughed so hard I almost fell off the chair.

Barbie put a boa around her shoulders and used an ink pen as her cigar. "Say the secret word, and the flamingo will swoop down and give you a prize." She waved one of the funny looking creatures above her head.

"You're nuts," Carrie Sue said.

Linc entered the office, and Barbie shoved him his future bride.

"*Nuts* is the word, and here's your prize."

A befuddled Linc backed away from us. "I'll come back later." His hasty retreat and slamming of the door left us three pink, fuzzy women laughing hysterically like grade school girls who had just squirted chocolate milk out of their noses.

"I better quit laughing so much." Carrie Sue's jolly mood turned maudlin. "My mom says 'laugh in the morning, cry at night.' Somehow, I always found that a true statement."

"Oh, that's terrible. We've all laughed so much today, we won't even be able to smile for at least three full days." Barbie took Carrie Sue's statement way too seriously. Her frown made my face hurt.

"Okay, if you two insist, I won't find anything funny ever again." I put on my sternness expression.

Linc stuck his head back in the office. "I hate to interrupt, but I have to go pick up a part from Joe for the car I'm working on. Carrie Sue, you'll have to take any calls that come in while I'm gone."

"No, problem. We're through here," I said.

His brow furrowed. "But she's covered with pink fuzz. Do you think that's good advertisement for the garage and towing service to have a driver covered with pink fuzz? Customers may balk."

"Linc, I'm surprised at you. I never realized you were chauvinistic. Would you feel better if she was covered in blue fuzz?" I was having a good time at my poor driver's expense. He sputtered like a badly running car.

"I'm just yanking your chain," I confessed. "This will all dust off." The three of us shook like wet hound dogs, and sure enough, all the residue from our afternoon crafting project floated to the floor. "See, we're back to our usual grease-stained coveralls. Ready to handle any call that comes our way. Feel better?"

"Yes." Linc gave his betrothed a shy smile. "By the way, the pink vultures look nice." He backed out and closed the door.

Carrie Sue, Barbie, and I stood in stony silence staring at the lovely flamingos. He thought they looked like vultures. My resolve to not laugh any more that day dissolved completely.

Through diehard laughter, I managed to tell my two cohorts, "Save yourselves. I'm a goner." My deep laugh mixed with Barbie's shrill squeals and Carrie Sue's donkey braying. The horrific sound ricocheted off the paneled walls. The more we heard it, the more we laughed. I feared we were going to need oxygen. I knew for sure I needed a bathroom.

Howie, the mailman strolled in. "Here's your mail, Bert." He looked at Carrie Sue and Barbie. "I call her Bert."

"Yeah, don't do that." I said it, but I wasted my breath. I'd been telling him for years not to call me that, yet . . .

"I got a great deal for you, Bert." Howie pulled a sheet of paper from his back pocket and spread it out on the counter. It was a flyer advertising brick mailboxes. "My cousin builds these. I thought you might be interested in one for here or your house or both."

I read over the literature. "They're nice looking. The price is a little steep though. I'm not sure I want to put that much out right now."

"I knew you'd say that. My cousin, you remember him, Bertram, he said he had some old cars in his yard he needs towed away."

I remembered Bertram very well. He was the same age as my brother Bobby and had the same temperament. He loved playing tricks on unsuspecting school kids like me, for instance. Worn-out tricks like hand buzzers, whoopee cushions, tainted chewing gum. Of course, those things only worked once on me, because I really was a street-smart third grader. After a few "gotcha's" from them, I learned to never be alone with them, never take anything they offered, and if all else failed I'd scream bloody murder. When an adult arrived, I'd point at Bertram. I didn't have to say a word. Everyone knew the things he did, so he would be hauled to the principal's office, saving me from being tricked or maimed.

The next I time saw him, I'd scurry by him and whisper "gotcha." After a few trips to the principal's office, his high jinks stopped.

"Well? Would you like to barter for a mailbox?" Howie interrupted my trip down memory lane.

"I'll give Bertram a call and see what we can work out. I think one of these would dress up our yard. Thanks."

After Howie left, I helped Barbie carry the wedding decorations to her car. The invitations were all done. She would drop them in the mail on the way home. Linc had returned with the part he needed. He and Carrie Sue finished the repairs he had been working on.

I called Bertram. "Well, Bertie Byrd, it's been a long time, no see."

"Yeah it has, but it's Bertie Fortney now. I'm married and have two girls."

"I think I remember Howie telling me that. So, did he talk to you about trading a mailbox for a few tow jobs?"

"Yes, he did."

"I got an estimate from that guy who works for you about how much it would cost to haul four cars out of my yard. For that amount I can put you up a fully-guaranteed brick mailbox and I have three colors you can choose from."

"I like that idea. It would be one mailbox, right?"

"Yeah, but if you want a second one, I'd be willing to give you a good deal on it."

"I'll tell you what, put one at the house in exchange for towing services. I'll see how I like it, and I might have one put in at the garage, too."

"When do you want this done?"

"As soon as you can. When do you want the vehicles towed?"

"I want to strip some parts off the cars before I get rid of them. I'll do that over the next couple of weeks, and I'll call when I'm ready to move them. In the meantime, I can put up your mailbox over the weekend."

"Sounds like a deal. Thanks, Bertram." We hung up.

I walked into the garage. Linc and Carrie Sue were cleaning up the bays. "Hey, guys, I just made a deal with Howie's cousin, Bertram, to move some vehicles from his yard to here for disposal in exchange for a brick mailbox he's going to put up at my house. He isn't ready to move them yet, but I wanted you aware so when he calls you'll know what's going on."

"Sure thing, boss." Carrie Sue slapped my back. "By the way, thanks for all the help with my wedding. Barbie has had some really cool ideas, and you've helped make them all happen."

"I'm actually having a lot of fun pulling it all together." Yes, it was fun, but exhausting. Her wedding plans, Petey's banquet, getting ready for the big debate coming up the next night, and packing for Arch and I to spend the weekend on a houseboat with my two brothers and their wives pulled more energy from my storage tank than I had in reserve. That was only outside activities. I still had a business and a house to run, plus somewhere in there were two precious girls and a husband. Just thinking about it made me tired.

After dinner that evening, Petey and I laid out her clothes for the banquet the next night. I took about an hour to get myself ready, giving special attention to pressing my new outfit and doing my nails and giving myself a facial.

I prepared a plan of action. Here's how it would work: the next day when I got home, Arch would have dinner ready. We'd eat, and I'd help Petey get dressed. I really wanted to spend a few minutes with her before the banquet, so Arch would watch LoJ while I took my beautifully coifed daughter to Millie's house. Then I'd hurry back, take a luxurious bath, Mary Lou would fix my hair, and I'd arrive at the debate relaxed and looking like a model.

I usually run helter-skelter and things go awry, but when I organize my thoughts, my movements, my plans, things are perfectly executed. Well, most times . . . sometimes . . . okay, seldom. But tomorrow would be a good day, and everything would be just right. I would set my Byrd determination in action and make it come out that way.

Nana Bryd used to tell me if there was enough blue in the sky to make a pair of britches, it wouldn't rain. Thursday morning, the sun shone brightly, a pleasantly cool breeze blew, and I could make a whole suit out of the blue in the sky. What a gorgeous day.

Other than a phone call from Tim Tuten to remind me not to be late because I would forfeit the debate, time dragged by. Finally five o'clock came, and I went home. Right on schedule, Arch had dinner on the table. Petey had already bathed. Soon she looked like a princess on her way to the ball.

When Arch hugged her goodbye, I think I saw mist in his eyes. I squeezed his arm to let him know I understood exactly what he was feeling. His baby girl was growing up. I felt the mixture of joy and sadness tugging at my heart just as he did.

At Millie's, I walked inside with Petey. M&M were ready to go. Just as I knew they would, they both looked lovely. The two may be slightly off balance in their wayward thinking, but they knew how to dress like they just stepped out of a band box.

"You ladies look very nice." I entered their living room.

"Why, thank you, dear. I'm wearing Mavis' clothes, and she's wearing mine. Thought we'd shake things up a bit." Millie made a dramatic spin, staggered a little, but caught herself on the arm of the sofa.

"Easy there, Millie. You know your reflexes aren't what they used to be." Mavis helped her to her seat.

Once they were through, I announced, "Presenting Princess Petey Fortney." I made a grand gesture and bowed at the waist.

"Oh, my." Mavis rushed to Petey. "You're the prettiest thing I've seen since Mickey showed me his 'Longfellow' tattoo across his—"

"Mavis," I shouted so loud everyone jumped. "Sorry, but I don't think we need to hear about anything pertaining to Old Coach Henderson, especially his tattoos. Understand?" I raised my eyebrows hoping she would get the idea such talk was not appropriate in front of little pitchers. Or me, for that matter.

I didn't slow her down a bit. "It's just across his chest. You have a dirty mind, young lady. You better go on home and wash it out with soap."

"You don't wash your mind out with soap for having dirty thoughts. You wash your mouth out for saying bad words."

"Well, of course you do, so run on home and do that."

Petey tried not to burst out laughing.

"Okay, whatever. I do have to run. Now, you are walking to the church, not driving the Caddy, right?" I didn't want to worry about Mavis driving with my precious cargo in the car.

"Yes, just to make you happy, we are walking the short distance, but if I throw my back into spasms, it will be your fault."

"I'll take that responsibility." I turned to Petey who was still giggling under her breath.

"You three are so funny. Some day I'm going to write a book about my childhood," she said.

"Great. What part will I be? Surely not the wicked stepmother?"

"No, ma'am. I think I'll make it about a mama bear and two chipmunks and change the names to protect the innocent, but you'll know who you are."

"We'll be like Chip and Dale," Mavis announced proudly.

"Oh, oh." Millie must have had a thought. Stand back. "That reminds me the dancers are going to be at the Round-Up in Lumpkin next Saturday. Want to go with us, Bertie?"

"Let me think about that. No!"

Shortly, I was on my way home, clearing my head of thoughts of

M&M and how good or bad an influence they really were on Petey, when traffic came to a dead stop. I fished my cell phone out of my pocket and called Linc's number.

"I'm stopped on 440. Are you working an accident around there anywhere?"

"Carrie Sue and I both are. We're at Bishop Road."

"I'm just a few blocks away. I'll see if I can work my way up there."

I pitched my cell phone on the passenger's seat and drove along the shoulder and managed to get within hiking distance of the crash scene. A tractor/trailer hauling live chickens on their way to be slaughtered had turned onto its side. Chickens were squawking and flopping inside wooden crates. Some had escaped and were running around like chickens . . . well, you know.

The company officials were on the scene, and they were loading the crates onto an empty flatbed. Carrie Sue and Linc chased the loose ones and re-caged them. I helped for about ten minutes.

"Bertie, you're going to be late for the debate." Carrie Sue took the two chickens I had in my hands. "Look at you. You have feathers all over you, especially in your hair. They've stuck to your hair spray." She gently shoved me toward my car. "We can take care of this. Get out of here and knock 'em dead tonight, Mrs. Councilwoman."

"Thanks." I hurried on my way. It was late. I would have to settle for a quick shower instead of a luxurious bath, but that would be okay. Mary Lou would already be waiting at the house for me so she could fix my hair. My new purple outfit awaited me, and I would look very distinguished.

The faster I drove, the more I realized I wasn't going to make it all the way home without having an accident, and I didn't mean a car crash. I had to pee, and I had to pee now. Where would be the closest bathroom? A brilliant idea came to me in my time of need. In the next block was Karo Stevens' home. I set up his outhouse so many times surely I deserved to use it at least one time.

I skidded to a stop in front of his house and scurried across the grass to the little brown shack out back. Luck was with me. It was unlocked. I hurried in, unzipped my coveralls, and am glad to report I made it in the tick of nine. I mean, in the nick of time.

Relief had just washed over me when I heard a loud noise at the door. "Someone's in here," I said.

"I know you are and that's where you're staying until the sheriff gets here to take you to jail. I'm through having to pay that towing shyster every time she has to set this back up just because you hooligans think it's fun to destroy property. Well, I got you now, and you're going to pay."

I hurriedly finished what I'd come there for and got my clothes back on. "Mr. Stevens, it's me. Bertie Fortney. I just stopped by to use your toilet. I didn't think you would mind."

"You can't build a fort in my toilet, you ingrate. You just find you a seat in there, and the police will be here soon."

I glanced at my watch. I hoped it would be soon. Tim said I'd forfeit the whole debate if I was late. I still had all that girly stuff I wanted to do to look good for my constituents.

I pounded on the door of the outhouse. Not something I ever remember having to do in my lifetime, but I could now mark it off my life's list of things I wanted to do before I died.

"Mr. Stevens, dear, you have to let me out of here. I'm going to be late for a debate."

"You're crazy if you think you can spew that rap crap at me and make me open the door. Deer out of here. Late for a debate," Karo chanted like the rapper Snoop Dogg on prune juice.

Is it required that when old age sets in, you must go crazy, too? By the behavior of the senior citizens I came into contact with, it seemed that way. Was there a pill I could take to keep it from happening to me? I'd worry about that later. Right then I had to get out of the trap Mr. Stevens had set for the boys who'd been harassing him.

I dug in my pocket for my cell phone. "Dang." It was in my car. If I could call Tim, he could come and get me. The sun was fading fast. Luckily, my watch had a lighted dial. Six-twenty-three. Why were the police taking so long? Oh, yeah, the chicken wreck had all of them tied up. Oh, no. It could take hours before they responded to Mr. Stevens' call.

I plopped down on the seat and hung my head. All the hype of Sweet Meadow's big debate was in the toilet. Pardon the pun.

For the next twenty minutes, I begged and pleaded with the bullheaded old man on the other side of the door. I couldn't believe I'd given him the idea to put a lock on the outside of his toilet and it was being used to hold me captive.

Alone, except for a pesky flying bug, I paced the small confines of the dark room. I could feel the time tick away and my chance to come face to face with my opponent and argue the pros and cons of our platforms dissolve with each passing minute.

"Ouch!" Without notice, the insect stung my right cheek.

Being held prisoner, in excruciating pain, and quickly becoming despondent, I began to have a hissy fit. Obscenities filled the small room and hung like blue smoke overhead.

"That filthy mouth of yours is not helping your situation. Young people today have no respect for their elders, or else they wouldn't use such language in front of women, children, and old people."

You might know that old Karo hadn't heard a word I said to this point, but let me use language I wouldn't want anyone to know I'd uttered, and his hearing magically reappeared. I parked my exhausted body onto the toilet seat and buried my aching, bug-bitten face in my hands and tried not to cry.

At six forty-five, I heard male voices outside and the two-by-four barricade slid from the brackets that held it. The door swung open and a bright light blinded me. Shading the glare as much as possible, I stepped out into the cool night air.

"Bertie?" Carl Kelly lowered his flashlight so it didn't shine directly in my eyes.

"Oh, yeah. It's me."

"What are you doing in there?"

"I had an emergency. I didn't think this old goat would mind if I used his toilet. After all, I spent a lot of time and energy keeping it in an upright position, but evidently I was wrong. Here." I held my hands out in front of me. "Put the cuffs on if you're going to. I might as well go to jail. It's too late for me to go to the Garden Club to debate Booger."

Carl looked at his watch. "You're not going to press charges on her, are you, Karo?" Mr. Stevens appeared to be thinking about it. "Karo, you remember that little matter of you relieving yourself in the courthouse bushes that I chose to ignore and not run you in for?"

Mr. Stevens nodded. "Okay, I don't know why she just didn't

tell me it was her, and I'd have let her out."

I'd just escaped being arrested for trespassing. I didn't want to up that charge to assault on a senior citizen, so I didn't try to explain I'd hollered until I was hoarse, nor did I slug Karo like I really wanted to.

"I am supposed to be at the Garden Club in ten minutes, but since I can't get home, get dressed, and make it back there in that amount of time, I just forfeited the debate and probably the election."

Carl took my hand and dragged me down the slight embankment to my car. He opened my door and shoved me in.

"Follow me." He ran to his car, started it, and turned on the lights and siren. We were off so fast I didn't have time to think of how I looked. I just saw an opportunity to get there. It was all that mattered. No, actually, chasing Carl Kelly at a high rate of speed gave me an even bigger adrenalin rush.

Chapter 13

I made it to the Garden Club with five minutes to spare. All the
bits of information, facts, and statistics Tim had been feeding me
all week began to bounce around inside my head. Sweet Meadows
population was 8,302. Or was that for all of Shafer County? I could
just about name everyone who lived in Sweet Meadow and count
them out, but, of course, that would take a while.

At the entrance of the mansion, Tim and Arch, pushing LoJ in
a stroller, paced like expectant fathers. When they saw me being
escorted by one of Sweet Meadow's policeman with lights flashing
and sirens blaring, they ran to meet me.

Arch yanked open my door. "Are you okay? I've been worried
sick."

I hurriedly exited my car. "I'm fine. Just a misunderstanding.
I'll tell you about it later."

Tim looked like he'd been hit between the eyes with a two-by-
four. "Couldn't you have at least fixed your hair? Maybe plucked a
few chicken feathers out of it?" He looked me up and down. "Wait
a minute. You know, Arch, your wife is pretty smart. Good idea to
let the voters see what you look like at the end of the day because

you are a hardworking business owner who isn't afraid to get her hands dirty. In your case, they'll see you smudged from head to toe. Personally, I would have foregone the feathers, but the rest works for me."

I didn't have the energy to argue with Tim. I would need what little bit of fight I had left to go toe-to-toe with Booger. Tim dragged me up the walkway, and Arch followed.

"Remember, make eye contact with people in the audience. You want them to feel like you are talking directly to them and that you understand their concerns. Don't let Booger rattle your cage about anything. I listened to his talk at the Garden Club a few nights ago. When he was asked something he didn't have a solid answer for, his demeanor became belligerent. Don't let that catch you off guard."

"And for heaven's sake, don't resort to childish behavior like shouting *nana nana booboo*," Arch said.

"Yes, for sure, and it goes without saying that sticking out your tongue at your opponent is totally off limits," Tim added.

"I'll try to behave myself." My pores exuded sarcasm. Who did these macho guys think they were dealing with? I could be as adult as the next person when it was required. I hoped.

I ran into the Garden Club ballroom, raced up the stage steps two at a time, and stopped when my body slammed into the podium. I righted the microphone and made it squeal in protest.

Arch and Tim took their seats in the front row. Tim started patting the side of his head. It finally sank into my befuddled brain that he was trying to tell me something. Instinctively, I touched my own hair. My ponytail, which had started out at the back of my head, had moved itself to the side. I ducked behind the podium, pulled the rubber band free, and fluffed my hair. Feathers floated to the ground.

Standing up quickly, I flipped my mane back in a *Charlie's Angel* move. All the rapid motion unbalanced me. I held onto the dais to keep from falling and tried to look composed.

Cy Linder, the moderator, introduced the candidates.

"Before we start, I'd like you to meet Roberta 'Bertie' Fortney and opposing candidate Jasper 'Booger' Bailey."

The audience offered obligatory applause. I could tell by the stares and Tim's actions that there were other things wrong with my appearance. Suddenly, Mary Lou appeared from backstage. She handed me a compact mirror. With my flair for the dramatic, I'd caused my auburn locks to stick straight out.

I pulled my grease rag from the back pocket of my coveralls and removed a streak of something black from my cheek. While I used the compact powder to cover the horrendous bee sting on my other cheek, which was swelling bigger with each passing moment, my dear friend beat my hair into submission. Just as she ran from the stage, the bell rang, and the debates were on.

"In a coin toss, Booger won the right to bring up the first item for discussion." Cy retreated backstage. I wanted to go with him, but, of course, I couldn't.

"Well, missy, so you believe you're the best man for the council?" Let the games begin.

"I believe I'm as qualified as you are, Mr. Bailey." I crossed my arms and tapped my fingers on my elbows.

"It's my understanding you wanted the council to dip into their Christmas Fund to buy a traffic counter. That shows lack of respect for the hard work the men on the council do during the year. I believe they should have their once-a-year time to relax and let their hair down."

If they had any.

"Then you waged a war against them and compelled them to spend the reserved money on a stop light. With that happening, they've been forced to forego their usual upscale barbeque or Chinese buffet and settle for Billy Bob's Fried Chicken. What do you have to say about that?"

Tim Tuten had worked hard at gathering tidbits of knowledge and relaying them to me. Pumped by the fact I could retain more than water, I faced Booger with confidence.

"Is it true that one of their choices, the barbeque to be precise, would have been supplied by you, at a price, of course? Now that they have gone in a different direction, you are left out in the cold. Is that the reason this issue is first on your hot-topic list?"

"Well . . . of course not. I'm thinking of the councilmen."

"Yeah, right."

I glanced at Tim who was slowly shaking his head to remind me to stay in control. I forced a smile and waited to see if Booger had more to say on the subject. Of course, he did.

"I didn't see the need for a stop light at Oak and Haverford when a stop sign would have worked just as well."

"We already had a stop sign on Haverford, but the heavy traffic flying by at a high rate of speed made pulling onto Oak dangerous. The stop light gives everyone the opportunity to go about their business in an orderly fashion."

"I'm eyeball-to-eyeball with that kind of thinking." Booger

pointed a V-shaped finger formation at my face and then back to his. He was either saying he could relate to my opinion or he was putting a curse on me. I couldn't be sure.

Grasping both of his lapels, sucking in his gut, and hefting his stout body to a straighter stance, he looked into the audience. "I believe there could have been a less costly answer to the problem. It just takes logical thinking."

"And what would that be, Mr. Barking Goats?"

Snickers rose from the crowd. I looked out over them and rolled my eyes.

"A more reasonable solution would have been to put in a school zone. Therefore, the people on Oak would be going slow enough to allow Haverford traffic to ease out."

He wet his finger and marked an imaginary tick for his side in the air.

"There's no school within five miles of that place." Mark one up for me.

"I know that, but they'd still have to slow if the signs said so. Sure would be a lot less costly than the full-fledged traffic light." He did a short victory dance. His son Art called out, "Go, Daddy. It's your birthday. Go, Daddy."

I dusted a few feathers from my coveralls and pretended not to pay any attention to the overgrown toad on the stage with me.

When the natives calmed, Cy told me to present my first topic for discussion. I glanced at the comprehensive notes Tim had made for me.

"Since we're on the subject of unnecessary costs to the city, I'd like to address the matter of the water management project near

Councilman Linder's house. I'm sure we've all seen the site. There's a sign announcing the project which, according to my findings, cost the city four-hundred and fifty dollars. The sign is placed at the beginning of a ditch which runs along side of Cy's property.

"On two occasions I've seen no fewer than two city workers out there digging in the ditch to drain the standing water. It's also been brought to my attention that an engineer was sent out there to evaluate the situation before the digging began. The engineer is the project manager. Are you seeing the dollar signs dancing above my head?"

"I thought those were chicken feathers," Dr. Johns yelled from the audience. I made a mental note to charge him double next time he needed a tow.

"When the council was approached about why this elaborate and costly project was approved, we were told Mrs. Linder complained because the standing water was a breeding hole for mosquitoes, and the insects had bitten her poodle on the nose.

"I find this a very foolish waste of money, and if I'm elected I'll do my best to see a more sensible approach is taken to remedy situations like this."

I paused to take a deep breath. Booger took it as a cue for his rebuttal.

"So what would you have the officials do? Grab a can of bug spray and run out there every few days?" I think Booger mumbled *women* under his breath, but since the room erupted with jeers and laughter, it was hard to tell.

"That's pretty close to the solution I would recommend." I had everyone's attention. "I have ditches laced with mosquitoes near my house. Don't you, Ethel?" I motioned to the elderly lady in the third row. She nodded.

"What about you, Elton? Do you have a ditch with standing water?"

"Sure do."

"If we all complained, it would not be feasible to set up a water management project complete with engineer/manager and workers to dig every ditch in town."

"Don't forget the four-hundred-fifty dollar sign," Elton reminded us.

"Right. In my investigations." I felt like a liar saying that. It wasn't *my* investigation at all. Tim did all the work, and I took the credit. The words didn't taste right. "I should say in the investigation completed in this matter, it was pointed out to me the city owns a mosquito control truck which could go up and down the streets on a regular basis and spray all the areas to rid them of insects. However, no one could tell us why it was no longer being used."

"I can." Jacob Winchell stood. "There's a problem with the motor. The city council won't allot the money for it to be repaired."

"I guarantee fixing it would take less money than the major production going on at the Linder's house. It would also benefit the whole town." I turned to Booger. "What is your take on this matter?"

"I don't really know anything about it, but I have a bit of video tape I think the fine citizens of Sweet Meadow might find interesting before they make their final decision on which of us would serve them better." He pointed to the back of the room. "Kill the lights."

Suddenly the room went dark and someone projected a home video onto a large screen behind the stage. I stepped aside, expecting to see an advertisement about and produced by my opponent. In a perfect world where life flows smoothly from alpha to omega, that would be what I saw. But life never flows smoothly in my world.

Instead, before my blurry eyes appeared the movie Alice from the *Old Bat's Antiques* had taken of me the day I was counting cars. The one where I waved at passing cars, snagged a potato chip from a bag, popped in my mouth, and then wiped my greasy fingers on my pants. I did that over and over and over until the whole crowd was lost in a world of tormented laughter.

I raised my hand. Soon they quieted. "I know that was good comic relief, but I have a short closing remark I'd like to make." The lights came back on. "I'm sure some of you wonder why I'm dressed in this manner, when my opponent appears to be dressed more professionally.

"The truth of the matter is I'm a mother, a wife, and a business owner. I work hard every day providing a service almost every one of you has required at some time or other. Although I may look a little worse today than usual, the fact remains that I take my jobs, all of them, very seriously. And if I'm elected to our city council, I'll work just as hard for you.

"Thank you for your attention. I'm going home." I stepped down from the stage.

To my surprise, I received a standing ovation from over half the audience. I acknowledged them with a few silent *thank yous*. Although I appreciated their encouragement, all I wanted to do was collect my little family and go home and lock the door behind us.

Several people came to shake my hand and congratulate me. Once I made my way outside, I found Tim and Arch waiting for me.

"You did really well." Tim gave me a light kiss on my cheek. Years ago, I would have wiped it off and yelled at him for giving me cooties. Today, I welcomed it.

Arch hugged me. "I'm so proud of you."

Suddenly, it all seemed worthwhile. Maybe I had made a better showing than I first believed. Maybe this was something I could do to help the community. Maybe.

Arch opened the door for me. "You go on home and take a nice hot bath. I'll pick up Petey, and we'll be home shortly."

"I'm not sure I have the energy for a hot bath."

Arch sniffed me. "Sweetheart, I think you should find the energy. Your new cologne has lost its appeal."

"You're right. A nice hot bath will do the trick."

"And about a cup of that smelly bubble bath you bought last week will help, too."

I drove away. Tomorrow I would pick out only the good stuff from this day and concentrate on it. How beautiful Petey looked; Arch was proud of me; Tim said I did a good job; the majority of the audience was in my camp; and my *eau de chicken poop* cologne would be gone. I hurried home.

I'd just gotten out of the tub and slipped into a warm, fuzzy robe. At the front of the house I could hear my family coming in the door. After the day I had, nothing could have brought me more pleasure.

"Mom? We're home." Petey yelled like a fish wife.

I joined them in the living room. "So I hear. How'd it go? Did

Millie and Mavis behave themselves?"

"Yes, ma'am, they were perfect ladies." Petey had something behind her back.

"What'cha got there?"

"It's a surprise for you. Sit down."

I slowly took a seat on the sofa and looked up at Arch who was holding LoJ. I couldn't name the look on Petey's face. "Will it bite me?" I asked.

"No, silly." She pulled a plaque from behind her back. "You were picked as Mother of the Year."

Paralyzed with emotions only a mother could feel, I simply stared at the words on the plaque: *Presented To Roberta "Bertie" Fortney, a well deserving Mother of the Year.*

Not long ago I was thrilled just to be a mother and now this. "Oh, my goodness. I don't know what to say."

"You don't have to say anything. I told them 'thank you' for it."

"Did they give you any idea why they chose me?"

"Each one of us girls had to write an essay about why we thought our mother should be Mother of the Year. Mine won."

Amazing how cosmic forces balanced the good and the bad. On one hand, my day had been one of the worst ever, but that night, life flooded my heart and soul with a kind of happiness I'd never experienced. I loved the way it made me feel.

"Oh, my. I may cry." I did!

Petey wiped a tear from my cheek. "It looks like you already are. I have the letter for you to read, but Dad said you'd probably rather read it while you're alone because you don't like to cry in front of other people."

"He's . . . right," I managed to mumble through sobs.

"My teacher framed my letter and gave it to me." Petey handed it to me.

I hugged her and held on for a long time. "Thank you. I love you so much. How did I ever get so lucky?"

"I love you, too. I hope you don't drown in all those tears. Maybe I shouldn't do anything nice for you again."

I drew back to look at her face. She started laughing.

"I guess that proves you don't have to be born with a dry wit, doesn't it?" Arch commented. "Apparently, you can catch it from your stepmother." His wide smile wormed its way into my heart and electrified my whole body.

"Bedtime, Petey," he said. "You go get ready while I put LoJ down. Mom and I will be in to say goodnight in a few minutes."

He turned to face me. "I'm so proud of you. You handled your-self so well under difficult and unfamiliar circumstances at the debate tonight. I believe you have a real chance of winning. And I'd really like to tell you how much I appreciate the job you are doing raising our girls, but I don't think you need to see me cry, too." He left.

Tomorrow, when my emotions were on steadier ground, I'd be sure to tell him that without his love I wouldn't be the person I was.

I ran my hand over my Mother-of-the-Year plaque. The cool wood and its beautiful lettering took it all from surreal to reality. I, Bertie Bryd-Fortney, who, a couple of years ago thought marriage and chil-dren were never going to happen for the female grease monkey and tow truck driver I was, now held in my grubby little hands validation that of all the hats I wear, motherhood was my best endeavor.

I lay the plaque aside. I couldn't wait another minute to read the letter Petey had written.

I'd like to nominate my mom for Mother of the Year because she works hard every day and always shows my dad, my sister, and me how much she loves us. My real mother died when I was very young. The mom I have now is the only mother I've ever known.

She lets me do neat stuff as long as she knows what I'm doing and who I'm with and when I'll be home, and who the chaperons are. She has to know all that stuff because she loves me. My friend Randy says she loves me too much, but I don't mind because I've missed out on a lot of years of my mother's love, so I'm making up for lost time.

My mom started loving me even before she and my dad got married. She says that just because she didn't grow me in her tummy didn't mean I couldn't grow in her heart.

I tell everyone my mom is a good mother and Dad says she's a good wife. She owns her own business and is racing with that Booger guy to be the only woman on our city council. And even though she is that busy, she tucks me in every night.

The thing I love my mother the most for is giving me a baby sister that some day I can boss around. I hope you pick my mom for Mother of the Year. If she wins, I know she will cry.

Petey Fortney.

The good news is that my heart swelled with a kind of pride I'd never known before. My arms ached to hold the precious child who had put the pride there. The bad news was that, although I loved tucking Petey in, I'd have to do it while blubbering like Jimmy Swaggart when he got caught sinning. I hoped she hadn't made a bet with Millie about whether I'd cry or not because then I'd have to have a talk with my daughter about the pitfalls of gambling.

On my way down the hall to tuck her in, I suddenly felt confident that if the need for a talk arose, I'd be able to handle it. After all, I was Roberta "Bertie" Fortney, Mother of the Year.

The next day I left work around noon. After the week I had, Arch and I spending a weekend on a houseboat cruising Lake Reavis with my brothers and their wives sounded pretty good. Petey and LoJ were staying with Mom and Pop.

LoJ spent every day with them, but Petey seldom had the chance. She loved the opportunity to do crafts with my mom and jitterbug with my dad, the dancing fool.

By the time Arch and Petey came in from school, I was armed and ready to make my great escape from Sweet Meadow.

When we got there, Billy, his wife, Nancy Diane, Bobby and his wife, Estelle, were in the parking lot unloading their cars. Orange and yellow streaks of fading sunlight shimmered across the water. A cool breeze blew from the lake. I could already feel my muscles relaxed and my brain zoned to a level of barely functioning. My favorite state of being.

Once we hauled everything to the fifty-foot houseboat and plopped it down, my two brothers and I took one look at each other and quickly scattered like roaches when a kitchen light comes on.

Our spouses cleared a path, knowing full well bodily injury could occur when the Byrd kids decided to claim something for their own.

Billy climbed a ladder leading to a loft. At the end of the hallway, Bobby knocked his baby sister out of his way. In one leap, he bounded onto the bed in a tiny cubical.

"This is mine and Estelle's." Bobby stretched out on the bed and put his hands behind his head. "You get the sleeper sofa up front, Ro-Bert-A."

I climbed a couple of rungs of the ladder and found Billy also stretched out. "We still have to put everything away. Get your scrawny butt out here and help."

"I'm coming. I just want to mark my territory," Billy said.

Back in the front of the boat, Estelle and Nancy Diane were putting groceries into the galley. Arch carried our luggage to the sofa.

"Billy," Nancy Diane bellowed. "What are you doing up there?"

"He said he's marking his territory. I guess that means he's peeing on the bed." I loaded the cold stuff into the small refrigerator.

He jumped half-way down the ladder. "I was not. I was just making a smart remark, Bertie. Good Lord, you're going to be a barrel of laughs on this outing, aren't you?"

Nancy Diane shoved a gym bag against his chest. "Here, mark my territory, too. Take these things to our room. And make the bed while you're up there."

Billy dropped the bag, grabbed her, and blew a raspberry against her cheek. After she'd wiped away his slobber, he had the unmitigated gall to do the same to me.

"I hope you're happy. Now, I'm going to die of cooties, and it'll be your fault." I dried my face on a paper towel.

"Here," Estelle handed him a second gym bag, "take this to Bobby and tell him to make our bed. Sheets are in there."

He pitched one bag into the bedroom. I heard Bobby grunt when it hit him. Billy climbed a ladder and disappeared into an upper berth.

In no time at all, we were unpacked, beds made including Arch's and my sofa bed, and we were ready for the fun to begin. Since it was dark, we spent the night at the dock and planned to set sail at sunrise.

On the back deck, we all sat in lawn chairs, eating bologna and cheese sandwiches and drinking a cool, nutritious beverage. Okay, it was beer, but it was light beer.

"This is nice. You guys've done this several other times, haven't you?" Arch asked.

"Yeah, my company carries the policies on the rental business. As a perk, the owner lets me use one of the boats two times a year," Bobby explained.

"This is the fifth time we've used it." Billy pulled another drink from the ice chest.

"It's roomier than I expected it to be." My mind kept drifting back to Sweet Meadow and the girls. "We could have brought the kids and still had plenty of room."

"We brought them the first time we ventured out here, but three days in a confined area was a little hard at times," Nancy Diane said. "They like to run around and with so little space inside, or even here on the deck, it cramped their style. And, there's only so long they could swim."

"When they were up on the top deck, they had more room, but we constantly worried about them falling overboard." Estelle smacked a mosquito on Bobby's arm. She hooked her thumb at him. "He kept telling them to go outside and play like they had a yard to run in."

"The truth of the matter is that Bobby and I decided it wasn't good for the kids to see their mothers topless and drunk, so we just started leaving them at home." Billy received a love tap from Nancy Diane, one which would probably fade after a few days.

"Billy, that's a terrible thing to say," I scolded.

"Actually, the next year we took all the kids to Wild Adventures down in Valdosta for a whole weekend. They enjoyed themselves so much we've made it a tradition. First, we take them there and then we come here." Estelle made it sound like a neatly tied package, but I felt guilty my two girls hadn't been given a choice. We took them to Mom and Pop's and kissed them goodbye.

"I think I'll give Mom a call." Inside, I pulled my cell phone from my purse and took it to the upper deck.

Petey answered on the second ring.

"Hey, sweetheart, everything going okay?"

"It sure is. Grandma and I made pearls out of water, flour, and food coloring. I strung a bunch of pink ones together and made a necklace." Petey certainly didn't sound dejected for being left behind.

I was the one feeling a little like Gloomy Gus. I should have been the one who taught my daughter to make the flour dough necklace, just like my Nana Byrd had taught me. Suddenly, remembering the fun I had with my own grandmother eased some of my guilt.

My mom and Petey were building memories that would follow her for the rest of her life. When bad or sad times came, she'd pull from those fun times filed in her heart and make things a little better. Just like Nana Byrd had done for me.

"How's LoJ doing?"

"Happy as a clam. That's what Poppy said." Petey laughed.

"I suppose he showed you his clam impression, didn't he?"

"You should have seen him. He took out his teeth and scrunched his lips, noses and forehead all down and then stuck out his tongue. I don't know what a live clam is supposed to look like, but if it looks like Poppy, I would have to laugh in its face."

Her enthusiasm lightened my worried heart, and her description brought an instant smile to my face. "I have seen him, many times, and you're right, he always made me laugh, too." I imagined having Petey with them probably reminded them of when I was young.

Satisfied my girls didn't feel abandoned, I spoke to Mom just long enough to make sure she had things under control. Back below I found the rest of the group excitedly reflecting on the pleasure they were expecting during the next few days—cruising the shore line, fishing, reading, and napping.

The cool fall air kept swimming from being an option. I, for one, found comfort in that because I didn't think I could handle watching my sisters-in-law sunbathe topless. Surely, Billy was kidding about that. Wasn't he?

I moved my chair closer to Arch and snuggled in the crook of his arm.

"Everything okay?" he asked.

"I don't think the girls will need therapy because we left them, but Petey may need some to get over the look of my father imitating a clam."

I would need some if Estelle and Nancy Diane sunbathed topless.

Chapter 14

Bright and early Saturday morning, Bobby launched the house-boat for a day of puttering around the lake in search of the perfect fishing spot. For me, not having to deal with high drama or having to make a decision would make my day perfect.

By lunch time I read half of a novel I'd been wanting to read since before I was married. Our three sportsmen put their fishing poles away.

"Arch is the only one who even had a nibble." Bobby took a bite of his sandwich.

"I still say I just snagged something on the bottom."

"The end results are the same. We have nothing to fry for dinner," Nancy Diane evaluated the situation.

"Sweetie, the day isn't over yet. Is it, men?" Billy roused the other two.

"No," they shouted together.

"Finish those vittles, and get back out there," Estelle said.

"Right, and don't come home until your stringer's full." My turn.

"Everyone knows early morning and late afternoon are the best fishing times." Bobby took the last slug of his beer. "Just as fishermen go home for lunch and take a nap, so do the fish. Wake me when it's time to go back out."

Billy followed Bobby down the short passageway. "Me, too."

Arch eyed the sofa. "Me three."

My sisters-in-law and I took advantage of having the upper deck to ourselves. At night, autumn briskness filled the air, but the noon sun hovering overhead sent its warmth directly to the open area at the top of the houseboat.

Nancy Diane stared toward the shoreline, and I followed her gaze. The leaves were just starting to change color. I've never been sure which season inspired me the most. Spring, when flowers splashed patches of color next to the fresh green trees and shrubs. Or fall, when the landscape appeared to be on fire with bursts of orange, yellow, and red.

Probably fall because Thanksgiving and Christmas wouldn't be far behind. My favorite holidays because, to me, they brought families together, even if they were apart most of the year. My family, kooky though they may be, meant everything to me. I recognized how much like a huge chocolate sundae they were. They were sweet, made me smile, brought me happiness, and were filled with nuts.

When I looked at Nancy Diane and wondered what she was thinking, I really knew how lucky I was. Her life had not been as ideal as mine.

"Are you okay?" I asked.

She appeared to drag her thoughts back from a long way off and managed to force a smile.

"Yeah. It was twenty-five years ago today I lost my twin sister.

Guess I'm feeling a little weepy." She wiped away a tear.

I consoled her the only way I knew how—by squeezing her hand and remaining quiet. I'd heard bits of the story a couple of times since she and Billy married, but no one talked about it very much because it was so traumatic for Nancy Diane that she had spent several years in therapy.

Estelle lay stretched out on a bench seat. Sunglasses covering her eyes made it hard to tell if she was asleep or not. After a few moments of complete silence, she sat up and moved next to Nancy Diane.

"It's been a long time since you've talked about Nancy Denise. Twenty-five years is a milestone. You know Bertie and I love you, so maybe it might help if you tell us how you're feeling."

Estelle had an unquenchable thirst for knowledge and constantly took adult courses at her local high school. Wonder what she was studying at that particular time that made her think she could delve into someone else's psyche?

"Night school psychology?" My inquiring mind wanted to know.

"Correspondence course," she and Nancy Diane said together.

"You don't have to say a word if you don't want, but I was pretty young when you and Billy married, and I've only heard bits and pieces about your sister. If you think it might help to tell me about it, I'd really like to hear, but only if you want to."

"Actually, when I woke up this morning, I had an overwhelming desire to talk about Nancy Denise, but I've kept it inside for so long, I was afraid I'd fly apart." She smiled weakly.

"Ah, go for it." Estelle pulled Nancy Diane close to her. "We'll put you back together. Won't we, Bertie?"

"You bet. We can do our own private tribute to Nancy Denise.

Start by telling us how you two have such strange names." I shifted to get comfortable.

"Mom didn't know she was having twins, but she insisted that if she had a girl she wanted her named Nancy. She told Dad he could pick the middle name, but he couldn't decide between Diane and Denise. When we were born and there were two of us, the decision was made." My sister-in-law smiled.

"What's the best thing you remember about your sister?" Estelle asked.

"She was smarter than me. She could sing. And she loved chocolate cake."

"If she passed away twenty-five years ago, that means you must have been what?" I did the math. "Seventeen?"

"We were sixteen." Nancy Diane's voice faltered slightly. "We'd both had our driver's license for a few months. Mom sent us to the store for a gallon of milk. It's funny, but I haven't drank milk since that day."

I thought about that for a moment. With the way I loved milk, I wasn't sure I could give it up.

"What happened?" Estelle broke my short trip from reality.

"I wanted to go by my friend's house to show off, but Nancy Denise kept saying we would get in trouble. Mom had said for us to go straight to the store and back. I called my sister a fuddy-duddy and went anyway. We didn't stay long, but when we backed out of my friend's driveway, I was so caught up with impressing her with my driving, I didn't look for oncoming traffic. I pulled right in front of a full-size pickup." She sucked in a ragged breath. "Nancy Denise died instantly."

"I'm so sorry that happened to you." I couldn't imagine what she must have gone through.

"Me, too. It took several years of therapy for me to accept the fact I'd done something stupid, and my sister paid the ultimate price. I constantly prayed God would come into my room in the middle of the night and bring her back and take me instead."

"How were you able to come to terms with it?" I asked.

"Some days I still haven't. I had a very good doctor who convinced me I would eventually learn from the experience and go on to do greater things for mankind because I understood what it was like to lose half of myself. The best half, I might add."

Suddenly, the air hung heavy with misery. While I ran through my witty repertoire searching for a way to lighten the sadness, Nancy Diane took the problem out of my hands.

"Then I met Billy Byrd of the infamous Byrd boys, and all those hours of lying around on my doctor's couch became perfectly clear. Billy and I melded together like the chocolate and marshmallows in hot S'mores."

I covered my ears. "I don't want to hear anything about you two melding."

"You'll want to hear, so listen." She laughed out loud. "Billy and I weren't together very long until I realized how much he needed me to make him whole. And the best part was I am the best half of that deal."

It was my turn to laugh. "Actually, my dear sister-in-law, it all worked out for the best. Heavy therapy is the only way you would have ever been able to live with Billy in the first place. I'm his sister. I know these things."

"I'm his wife, and you speak the truth."

"Don't you two feel sorry for me?" Estelle asked. "I have the other brother, and I have to put up with him without the benefit of psychiatry." She did an exaggerated shiver.

I'd always felt close to my sisters-in-law, but us all hee-hawing like mules at my brothers' expense bonded us even more. They were the sisters I never had, but always wanted. Finally, the scales were tipped to my side. Life was good.

"Come on." I pulled Nancy Diane and Estelle to their feet. We went below to the galley where I cut four large pieces of chocolate cake and poured four glasses of cold milk.

Nancy Diane looked puzzled, and then the dawn of understanding crossed her face. We raised our red plastic cups. "To Nancy Denise. You are loved and missed," I toasted, and we all clicked our cups together.

Nancy Diane hesitated a moment and then took a drink of milk. Her first in twenty-five years. She smacked her lips. "Pretty good." We dug into the chocolate cake with gusto. "My sister would have loved this."

At that moment, Arch got up from his nap. He stopped at the end of the table and looked at the unclaimed cake and milk. I looked at Nancy Diane. She slid the plate and cup to him. "Here. Knock yourself out."

He gathered his prize and went outside. She watched him until he was happily dining on cake and milk. She looked back at us. "I didn't have the heart to tell him it belonged to my deceased sister."

Estelle and I waited to see if she'd meant it as a joke. Nancy Diane laughed until she snorted and we, of course, joined her.

By the end of the day, it became apparent the fish had gone home for a nap and wouldn't be back. The fearless fishermen gave up their quest and settled for watching a football game on the small, three-channeled television.

Estelle and Nancy Diane busied themselves fixing dinner. They used the excuse the galley was too small for three chefs, but the pattern of they-cook-I-wash had been established when they first married into the family. Since cooking had never been my strong suit, the old pattern worked fine for me.

On the back deck, I decided to drown a worm or two. Since the pros hadn't managed to hook a fish, I didn't expect to either. Boy, was I wrong. The bait barely hit the water before I was in a desperate struggle with what I was sure was a twenty-five pound bass. My squeals of exhilaration brought the rest of the group running.

"That's it, Ro-Bert-A, show us all up." Bobby hung a scoop net over the back of the boat.

"Good job, sweetheart." Arch sounded proud.

"Want me to bring it in for you?" Billy asked.

"Not in this lifetime, brother." I continued to pull and reel for several long minutes. My arms ached. The rod bent to touch the water. The fish broke the surface in what would have been a graceful leap. Unfortunately, I'd chosen that exact moment to yank the pole with all my might. The bass sailed straight at me, hit my chest, and sent me backward onto the floor. The fish and I both flopped around on the deck, each trying to get out of the other's way.

All the screaming going on gave me an instant ice-pick headache. I wished whoever was doing it would quit.

"Stop screaming, Bertie." With ease, Bobby lifted me to my

feet. "Are you hurt?"

"Yes. No. I don't know." I glanced down at my T-shirt with my company name and logo on the front. "That thing hit me right on my tow truck."

Arch corralled the demon fish. The first thing I noticed was it was far from a twenty-five pounder. Eight at the most. The second thing I saw were talons permanently attached to the fish's side.

"What is that?"

"An osprey," Bobby said.

"If you don't want to give me an honest answer, just say so."

"I swear that's an osprey's foot."

"You can tell because there are two talons in the front and two in the back. They swoop down and lock onto a fish. If its catch is too heavy for the bird to carry, it's pulled underwater and drowns," Arch explained in his science teacher voice.

That didn't make sense to me. "Why don't they just let go?"

"Because there is something that makes their sharp claws lock, and they can't let go." Billy beamed.

"You mean like Bobby when he's after the last Twinkie?" I loved the adrenalin rush I got from barbing one of my brothers.

"Exactly," Estelle said.

"You're so funny, Ro-Bert-A. You need to go on stage." Bobby lifted the fish. "Guess we better get this striped fellow back into the water before he croaks. Or, did you want to keep him?"

"Put him back. I couldn't eat an osprey killer. Yuck."

During the weekend, we had a variety of delicious foods, all cooked by my talented sisters-in-law. Unfortunately, none of it was fish. Oh, we knew they were in the lake. We saw them leap from the water with the grace of ballerinas and then they'd sail back in like Greg Louganis on a good day. Yet none chose to honor us with the presence of their bodies, cleaned and grilled.

I believe that one of the performing fish may have been my osprey killer. Mind you, I only got a glimpse of him, but I think he stuck his tongue out at me and something that sounded a lot like *nana nana booboo* skimmed across the water's surface.

I jumped to my feet and yelled, "Same to ya!"

Since Bobby was dozing, I startled him. "What the heck is wrong with you, Ro-Bert-A?"

He didn't wait for an answer. Instead he looked at Arch. "Don't let her have anymore beer."

"I'm sober as a toad," I shouted. "I haven't had one alcoholic beverage all day."

"Well, if I were you, I wouldn't admit to it. People who act like that are either drunk or crazy. I'd stick to the drunk, if I were you. And stay away from the railing. I don't feel like fishing you out of the depths of Lake Reavis." My brother thought he was so smart.

"At least then you could say you caught something," I ridiculed.

"Arch, please control your wife. She's giving me a pain in my butt."

"You're on your own," my dear husband announced. "I wouldn't want to break up a family tradition."

Bickering with Billy and Bobby *was* a family tradition, but I wouldn't trade either of my brothers for a million dollars. On the other hand, I wouldn't give you a quarter for another one just like them.

When noon on Sunday rolled around, my emotions were a little out of whack. Completely relaxed and rested, part of me longed for just one more day on the houseboat floating on beautiful Lake Reavis. The other part, the mommy part, missed the girls so much it hurt.

My bags waited near the front hatchway, and I sat on the lower deck soaking up a few more rays. The cool wind mixed with the heat of the sun stirred my enthusiasm to get underway for the dock across the lake. I'd been ready for about thirty minutes. The others were still gathering their belongings.

Finally, the engine started and rumbled roughly, vibrating the floor under my feet. Billy and Arch came onto the deck to pull up the anchor.

"Wait. There's something wrong," Bobby yelled from the helm just inside the door. "Put the anchor back down."

The engine accelerated to decibels that hurt my ears. The houseboat lunged forward. The anchor did its job and held tight causing the vessel to jerk to a stop. My chair pitched over backward, and I ended up flat on my back staring up at Arch, who had landed face down on a small table.

No time for chit chat, we scrambled to our feet and vied for who got to go inside first. I won. Bobby pulled himself to his feet. Frantically, he jiggled the key trying to kill the racing engine. He pushed buttons and flipped switches, but nothing worked. The motor got louder. He moved the throttle back and forth. The mechanism came free. He lifted it completely out of its home.

His eyes widened. He muttered, "Oh, crap. We're toast." After jamming the throttle back into place, Bobby raced down the passageway to the stern of the boat.

"I may have switched the controls to the bridge," he bellowed above the engine's roar.

Arch took his turn at the helm. Going through the exact same motions Bobby had just completed, my husband's luck wasn't any better. He, too, yanked the throttle from its cradle, replaced it, and then ran down the passageway. At the bottom of the ladder, he had to wait for Bobby to come down from the bridge before he could ascend the steps.

Much to my disbelief, Billy went through the same procedure he just watched Bobby and Arch do. All the while the large boat strained against the anchor, which relentlessly held it in one spot. As Billy made his trek down the passageway, he waited for Arch to clear the steps and then disappeared out of my sight to take a stab at turning off the engine where his companions had failed. I stepped up to the helm.

I refused to do any of the things Larry, Moe, and Curly had done. Since the anchor chain was stretched under the boat back to the propeller, my fear was that if the chain broke, it could get caught in the blades. Bobby's insurance company would be putting out big bucks for the damage to the boat. That didn't even take into consideration what would happen to the occupants inside. Surely the quick release would send us all flying like flakes in a snow globe. Heaven only knew where we'd land.

On the console, nothing worked but the helm. I turned it hard to the left sending the houseboat in a circular pattern. Around and around we went. Estelle sat in the horseshoe-shaped banquette slowly nursing a Bloody Mary. Nancy Diane had fear etched on her face.

"She's petrified." I pointed to Nancy Diane. "Help her."

Estelle slid next to our sister-in-law and put her arm around Nancy Diane and eased her drink glass to Nancy Diane's lips, who promptly took several big gulps. I wished I could have reassured them everything would be fine, but I couldn't. I needed a couple of shots of that drink myself, but I didn't have time.

At least the circular motion kept the chain from being directly under the propeller, but how long could we go around and around before we were all sick? The dinghy we'd pulled with us was following along nicely. Thank Heavens for small favors. If we needed to go get help, at least we had a way to do it.

I couldn't worry about any of that right then. The engine had to have a kill switch, and I had to find it.

Bobby and Arch were on the upper deck doing God knows what. Billy was in the head vomiting.

On the rear deck, I found the hatch to the engine compartment. Just as I opened it, Billy, looking a little green around the gills, emerged from the head. Smoke bellowed from below.

"We're on fire," Billy howled and then my macho brother screamed like a girl.

"We are not on fire, you dimwit. It's just smoke."

"Where's the dinghy?" Terror echoed in Billy's voice.

The pitter patter of big feet pounding against the upper deck sounded shortly before Arch and Bobby landed at the bottom of the ladder in a pile of thrashing body parts.

"We're going to flip and sink like the Poseidon." Bobby escalated the pandemonium. "We're going to drown. Bertie, you'll be Shelley Winters."

"You're not going to drown, Bobby, because I'm going to kill you first. Knock it off about my weight."

"You two stop fighting. Where's the dinghy?" Billy pushed past me.

I climbed down into the tight area that housed the engine. "I'm surrounded by dinghies. They're everywhere. They're everywhere," I yelled above the roar.

I would deal with Bobby Byrd later. "There has to be a kill switch here somewhere." I couldn't find it. Finally, after two burns to my body, I found the switch hidden away under the hot exhaust manifold. The engine sputtered to a stop. While the houseboat slowed to barely rocking on the choppy water, I lifted my exhausted body out of the hole and collapsed onto my back.

"Hey, sis," Billy stood over me. "If you'd gotten out of the way, I could have done that a lot quicker."

"Oh, I'm terribly sorry about that, but I'll tell you what. You stay out of *my* way, and I won't kill you. Deal?"

The owner of the houseboat towed us back to the dock where we unloaded our belongings.

"Thanks for inviting us, Bobby." Arch and my brother shook hands.

"Yeah, it was interesting and a welcome change of pace for us." I hugged my brothers and their wives. "And just think . . . someone towed me for a change."

"Can I talk to you for a second?" Bobby whispered and walked to the back of his car. Everyone stared at me, but I just shrugged. While they got in their vehicles, I joined my brother.

I looked up into his misty eyes. "Am I dying?" I asked.

He dragged me into his arms so quickly I didn't have time to unfold mine and wrap around him. After several seconds, my compressed arms began to go to sleep. I pushed away from Bobby.

"I am dying!" Panic set in.

"No, it's nothing like that. I just wanted to tell you how proud I am of you. Proud of the woman you've become. You're Mother of the Year because you *are* a super mother. You own your own business, you done good finding a husband, and now you're running for city council."

I kept waiting for the punch line, but it didn't come. It boggled my mind that my brother, whom I didn't believe even liked me, now sang my praises. I stared at him, dumbfounded by his proclamations. "Ah . . . thank you?"

"Another thing," he continued.

"Okay, here it comes. What's the joke? Do you have an exploding box you want me to open?"

"No, I've never been this serious about anything in my life. You astounded me back there on the boat when you were able to keep your head while the rest of us were flying around like rats on a sinking ship."

"Oh, wow, that's so cool of you to say, but don't forget, mechanical things are what I do all day long."

"Yeah, but I couldn't have done what you did."

"Maybe not, but if it had been on fire, you could write the insurance check to cover the owner's loss. I couldn't do that."

"Don't let this go to your head, sis, but I love you."

I put my arms around his beer-gutted middle. "Thanks. I love you, too, big brother, and always have even when I wasn't sure if my eyebrows would grow back."

Inside the car, Arch waited patiently. "Everything okay?"

"My brother loves me. I can die happy now." I gave my husband a toothy grin.

"I hope you don't plan on doing that soon."

"With you at my side, not for at least a hundred years."

Arch and I gathered our girls and still made it back to our home on Marblehead Drive before sunset. A very nice looking brick mailbox had been erected during our absence. Together with Arch's artistic landscaping, it gave our otherwise unassuming house a more stately appearance.

"Looks like Howie's cousin came through for us." Arch hauled our suitcases out of the trunk. "I like it. Do you?"

On both sides of the brick formation were signs advertising who put it up and the telephone number to call to get one just like it. "I'm not crazy about that." I pointed at one of the signs. "I forgot part of the deal was that for the first month we agreed to let him advertise. I just didn't realize the signs would be so intrusive."

"It's only for a month. We can live with it." Arch said.

While Arch and the girls went into the house, I checked to see if we had any mail. Inside the box I found one envelope. It was an invoice from the man who had built the mailbox. Did he forget I wasn't paying cash, but that we were trading services? He'd said he'd call when he was ready for me to remove the old cars from his yard.

"I better give him a call to be sure," I mumbled to myself.

Inside the house, Petey was checking messages. I caught the tail end of one.

"So I hope to see you and your family at my barbeque tomorrow night. It's at my house at seven. See you there." I quickly recognized Booger Bailey's voice coming from the answering machine.

"Did he say how much we had to pay for the barbeque?" I asked Petey.

"He said it was free and that he's expecting a big crowd. Come early."

Free? Booger didn't have the money to put on a free barbeque. I wondered who could be backing him with that kind of money.

"Were there any more messages, sweetie?"

Petey handed me a piece of paper. "I wrote them down."

Mary Lou called to see if we were going to the barbeque the next night, and Millie called to ask the same thing.

Arch had gone to put LoJ in her bed and returned to the room. "What barbeque? Where? Now, I hope. I'm starving."

"Booger is throwing a free barbeque tomorrow at seven. Evidently he's invited everyone in town including his opponent. He said for me to bring my whole family."

"At least I know where my dinner is coming from tomorrow night, but what about tonight? I'm hungry here."

I fixed the fastest thing I could—kielbasa sausage and mac and cheese—but all the while my mind kept pondering the question of who was backing Booger Bailey in his campaign. An open barbeque would cost big bucks even if he did smoke it himself. He still had to buy the meat and fixings.

After the girls were settled in bed for the night, I called Millie.

"Do you have any idea who's sponsoring the shindig tomorrow night?"

She hesitated. Maybe I awakened her, and she was a little more disorientated than usual. Was that possible?

"I don't have a clue, dear. Do you, Mavis?" Millie asked her sidekick who evidently sat nearby.

"About what?"

"Who is paying for the barbeque for Booger?"

"I don't have a clue." I heard her plainly.

"She doesn't have a clue," Millie relayed to me.

"Okay, I was just wondering. Are you two going?"

"Actually, the four of us are going."

"Four? Would that be you, Mavis, homeless Tom, and Old Coach Henderson?"

"That's right."

"That's what I feared. I'll see you there."

When Petey and LoJ become teenagers I would already have experience at handling people with raging hormones. Surely it wouldn't be as difficult as handling Millie and Mavis.

"Surely not."

"Are you talking to me, Bertie?" Arch stood next to me.

"Yeah, I said, surely you are ready to go to bed." No need to upset him by letting him know I was comparing his daughters with the two terrors of Sweet Meadow. His heart couldn't take the pressure.

Chapter 15

Monday morning, while Carrie Sue swept the office, I called Bertram. His wife answered the phone. He wasn't there.

"This is Bertie Fortney. Your husband built a mailbox at my house, and the deal was we were going to exchange services."

"Ahhhh, I see." Did I detect a condescending tone?

"Yes, I am going to pull his—"

"I used to be a prostitute, too," she said. "How long have you been one?"

The muscles in my throat constricted. I may have even quit breathing. "I'm not a . . . one of those. I own a towing company in Sweet Meadow. Bertram said he needed some cars removed from his yard, and I would do that in trade for a mailbox."

"That idiot. The people at the Piggly Wiggly won't allow me to barter for food. Believe me, I've tried."

"Well, I'm sorry, but I never would have agreed to him erecting the mailbox if it meant cash out of my pocket. My old metal, regular hardware variety one worked just fine."

"I suppose what's done is done. I'll tell him you called." She hung up.

"That crazy woman thought I was a prostitute. Can you imagine that?" I asked Carrie Sue.

Leaning on her broom, she laughed out loud. "No, that's the last thing I'd mistake you for."

I didn't like her inference. "What does that mean? You don't think I could do it or I wouldn't be good at it?"

While she doubled over with laughter, I pulled my brain back from its trip to the dark side and made a mental note to have my neurosis checked as soon as possible.

"Knock it off. I was just kidding." I think.

"You're as daffy as a duck. Only your call isn't 'quack' it's 'cracked'." Long after she rode off on her broom, her laughter lingered in my ears.

I had a lot on my plate and that plate got heavier with each passing day. Maybe it was taking a toll on me. Naw, you could ask anyone in town. I'd been cracked for years.

Speaking of cracked—Millie and Mavis pulled to a jerky stop just short of the concrete pole in front of the building. At least Mavis had mastered that part. Millie opened the passenger door and started to get out. As Mavis did the same, the car lunged forward and crashed into the pole.

Millie fell back into the seat. Mavis put the car into reverse and quickly backed up about three feet. Without hitting the brakes, she slammed the shift into park. Millie's head bobbled.

I didn't even bother to go check on them. I waited for them to get themselves together and come into the office under their own steam. By the time they made it into the office, I'd taken a seat in the waiting area.

"Are you two okay?" I asked.

"Sure, that's becoming a way of life for us." Millie closed the door.

"Unfortunately, it's probably going to be the death of you." I shook my head. "Or me."

"You are such a nervous Nellie." Millie sat down. "And, we think we know why."

"That's why we've come here to talk to you." Mavis took a seat next to me and took my hand.

What were those two talking about? Yes, I had a lot going on. Maybe too much, but I was handling it pretty well, I thought.

"Okay, you two, what's going on? What's the problem?"

"Mavis and I think you've taken on too much. We feel you're neglecting your family." Millie was quick and to the point.

"We know you don't mean to, but you've been channeling your energy into this council thing." Mavis backed her up. "When I was young, my dad was mayor of our town. Believe me, the campaigning is only the beginning of claiming your time. The meetings, listening to citizens' demands, studying the facts of those demands take even more time."

My gaze drifted to Millie. "Petey and LoJ need their mother, and you're not going to be there for them."

"I know what I'm talking about." Back to Mavis. "I remember spending very few evenings with my father. The city took all his time."

Millie: "Sweet Meadow will do the same to you."

The notion had been nagging me, but I'd thought it all through and felt confident to handle whatever came my way. Arch and

Bobby had both told me flat out they were proud of me for running for city council. Petey had even written about it in her nomination letter for my being Mother of the Year. Tim Tuten let me know at every turn how suited I was for the job. Sure I had a little sniggle of doubt, but their support made it seem right.

Since Millie and Mavis were older, could they also be wiser? I studied them for a moment. Mavis' one eye was stuck cocked to the side, which she rectified by pounding on the side of her head. Millie had lifted her blouse and dug lint from her bellybutton. There's a myth buster for you.

"I appreciate your concerns, but I really have looked at all the job would entail, and I'm positive I can handle it."

Millie rose. "Come on, Mavis. We've done all we can do. We better get out on the highway and get set up. Our nuts are hanging out there in trunk getting cold."

I opened the door for them. "I'll see you ladies tonight at the barbeque."

"You sure will," Millie said.

I gave them both a quick hug. "Thank you for caring."

They were outside, but I hadn't closed the door so I easily heard their conversation.

"When she gets on that darn council, she'll never have time for us any more," Mavis said.

"You're right, my dear friend. We've lost her."

I eased the door shut and went to my desk behind the counter. So, that was the real reason for their visit. They thought I wouldn't be able to ease them into my busy schedule. Until that moment, I hadn't realized the significance of our friendship. I'd always thought of them as wacky senior citizens who had somehow become my wards. That I might be important to them had never entered my mind.

I would just have to make sure I saved time for them. I could do that. I would do that.

At least two hundred people milled around Booger Bailey's front and back yards. Huge timbers were stacked teepee fashion in the field next to the house ready for a bonfire to be lit. His barking goats roamed freely among the guests.

Tantalizing smoke filled the air. Tables loaded with ribs, chicken, and shredded pork butts lined the walkway leading to the porch. Another grouping held several types of salad. Spotlights and tiki torches lit eating areas scattered everywhere.

Utterly bowled over, I looked at Arch. "Who is backing Booger? I know he can't afford all this."

"There he is. Go ask him." Arch took LoJ from me and placed her in her stroller. "I'll be right there."

Petey went with me. "This is quite impressive, Booger." I extended my hand, but he bypassed it and gave me a big hug. My nose went directly to his armpit. Even though the evening air chilled me, standing over the barbeque pit had caused his five-day deodorant to give up after three days.

"Glad to see you, my worthy opponent." Booger released me.

"Yeah, same to ya. Who's footing the bill for all this? And do they know you are running for city council and not for Leader of the Free World?"

"You're very funny, Bertie. Ho ho ho." He rubbed his substantial stomach.

"I know who you are." Petey piped up.

"Santa Claus? Is that because I'm so giving?" Booger asked.

"No, the Jolly Green Giant because you are so big."

"Petey! Here, you push the stroller, and we'll go put some food in your mouth." Arch herded our little family away.

"Cute kid," Booger said.

"We think so. Back to my question. Who's your sponsor?"

"I'm not at liberty to say. They wish to remain anonymous."

"You're kidding, right? You mean to tell me someone in our town has enough money to put on an affair like this, but no one is allowed to know who it is?"

"Well, *I* know who it is, of course, but no one else can." Booger waved to someone. "Nice talking to you. Enjoy yourself." He fluttered away leaving me to speculate who Mr. Anonymous could be.

I loaded a plate and then joined Arch and the girls at a table in the backyard. Millie and Mavis along with their sidekicks, Tom and Coach Henderson, were also there.

"Did you find out?" Arch asked.

"No, he said the person wishes to remain anonymous, but I'm not giving up that easily." I ripped a chunk of meat from a chicken leg.

"Maybe that's not something you really need to know, dear," Millie said.

"I agree I don't *need* to know, but I want to know. It's not simply a matter of someone wanting Booger to win so badly they'd help him get attention by feeding the people who will ultimately vote for him."

"If it's not that, then what is it?" Mavis asked.

"It's the fact someone would go to this extent to keep me from being picked for the council."

"Oh, my. Who in the world would have anything against you?"

"No one," I answered a little too hastily. "Well, I can think of one or maybe two or three, four at the most."

Arch took my hand and squeezed it tightly. "Don't work yourself into a state. As hard as it may be to hear, some things are out of your control."

"Are you insinuating I am a control freak?"

"There you go jumping to the wrong conclusion."

"Some days that's the only exercise I get. Don't take it away from me." Arch looked me straight in the eyes and plastered a sour grin on his lips. "People are looking at us. Calm down."

I knew he was right, and I was not acting in a professional way. I nodded to acknowledge he was right. "I'll be a good girl," I said slowly and softly. "But I am going to get to the bottom of this if it kills me." I took another bite from the chicken leg.

Something large hit me square in the back causing me to swallow a hunk of chicken which lodged in my throat. I couldn't force it down or back up.

Distracted by whatever freight train had hit me, no one noticed I couldn't breathe and was slowly, but decisively dying. I waved my arms frantically trying to get someone's attention.

Where was my loving husband? My children? Millie? Mavis? They'd all moved too far from me to notice my distress. Somehow I managed to get to my feet, but lack of oxygen left me weak. I melted to a sitting position on the ground. My vision blurred and objects around me squiggled into distorted shapes. I was fading fast.

My life flashed before my eyes. When the images got to the chapter of my breakup with my old boyfriend, Lee Dew, someone slapped me sharply between my shoulder blades, snapping me back to the hard reality that I still couldn't breathe.

Arms wrapped around me from behind, locked under my breast, and jerked upward. The chicken projected from my mouth and landed in the grass several feet away. I sucked in the substance of life and promptly lost consciousness.

Still lost in darkness, I heard Arch. "Bertie, are you okay?"

"Mommy, wake up," Petey cried.

Fully expecting to see their smiling faces, I opened my eyes, slammed them closed again, and prayed I wasn't in Hell. Slowly I dared to look again. Inches from my face, I found Tom, the home-less man, and Booger's barking goat staring at me. Too weak to shuffle away from them, I just closed my eyes and waited for what-ever fate had been appointed to me.

"I saved your life."

"Who said that?" Was it Tom or the goat?

"I did. Tom Barrs."

"Thank you," I said, but I couldn't help wondering how he'd done it. I remembered the Heimlich maneuver being administered, but was artificial resuscitation also used? If so, would I have rather it had been done by Tom or the goat?

Tom and Arch helped me to my feet. "Maybe we should get you to the hospital."

"No, I'm all right. A little lack of oxygen never hurt anyone."

"That's always been my theory," Millie announced.

"I think we should get to the emergency room right away." Poor Arch hit panic mode.

"I promise I'm just fine. I do think we should go home, though."

Booger apologized for this goat's behavior and helped me to my car. "I guess the next time I see you will be at the council meeting next Monday night."

"I guess so. Good luck." Quickly, I rolled up the window to thwart his attempt to hug me again. Seconds before we drove away, the bonfire erupted into a brilliant pyramid of flames.

"Take this chariot home, James. The villagers are restless and will soon be storming the castle." I jabbed an imaginary sword into the air.

"Are you sure we shouldn't swing by and have Dr. Johns take a look at you?"

"Most definitely, *mon cher.*"

"Bertie, you don't speak French."

"Is that what that was? Sorry, I won't let it happen again."

We left the emergency room around one in the morning. Dr. Johns had declared me as stable as ever, but when he wrote it in my thick chart, he snickered.

The next morning, except for a sore throat, I felt good as new. Last evening's events may have temporarily kept me from uncovering Booger's backer, but with a new day ahead of me, I was determined to solve the mystery.

After dropping LoJ at Mom and Pop's, I checked to make sure

all was right with the world at the garage. Linc and Carrie Sue had things under control, so I drove to the sheriff's office to have a little talk with Carl Kelly. Since he was tied up, I had to wait for a few minutes.

Newspaper editor, Jim Ed Swain, came out of the restroom just down the hall from the waiting room.

"Good to see you, Bertie. I planned to come by your garage today." Jim Ed took a seat next to me.

"What can I do you for, Mr. Newspaper Man?"

"I'm doing an article for tomorrow's paper, and I wanted to get your comments about the campaign barbeque held in honor of Booger Bailey. I saw you there, but I never had a chance to talk with you. So, what would you like to say?"

"It was a nice affair. The food was good, what I got to eat of it. Do you know who paid for it?"

"As a matter of fact I do, but that was told to me off the record, so I can't divulge the info."

"That stinks." Anger hooked its ugly fingers in my heart. Or could it be jealousy? After all, someone liked Booger better than me.

"Come on over, Councilwoman." Carl motioned from his desk.

"Are we all through here, Jim Ed?" I asked.

"Sure."

At Carl's desk, I didn't wait for him to tell me to sit down. I plopped onto the hard chair next to his desk. "Who's backing Booger in his campaign?"

Carl smiled. "I can't answer that."

"You mean won't or you don't know?"

"I know, but I can't tell you." Carl put his finger to his lips. "It's a secret."

"Knock it off, deputy. Word on the street has it that you are going to be running for sheriff in the next election. If you don't tell me who it is, I'll tell my backers not to vote for you."

"With the amount of money being spent on Booger compared to what is being spent on you, I'd say he has more people in his court. I think I'll take my chances with him."

"You wound me, my dear friend. You wound me deeply."

"Sorry, my lips are sealed. Anything else I can do for you today?"

I left Carl in his little dark hole next to the jail cell and wished Nana Byrd had taught me how to put hexes on people, because ol' Carl surely would have gotten one that day.

Back at the garage, Carrie Sue carried on a heated debate with someone over the telephone. "It's a groom's cake. It can be in any shape I want. Do you agree with that?" Stress lined her face. "Okay then, I want a tow truck. Make the truck red. Are we clear on this now?"

I stuck my purse behind the counter and gathered bills and the checkbook.

"Hold on a second." Carrie Sue pulled the phone from her ear. "Will you please explain to this person from the bakery what I want?"

"I thought you ordered the cakes awhile back."

"I did, but they just called. The woman who took the order didn't make it plain what I wanted. She no longer works there, and I can't make this person understand. Maybe you'll have better luck."

I took the phone. "Hello."

"Halo," a voice with a heavy accent answered.

"Mrs. MacMillan ordered a groom's cake several weeks ago, and she even gave a picture to the lady who took the order. Have you looked around there to see if you can find it?"

"Yesss, I look, but she no here no more. She have bun in oven and time to come out."

"No, I'm not looking for her; I want you to look for the picture of the tow truck. Understand?"

"Yesss, tow truck. Other lady tell me that. What's new with you?"

"Nothing's new with me. We want a groom's cake in the shape of a tow truck. Chocolate cake, tow truck on bed of green coconut grass. Truck red. Understand?"

"Yesss, tow, red truck on coconut green grass. Sure thing. Bling bling."

"Okay, bling bling to you, too. Now, both cakes must be delivered to the Garden Club by four Saturday afternoon. Okay?"

"You want two tow truck cakes?"

"No, one wedding cake and one groom's cake. That makes two cakes total."

"Oh, ha ha ha. I make funny. I got it now."

"Good going. Bling bling and all that jazz." I hung up the phone. "Good luck. I did the best I could."

"At least you got further than I did with her." Carrie Sue scratched an item off her to-do list. "The flowers will be delivered to the church, cakes to the reception hall, and then Elton has assured me the food will be ready when we are. Can you think of anything

I've forgotten?"

"Sounds like you have it all under control. What time is the rehearsal?"

"We'll meet at the church at six. We should be done and at the Bull's Tail for dinner by seven. Saturday morning, my sisters will go set up the Garden Club for the reception. I'll meet you and Barbie at the church at nine to decorate with all the tulle braids and flamingos we've made."

"I'll be there. By the way, do you know who paid for the barbeque at Booger's last night?"

"Nope." Carrie Sue made a hasty retreat into the shop.

I hated to think she'd lie to me, but I had a sinking feeling she just had. Why? What was the big deal? Why did everyone in town know but me?

The next morning, I went to work early. Bills were stacking up, and I wanted a few quiet minutes to think about what lay ahead in the next few days. By Saturday evening, the wedding of the year would be over, and I'd be two days away from finding out if I would be the next member of Sweet Meadow's city council.

The more people I learned knew the secret of my opponent's supporter, the more my feelings were hurt. Since I didn't dare to voice my sentiment, I decided to let it go. In the tranquil surroundings of my office, I declared my intention.

"I will let it go. I will let it go. I will let it go."

"Let what go?" I hadn't heard Linc enter.

"Nothing, I've already let it go. So, are you excited about Saturday?"

"I'm more nervous than excited. I've never been married before."

"Everything's going to be perfect. You'll see."

He frowned and appeared to have something weighing on his mind. If he did, I didn't want to know what it could possibly be. I did not want to take on his problem when I'd just kicked mine to the curb.

Let it go. I told myself. *Let it go.*

"Is something bothering you?" Jeeze, couldn't I control my mouth at all?

"Well, I don't know how to tell you this." Linc tapped a newspaper in the palm of his hand.

"You've changed your mind about getting married?"

"No, it's not that."

"You've found a better paying job?"

"No, it's not that."

"Well, for crying out loud, what is it?"

"Just promise me you won't get upset."

"Okay, I promise."

"You made the front page of the morning paper." Linc held up the News-Leader.

"Ah, no," I groaned in my ever-present defeatist tone. A very unflattering picture of me lying on the ground with Dog, Booger's barking goat, standing over me. My eyes were closed so I was probably still unconscious. Why couldn't I have stayed that way?

"Do I want to know what the article says?"

"Actually, that part's not too bad." He sat down and spread the paper onto the waiting area table.

"Just give me the highlights."

"Over two hundred people. Mr. Bailey smoked the meat which, along with the rest of the food, was donated by an anonymous source. Big bonfire ended the evening's activities."

"What did the article have to say about me?"

Linc looked at me like I'd kick his family jewels. "Maybe you better read that." He handed me the paper.

"Mr. Bailey's opponent, Roberta 'Bertie' Fortney of Sweet Meadow, attended the gathering. Although alcohol was not served, Mrs. Fortney may have made a stop on the way. Sometime during the evening she landed on her back and had to be helped to her feet. When asked what she thought of the food, Mrs. Fortney replied 'it stunk.' Could that be a case of sour grapes?"

"How long will it take me to squash Jim Ed like a grape?" I folded the newspaper. "Can I keep this? I may need it for evidence." Before Linc had time to answer, I hit the door running.

On my cell phone, I called the sheriff's office to see if Jim Ed *Slime* happened to be there.

"He's here," Carl said. "Do you want to talk to him?"

"No, just keep him until I get there." I slammed the phone into the seat and gunned my car into Daytona 500 speed. "I'm going to kill him." I spoke to the irate woman looking back at me from the rearview mirror. "I've let that old man get away with too many things. When they beg me to remove my fingers from around his scrawny neck, I'll tell them I can't *let it go.*"

Carl met me at the door of the jail and blocked my way to Jim Ed. "Get out of the way. I'm going to kill him."

"You know I can't let you do that."

"Well then, you do it. Take that gun from your hip and shoot him."

"Bertie, you can sue him for slander, but you can't kill him."

By that time, Carl had lifted me off the ground. My arms and legs were whirling like pinwheels. My head spun just as fast. Finally, I ran out of gas and hung from Carl's big frame like a rag doll.

"Can't I maim him?" I begged.

"No."

"You win. I give up."

My feet hit the floor. Carl pointed a warning finger at me.

"Okay, just let me talk to him."

As I walked to Jim Ed, he ducked.

"Why did you write those terrible things about me? You know I hadn't been drinking. You also know I didn't say the food stunk. Now, I'm going to give you the chance of a lifetime. Explain your actions, and I won't lie in wait in the shrubbery and kill you when you least expect it. Make it a really good reason, and I won't sue you and take everything you own." I forced a smile that made my face hurt. It must have come off more as a snarl because Jim Ed leaned back out of my reach.

"Talk, Bozo," I demanded.

Behind me I heard Carl snort. I spun around and pinned him with a glare that could have killed a lesser man. He staggered back a couple of steps. I turned back to Jim Ed, who had taken advantage of my lapse and jumped over the counter dividing the public from the deputies.

"You can't get away. Tell me what I want to know. Why did you say those things about me in the paper?"

"Because they paid me to. I couldn't turn the money down."

"Who paid you?"

"The same people who paid for the barbeque and, since it's off the record, I can't say who that is."

I don't know where the energy came from, but like Wonder Woman, I bounded over the counter. Jim Ed turned to run, but I grabbed him by his suspenders and dragged him back to me. "Who is so determined to keep me off the council?"

Carl didn't make it over the counter as gracefully as Jim Ed and I had. His deputy paraphernalia tripped him up sending him on top of a desk and caused a heck of a racket.

I wasn't about to let Jim Ed get away. I held tight to him with one hand and with my other I tried to help Carl to his feet.

"Okay, I'll tell you," Jim Ed screamed.

Carl and I stared at the shaking editor.

"Oh, Lord, Jim Ed. If you think she's something to deal with, wait until they find out you told." Carl crossed his arms.

"Who is it?" I demanded.

"It's Millie Keats and that Mavis friend of hers. They used the money they made selling boiled peanuts. Now, you promised you wouldn't kill me or sue me, right?"

Stunned, I released the slimy editor. Millie and Mavis went to that extent to keep me from being on the city council. Why? I thought they supported me, but instead they used money they made from a business I set them up in to go against me.

I looked at Jim Ed. "Yeah, you're in no danger from me. Thanks for telling me."

He started to leave.

"Wait." I stopped him again. "I'll make sure Millie and Mavis don't bother you either." With the heaviest heart I'd had in a long time, I left the jail. I'd been betrayed by two people I thought, in a strange way, were very good friends. I guessed I was wrong.

Chapter 16

Millie and Mavis betrayed me. For the rest of the day, I thought of every conceivable excuse to soothe the open wound left in my heart by their disloyalty. Nothing helped. I could not manufacture an acceptable reason, but somehow I held it together.

For the rest of the afternoon, it was business as usual at Bertie's Garage and Towing, but for me, my heart held a hole as big as Lake Reavis. Several times, I had to force my mind away from the subject of Millie and Mavis.

When the work day ended, I secured LoJ in her car seat behind me and drove down the highway headed home. All day long, the tears had pounded at the back of my eyeballs, but once I was locked inside my car, the dam broke, and I cried harder than I ever remember.

The last thing I wanted to do was hit the door and crumble into Arch's arms in a blubbering mass. He didn't deserve that, and I'd be darned if I'd do it.

I parked behind ET's Donut Shop and wiped my wet face with a sleeve of my coveralls. After I climbed into the back seat next to my sleeping baby, I closed the car door and dug through her diaper bag. A rattle with a small mirror gave me a mini view of my face. I needed something to clean it. Diaper wipes worked well to remove tears and refresh my skin. When I took another peek, I could only see one eye at a time. My right one looked like it was rimmed with a cherry Lifesaver and the other with tangerine.

I needed something cold to reduce the swelling. In the diaper bag, Mom had packed two bottles of formula which were ice cold. I pressed the bottoms against my swollen eyes and leaned back against the seat.

"Just relax. I am on a tropical isle in the South Pacific watching the blue surf roll in and feeling the whitecaps at my feet," I spoke aloud. "As each wave goes out, it washes my heavy heart clean of sadness. The coolness of the baby bottles is sucking the redness from my eyes. I'm invincible. I can, and I will handle this disappointment by myself. I will not drag my husband or my girls down into the hog wallow I've been in all day." I stopped for a moment trying to remember what it was called when you tell your subconscious what to think.

"What is that called?" I whispered. "I know. Auto suggestion." I chuckled. "I'm making an *auto* suggestion in the car. That's funny, isn't it, baby girl?" I removed the bottles from my eyes.

"Aaaah!" In front of my car, police lights flashed. Carl Kelly stared at me through the windshield and Elton through the side window. I opened the door.

"You scared me to death."

"You didn't do much for me either. I brought the trash out, and you were sitting there talking to yourself and laughing like you were crazy." Elton formed glasses with his fingers. "You had bottles on your eyes with your nipples sticking out."

"Don't you dare tell anyone my nipples were sticking out."

"I didn't know what was wrong with you so I called for back-up." He pointed to Carl who came around the car and joined our little party.

"Everything is fine," I said. "You know I've had a bad day. I just wanted to compose myself before I went home. This is a public parking lot. I wasn't breaking any laws, was I?"

"No. Do you want me to go get Arch so he can drive you home?" Carl asked.

"That won't be necessary. I can drive myself." I made my way to the driver's seat. "Thanks anyway."

By the time I arrived home, I had my act together and decided not to tell Arch about Millie and Mavis. I didn't know how he'd react, and I'd already caused discord in his family when I inadvertently talked Mavis into leaving Arch's uncle. As a matter of fact, I wasn't sure how *I* felt about the matter. So, until I came to grips with it, I'd keep it to myself.

The next couple of days, I did everything in my power to keep my chin up and not let on that anything was eating at me. I managed to fool everyone but Arch. He asked a couple of times if something was wrong, but didn't push when I declined to talk about it. However, he did appear relieved when I assured him it wasn't him.

Since I hadn't gotten to wear my new purple suit during my debate with Booger, I planned to wear it to the wedding. I would probably stand out against the splashes of opossum pink and pond scum green, but it would have to do.

By Friday afternoon, I'd avoided Millie and Mavis completely. Some of my disappointment had waned, but I still searched my soul for the motive behind their disloyalty. Maybe they didn't realize what they were doing. Lord knows they were plagued with a heavy dose of senility, not to mention the inability to think like rational human beings.

On my way home from work that evening, I talked myself into giving the elderly women the benefit of the doubt. Surely they wouldn't deliberately hurt me, and as hard as it was for me to reason it out, I had to believe that was true. Since there wasn't time for me to talk to them before I had to be at the rehearsal dinner, I'd put it off until after the wedding.

In my driveway, I lifted LoJ out of the back seat. Something called my attention to the edge of the yard near the road where our mailbox used to sit. The fancy red brick letter receptacle no longer stood in its stately place. As a matter of fact, I had no mailbox at all.

When I got into the house, I found Arch watching the evening news. He rose and took LoJ's carrier from me.

"What happened to our mailbox?" I asked.

"I hoped you would know. It was gone when I came in. The mail was sticking out from under the welcome mat." He gave me a kiss.

"I'll see if I can find out." I picked up the phone and called Bertram.

"Why did you take my mailbox?"

"Because my wife said you weren't going to pay for it."

"You told me I didn't have to. You were going to call me when you wanted me to remove vehicles from your yard at no cost to you. That was to square us even up."

"I guess that slipped my mind. I got an order from someone who would pay me cash if I could get them one today. I went by your place and winched it up onto my flatbed and had it set up at my paying customer's house in less than forty minutes. That may be a record."

I'd spent a week feeling beaten, and I had just pulled myself out of a funk. I had no intention of letting a baboon named Bertram put me back in it.

"Okay, just bring back the mailbox I had before you put up the brick one and reinstall it, and we'll forget the whole thing."

"I don't have your mailbox anymore. I remove them and then take them to the dump about once a month. I did that yesterday."

"You'll just have to go buy me a new one and put it up. Please take care of it tomorrow."

"I'm not going to buy you a new one. That's your responsibility."

My blood pressure climbed. "You mean to tell me I now have to go buy another mailbox? That's not a very good way to run a business. I hope you don't expect me to do any favorable advertising for you."

"Actually I got several orders because people saw the advertisement on the side of the mailbox while it was in your yard. Technically, you already did advertise for me." He brayed like a donkey.

If it were possible, steam would be coming out of my ears. "You lop-eared ape. You have a lot of nerve. You used my yard as a billboard, and you're going to pay for that. Expect a bill in your own mailbox in the next few days for the service. I'll expect payment in full in ten days." I slammed down the phone.

"Did you find out what happened?" Arch asked.

"Yes."

"May I also know?" He waited patiently.

Overwhelmed with events of the past week, the absurdity of the conversation I just had, or maybe I'd simply lost touch with sanity, whatever the case may be, I laughed so hard I had to pee. Walking cross-legged down the hallway, holding my aching side, I managed to say to Arch, "We've had our mailbox repoed."

He followed me. "Are you kidding?"

"Nope. Call Mr. Ripley. I'm sure he'd be interested. Believe it or not." I slammed the bathroom door and answered nature's call.

When I opened the door again, Arch still waited.

"The best part of the story is we now have to buy a new regular mailbox because Bertram disposed of our old one."

"No, the best part is that for a few moments I get to hold you." My husband kissed me long and slow.

Being so close to the love of my life and absorbing his warmth, my strength renewed making me ready to face the out-of-control events which had been consuming my life over the past weeks.

"It'll all be over in a few more days." Arch stepped aside. "You better hurry, or you'll be late for the rehearsal dinner."

"I wish you and the girls were going with me."

"I know, but we'll be with you at the wedding tomorrow. Petey's next door borrowing a movie, and when she gets home, she and I are going to watch it and eat popcorn."

"Thank you for understanding."

I showered and dressed in a pantsuit I hadn't worn since LoJ was born. It fit nicely. Sucking in my tummy, I looked in the mirror. Apparently, all the hectic running I'd been doing had knocked a few pounds from my frame. Knowing I looked pretty good gave me an extra boost of confidence. I was as ready as I'd ever be.

Petey rushed through the front door. "I got the movie," she shouted. "Barbie is waiting at the car for you, Mom."

"Great." I spread kisses all around and raced outside. Barbie tucked her notebook, which held all her lists, under her arm and got into my car.

"This is the beginning of the end," she announced.

"What do you mean?"

"Well, the highest excitement for the bride and groom starts tonight and goes through tomorrow climaxing as they ride off into the sunset. It'll all be over and the anticipation and the exhilaration will be gone. Most people think that just applies to the couple, but the friends and family who have been involved in executing the details of the wedding are also left a little disheartened when it's all over." Barbie certainly was on a roll.

"You mean like Thanksgiving turkey. You spend hours cooking and in twenty minutes it's over."

"You're not listening to me. I'm talking about the aftermath of a wedding. I said nothing about turkeys."

"Excuse me. I stand corrected."

Just my luck. Barbie was in one of her moods. Which one? I hadn't figured it out yet. I was leaning more in the direction of Arrogant Barbie, but one thing for sure, if she kept up that attitude, she'd be voted Most Likely to Get Smacked before the night was over.

Barbie and I beat the wedding party to the church. The rest dribbled in a few at a time. Carrie Sue floated around on a love cloud. Linc looked like he'd been sucker punched. His family—mother, aunt, and sister—had driven in from Atlanta late that afternoon. Although I talked to his mother on the phone a few times, I'd never had the privilege of meeting her.

I immediately saw the family resemblance: a kind face, tall, corkscrew curly hair, kept brown by Lady Clairol. The major difference, besides the obvious, was Linc's mother made three of skinny Linc. When we were introduced, Maureen Johnson crushed me to her ample bosoms, realigning every vertebra in my back. *Snap, crackle, pop* sounded through the vestibule.

She finally released me. "I'm really happy to meet the woman who's been so good to my Lincoln."

A little scared, I mumbled, "It's very nice meeting you, too, Mrs. Johnson."

"Now, now, none of that. Call me MoMo. Mrs. Johnson was my mother-in-law. Just hearing her name said aloud sends chills up my spine." MoMo leaned in for a whisper. "She went to her grave hating me for taking her son away. I never understood why. He was such a pain in the rear. I thought I did her a favor." A gurgling laugh erupted from deep inside MoMo. She slapped me on my back so hard I took two steps forward.

While I recovered, she scanned the group gathered at the front of the church. "Oh, let me go, dearie, I see my sweet Lincoln up there with that hussy who's trying to ruin his life." She disappeared on the crest of a mission.

That didn't sound good. Carrie Sue had met her future mother-in-law once when Linc took his fiancé to Atlanta a few weeks earlier. According to Carrie Sue, she'd gotten along famously with his whole family. I hated the fact her love for MoMo wasn't returned.

Just then, she hurried past me dragging Judy Craig, the daughter of the Redneck Mafia's boss, by the scruff of her neck. In short order, MoMo put Judy through the door and out into the church yard. I followed them.

Linc's mom shook her finger at Judy. "This is the Lord's house where my son is going to marry the best woman in the world. There is no room for the likes of you in this church, in this town, or in his life. Go on with your bad self, and leave Lincoln and Carrie Sue to have a happy life."

Thrilled to find out how much MoMo thought of Carrie Sue, I used every bit of strength I had to slap Linc's mother on her back. "Good job, MoMo." It was like hitting a large refrigerator. I didn't budge her a fraction of an inch. While I was rubbing my hand to see if I'd broken it, Judy waved to me like we were old friends.

"Go home, Judy. Linc is happy. Don't ruin that for him," I said softly. She nodded and disappeared into the darkness, and everyone went back inside except me. I wanted to be sure Judy was gone.

Someone walked up behind me. "I know how she feels," a man said.

Instantly I recognized the voice. Lee Dew, my old boyfriend who left me for Carrie Sue's sister. I turned. "No, you don't. It was different with us. You're the one who abandoned ship, so you can't possibly know what it feels like to be left behind."

He didn't have anything to say that I'd want to hear, but I had something I wanted to tell him. "You're leaving me was the worst and the best thing that could have happened."

"How's that?"

"The worst because, at the time, you broke my heart. The best because you freed me to find and marry my soul mate. Thank you for that." I left him standing in the dark and joined the rehearsal for the wedding of two people who were my employees, but also my friends.

Back inside the church, as the wedding coordinator, I told everyone where to go and what to do. Lee, serving as Linc's groomsman, said he knew from personal experience I was very qualified for the job. At one point in my life, that would have been a painful barb, but I'd grown past having to verbally lash out or in some way exact revenge on the warthog. Instead, I continued with my task at hand.

"Lee, you need to take a few steps back." I pointed to a place precariously close to the edge of the riser he was standing on which led to the pulpit.

"Elton, as the Best Man, you'll stand here." I used his shoulders to steer him where I wanted him.

Upon examination of the pyramid made by the bridal party, I found it needed a little more tweaking.

"Lee, you need to move back just a little."

Off the step he went and down on his butt.

"Oops. My bad," I said and pretended not to notice the glare he and his wife, Annie, gave me. All in all, the rehearsal went well.

The wedding party caravanned to the Bull's Tail, a barbeque establishment opened in an old McDonald's. The arches had been covered with metal to look like the hind end of a bovine. The wait staff wore fake bull's noses with rings in them. Not very appealing, appetite wise, but the barbeque was the best in three states.

Linc's mother had worked on the menu with the Chef Wachee, who was no more a chef than I was the man in the moon. Wachee, a burly man, liked to cook and, even more, liked to eat what he cooked. He started his barbeque business in his backyard when I was not more than ten or eleven. Eventually, the health inspector shut him down. The demand for Wachee's tasty pulled pork and baby back ribs was so great he opened the Bull's Tail. He's been smokin' ever since.

Wachee personally showed us to our seats in a room used for a small banquets or parties. While we crowded in, he held the chair for MoMo and then motioned for someone at the door to come in. Two waiters carried a big tray and set it in the center of the table. A huge, roasted pig with a big apple in his mouth looked at me with pimento-stuffed olive eyes.

"Bravo. Bravo." MoMo applauded. "You've done a beautiful job, Wachee."

After we showed the proper amount of appreciation for the artistry displayed in the presentation of the hog, the waiters whisked it to the buffet table to be carved. It *was* like a piece of art whose eyes appeared to follow my every move. I stared back. No pig could intimidate me. Especially a dead one. *Jeeze. How much would an hour of therapy cost?*

"If you don't mind my inquiring, what kind of name is Wachee?" MoMo asked.

"I originally got the name because I *watchie* the fire," the master of the coals explained. "But from now on, I think it will mean I Wachee you." He winked at MoMo who promptly blushed a bright crimson and looked away shyly.

Linc choked on his brew. Few heard what Wachee had said. They were all running for the buffet and quickly loading their plates with fresh, roasted pig, corn on the cob, slaw, and cheese grits. But I found it heartwarming to see flirtation between the older members of the party.

Mavis and Millie and their new beaus came to mind. I'd tried to discourage them from becoming involved with Tom Barrs and Old Coach Henderson. But why? What if it was their last chance at love? Could that be the reason they had gone against me in the council race? To pay me back for trying to deprive them of companionship during their senior years?

On Saturday, after the wedding, I would have a long talk with Mavis and Millie and get everything out in the open. I had to know what exactly I'd done to force them to betray me.

For some unknown reason, my alarm clock didn't go off. I opened one of my peeper toms and looked to see what time it was. Eight-fifty.

"Oh, no. I'm late." My butt must have grown wings, because I leaped from the bed in one bound. I had ten minutes to dress and meet Carrie Sue at the church.

Quickly, I threw on jeans and T-shirt and ran a brush through my hair. It had absorbed the smell of barbeque from the night before, but I didn't have time to shower or eat breakfast. So, until then, the smoky aroma would trail along with me reminding me how hungry I was.

As I raced toward the front door, slipping on shoes, grabbing my keys and my purse, I found Arch at the front door with a cup of coffee in one hand and a blueberry muffin in the other.

"Sorry, you didn't tell me you had to be up at a certain time, or I would have awakened you. I heard your battle cry and thought you might need these."

I took my breakfast and gave him a kiss. "What would I ever do without you? I love you."

"I love you, too. I'll see you when you finish at the church." Arch held the door for me and I hurled myself into a day that held heaven only knew what.

I did a petite halt at the stop sign near the church and pulled right in front of a police car. Carl zipped around me, shook his finger at me, and sped away. That worked out well. I didn't get hit, and I didn't get a ticket. Maybe the day wasn't going to be too bad.

At the church, the minister's wife had unlocked the door, and Carrie Sue waited out front for me.

"You're ten minutes late. Where's Barbie?" She looked in the back seat like I had her hidden. Which of course I didn't because in my hurry to get to the church on time I'd forgotten Barbie.

"I'll be right back."

When I pulled into Barbie's driveway, she was sitting on her front stoop with several boxes of wedding decorations next to her. I jumped out and helped her load the things into my car. "I'm so sorry. I was late, and I just forgot to pick you up. Can you ever forgive me?"

"If I forgave my mother for forgetting to take me to the church

281

on *my* wedding day, I'm sure I'll eventually forgive you, too." Suddenly, she started laughing. "It was *déjà vu* all over again."

Barbie was a big slice of my fruitcake life, and I cherished her. "Thank you." I reached over and squeezed her hand.

"For what?"

"Just for being you."

"Rick says that to me all the time. Someday I'm going to figure out what it means."

If she ever did, I hoped she'd take it in a good way. That's how I meant it, and Rick did, too.

Barbie and I found Carrie Sue setting flower arrangements around the pulpit. Pink and white posies with light green ribbons formed a beautiful bridal bouquet. The two attendants would carry baskets of just the darker pink flowers.

We strung braided pink tulle from the chandeliers and over the railing in front of the choir loft. Single layers of what I originally called pond scum green tulle filled in empty places for contrast. On the end of the first four rows of pews, we attached bows made of layers of the green tulle. In the center of each, we attached pink marabou covered plastic flamingos.

From the back of the church, we looked at our handiwork. Beyond my wildest imagination, the colors, the flowers, and the yard ornaments had gone together to form a magical setting for a fairy-tale wedding. It took my breath away.

"It's even prettier than I thought it would be." Carrie Sue stared misty-eyed at the end results. "Thank you both."

"All I did was what I was told. You two were the geniuses behind the plan. I gotta admit I was a little skeptical, but I think it'll be the prettiest wedding Sweet Meadow has ever seen," I proclaimed.

"If Fletch doesn't ruin the whole thing." Sadness threaded through Carrie Sue's voice.

"Who's Fletch?" Barbie asked.

"That's Carrie Sue's ex. Is he giving you trouble?"

"His brother told me he was going to show up at the wedding and make a scene. I don't know why. He didn't want me when he had me. Why would he want me now?"

"His brother said Fletch wants you to come back to him? That's crazy." Of course, so was Fletcher MacMillan.

"No, his brother said he was coming to make a scene. Wanting me back was the only reason I could think he'd do that." Carrie Sue shrugged. "Bertie, you have to promise me if he shows up you won't let him ruin my wedding. Please."

"Of course I won't let him."

She hugged me. "Thank you."

At least I could cross off another thing from my must do before I die list—be a bouncer.

The plan was for me to be at the church an hour before the ceremony to make sure everyone was in their right place. Arch and the girls would get there just before it all started. I almost made it to the church when my cell rang.

The caller ID told me it was Donna Carson, Carrie Sue's bigger and scarier sister.

"Hello. What's wrong?" There had to be something for Donna

to call me.

"We have big problems at the reception hall. Please get over here right away," she bellowed into my ear.

"I have things to do here. Can't someone else handle it?"

"Get over here . . . now!"

"Just tell me, is there a ghost of old lady Martone hovering in a corner?"

"Uh . . . no. Bertie, don't make me come after you." Donna had such a sweet disposition it was hard to refuse her request.

When I arrived at the Garden Club, Annie and Donna zoomed past me. "We're late. We were supposed to be at the church fifteen minutes ago," she called over her shoulder. "Elton is inside. Help him and then get him to the church. He's the Best Man and should have been there forty-five minutes ago."

The ballroom looked spectacular. Elton's tables were laid out like we were expecting Queen Elizabeth. They were beautifully displayed with flair, awaiting platters of food, which he would put out before the guests arrived.

When tuxedo-clad Elton saw me, he pointed to a nicely draped, round table where the wedding cake should have been. "That's just wrong on so many levels." He swiped a tear from his cheek.

I agreed. Instead of an elegant, three-tiered, white-frosted wedding cake, I stared at a sheet cake resembling a football field covered with green tinted coconut. Right in the center stood a cake in the shape of a human toe. Balanced on top of that was a red pickup truck.

"What kind of mess is this?" Elton asked.

"That would be a toe truck."

"That's not funny, Bertie."

"I'm not trying to be. We'll have to go with it whether we like it or not. Let's get this one moved to the other side table and bring in the wedding cake. Where is it? In the kitchen?"

"There is another cake, all right. Come see it." Elton took my hand and pulled me down the hallway. In the kitchen, Clara Moore and three other ladies were busy setting up trays of food. On one of the counters sat another cake just like the one in the ballroom.

"Are you telling me there are two of those monstrosities and no wedding cake?" My heart pounded so loudly I didn't hear his response, but when he nodded, I may have heard his head rattle.

No time to melt down; I quickly formulated a plan. I handed Clara what money I had in my purse. "Take this and go find a wedding cake and get it back here before the reception starts."

She counted the cash in her hand. "I can't buy a cake for nine dollars."

"Use your own money, and I'll pay you back later. It's the least you can do after I helped buy your daughter those handy dandy things she needed." I shoved her toward the door. "Just get one."

I turned back to Elton. "Leave this cake in here. The one out there will be cute as a joke cake. Let's go."

He started to protest, but I stopped him. "We have to get to the church. Go." We scrambled for our cars.

In my absence as the coordinator, Barbie, had stepped into my place. Thankfully, everything appeared to be on schedule. I found Carrie Sue in the bathroom next to the minister's office. I expected her dress to be a bright, gaudy pink, but the embroidered satin, full-length gown carried only the slightest hint of pink mixed with champagne. To say she made a beautiful bride would be an understatement.

"Donna said there was a problem at the reception hall, but I wouldn't let her tell me what it was." Carrie Sue swayed and her breath smelled of whiskey.

"Have you been drinking?" I didn't really need to ask.

"Please tell me it's under control," she begged.

"It's all worked out. Don't worry another minute about it." I was doing enough of that for both of us. I smiled. "When he sees you, Linc is going to be blown away. You're beautiful."

"Oh, Bertie, don't make me cry." She belched.

We were saved by a knock on the door. Carrie Sue's dad stuck his head into the room.

"It's time, sweetheart." Mr. Barrow's words seemed to stick in his throat.

"Let's go," I said and led the way to the vestibule. All the work that went into pulling the wedding together was worth every moment when Linc first saw Carrie Sue. He glowed with pride and happiness. The congregation stood and everyone watched the bride march down the aisle. Everyone, that is, except for one particular pair of eyes I felt staring at me.

Arch. My heart flipped, and I knew he was remembering the moment we first saw each other when I walked down the aisle to become his wife. I placed my fingers to my lips and blew him a kiss. He smiled and winked.

Once the ceremony began, I quietly went to sit with Arch and the girls.

"If anyone present knows a reason Carrie Sue and Lincoln

should not be man and wife, please speak now or forever hold your peace." The minister spoke softly, matter-of-factly.

The man sitting next to me stood.

"I object."

Chapter 17

Without looking up, I knew the Neanderthal next to me, who had just interrupted Linc and Carrie Sue's beautiful wedding, had to be her ex, Fletcher MacMillan. With the force of the gasps and whispers going rampant through the church, it's a wonder the roof hadn't blown off.

Not only had I screwed up my bouncer job, but the man had been sitting right next to me. How lame was that? Carrie Sue or Donna or both were going to kill me. I had to redeem myself.

I stood toe-to-toe with Fletch. "You can't object. You're not in a courtroom. Sit down and be quiet."

Ignoring me, he climbed over two ladies into the center aisle. "This man has to be told what he's getting into." Fletch walked toward Linc. I followed him and grabbed him by his coattail.

"Stop," I shouted.

"I could not live with myself if I let this man dive head first into the shark tank known as the Barrow family and not try to warn him. This poor man is going down a path of misery and heartache. I know because I spent five long years married to this particular Barrow sister. Not only is she a force to reckon with, but she comes complete with bodyguards. Granted, they are usually her sisters, but if you look closely you'll see I have one hanging on my backside."

"I'm not on your backside. I'm just trying to stop you from ruining this wedding. We all know what put an end to your marriage." I didn't want to say it out loud, so I made a motion of drinking and whispered just for Fletch's ears. "Alcohol."

Just then Carrie Sue hiccupped loudly. The minister's microphone easily picked it up and broadcast it through the whole church. She slumped onto the step she'd been standing on and started laughing hysterically.

I got between her and Fletch. "This wedding is going to happen even if it means I'm going to jail for your murder."

Someone stood very close behind me. "Get him, Bertie. I got your back," MoMo said. "We can't let him ruin my precious son's wedding."

The commotion had to stop before it became a brawl in the Lord's house. I took the minister's mic. "The show's over. Fletch has had his say. Please, let's settle down and get on with this wedding."

Donna and Annie helped their sister to her feet and back into her position as the bride. Linc held her up. The rest of us shuffled back to our seats, including Fletcher MacMillan, who sat back down beside me.

"What do you think you're doing?" I glared at him.

He crossed his arms and stared defiantly at me. "I'm waiting for the wedding to be over so we can go to the reception. You don't think I'd pass up free beer, do you?"

Give me strength.

Somehow we made it through the ceremony and all the way

to the reception. There I found a magnificent wedding cake in its rightful place on a beautifully-draped table in a corner. On a smaller table the toe truck cake received a lot of favorable attention. Most thought it was a deliberate comedic statement of the bride and groom's occupation.

I found Elton in the kitchen working frantically alongside his help. "The cake looks good." I smiled widely.

He continued to place chicken puffs on a huge platter. "Don't cut the cake, Bertie."

"Why not?"

"It's a Styrofoam display, and it has to be returned to the bakery first thing Monday morning."

I would have asked Elton if he jested, but of course that would require him having a sense of humor.

"For the pictures, they'll have to pretend. We'll serve the other two cakes." At least he had a plan.

"Won't the guests notice there's no white cake being served?"

Elton stopped and looked at me over his puffs. "How about you come over here and load these trays to feed the starving masses out there, and I'll go over there and harass you with useless questions?"

"Okay, I'm out of here." I made a quick retreat to the ballroom. In the center of the dance floor, Millie and Mavis shook their bon-bons to a Ricky Martin tune. Maybe I could find a few minutes to talk to them about their backing Booger. At one point they were free, but LoJ demanded feeding. By the time she became happy again, M&M were dancing again.

The evening grew to a close. As we sent the newlyweds off

on their honeymoon, I saw Millie and Mavis at the far side of the crowd. Yet, as quickly as Linc and Carrie Sue disappeared, so did my elderly friends.

My talk with them would have to be postponed.

In church the next morning, I saw Millie and Mavis sitting several rows away. Tom Barrs and Old Coach Henderson sat beside the ladies. Once, when I locked gazes with Millie, I used primitive sign language to tell her I wanted to talk to them. Presumably she understood and nodded.

Immediately following the offering, we bowed our heads in prayer. I heard a little shuffling across the room. I took a peek in that direction, just in time to see Millie, Mavis, and their two men friends disappear out the back door.

My heart sank. They were deliberately avoiding me. Whatever I'd done to bring on this reaction from them must be really bad. But what could it be? I hadn't come up with one idea on my own. Perhaps being so close to my heart made it hard for me to rationalize alone.

I still hadn't told Arch because I didn't want to upset the apple cart where Aunt Mavis and Little Archie were concerned. Still, I needed someone to talk to about the whole situation, and his ability to reason made Arch the most logical person. But did I really need that much brain power when dealing with the dynamic duo?

Where most people found themselves between a rock and hard place, I was between a high IQ and a head case. Just as the prayer was winding down, I made the decision to wait until after the election, which would take place the next night.

"Amen," I said in unison with the congregation.

At the Monday night council meeting, people crowded into the hall. They filled every seat, lined the walls, and packed the foyer. Chairman Cy Linder announced they would handle a few items left from the last meeting and then let the two candidates have two minutes for a final statement.

While I waited, I thought about what I would say. Should I mention the most important item on my agenda for the betterment of Sweet Meadow? I wasn't really sure what that would be without asking Tim Tuten. What was the number one thing I'd like the council to do for our town? Again, I'd have to confer with Tim on that. How many children attended Sweet Meadow schools and what were their needs? I had no idea, but I'd bet my last dollar Tim would know.

What kind of councilperson would I make? I didn't know my water management projects from a hole in the ground, but Tim did.

When Cy introduced me, I made my way through the crowd to the podium.

"Hi. It's nice to see this great turnout. I want to keep my comments confined to me and what I can do for Sweet Meadow. After much soul searching on the matter, I've come to the conclusion I can't do squat for our town."

The room rumbled with murmurs of expectation. "I've stood before ya'll on several occasions and quoted stacks of facts on what the community needs, doesn't need, and should have already had."

The audience applauded.

"Thank you," I said. "But I didn't gather all that information, and I seriously doubt I could repeat most of it just off the top of my head. A very adept attorney who was born and mostly raised here in Sweet Meadow compiled and spoon-fed the statistics to me. He knows that kind of stuff like I know the towing business. He's the one who should be in this race for a council seat. I should be in my truck seat."

I inhaled the wonderful aroma of getting my life back and exhaled the weight from my shoulders.

"If you came here tonight to vote for me because you believe I can do good things for Sweet Meadow, I assure you that gentleman sitting right over there," I pointed to Tim, "will do even more. Councilmen, ladies, and gentlemen, since this isn't a sanctioned election with rules to follow, I am pulling my hat out of the ring and throwing in the very capable one of Tim Tuten."

I started the applause and the majority of the audience rose and clapped, too. Tim looked a little shocked. I beckoned him to come up front. He went to the microphone.

"Thank you, Bertie. I believe I *would* like to serve on Sweet Meadow's City Council. That is, if I'm elected."

Tim escorted me back to my seat between him and Arch, where we waited for the voting to begin.

"We really hadn't expected this many voters." By pounding his gavel several sharp times, Cy called the meeting back to order. "Here's what we've decided is the best way to fairly collect all the votes. Everyone will go through the back doors into the outside courtyard. As you go out, you will be given a ballot with Bailey and Fortney on it.

"Now, this part is very important, so pay attention. You will mark your vote on the paper. Just remember that a vote for Fortney is really a vote for Tuten. Does everyone understand?"

Yes echoed around the room.

"Good. Once you've marked your ballot, come back in and place it in the box. The ladies sitting at the table will tabulate the votes as quickly as possible. With so many volunteers, we should be able to announce the winner in short order. Good luck to the candidates."

That night, several of us went home winners—Tim Tuten was our new city councilman, I took pride that, in the end, I would have beaten Booger even without the help of Millie and Mavis, and the biggest winner was Sweet Meadow because Booger Bailey wouldn't be governing our citizens. With that little bit of knowledge tucked away, I knew I'd sleep better.

However, I feared sleep would be hard to find until I had a heart-to-heart talk with Millie and Mavis. After we got home and tucked the girls in bed, I poured Arch a glass of milk, and we sat at the kitchen table.

"You don't seem as disappointed as you might have been by withdrawing from the race." Arch took a big gulp of milk.

"Several times during the campaign, I wondered when all of that had become a dream of mine. I never came up with an answer. Tonight, I tried to plan my final statement and realized I didn't know enough about anything to convince the people there to vote for me. If I wanted something to grab their attention, I'd have to ask Tim what it was.

"Like being hit between the eyes with Cy's gavel, I realized the wrong person was running for the position. Tim had done all the work, and he knows what he's doing. I think I made a wise decision."

"Well, now we can get back to our normal life." Arch chuckled. "Whatever that is."

For a moment, my mind drifted to a house across town where Millie and Mavis were probably getting ready for bed. My life couldn't go back to normal until I talked to them.

Arch took my hand. "Why don't you go over to Millie's? It'll do you good."

My husband knew, too. Why shouldn't he? Everyone in town did, except me. "How long have you known?"

"For a few days. Aunt Mavis came by school to talk to me."

"Why didn't you say something?" I tried to decide if I was hurt or just disappointed.

"I never mentioned it because you never mentioned it. When you were ready, you'd let me know." He squeezed my hand. "Go talk to them. Just promise me you'll remember they are old, and you'll be that way someday, too."

"With the way my life goes, do you really believe I have a chance of reaching old age?"

"I hope so. It's a journey I plan on us making together."

With a man like Arch, how could I do anything but grant him his wishes and at least give Millie and Mavis a fair chance to explain why they betrayed me. I think that's what Arch wanted me to promise, or maybe he was just concerned I might kill them.

I drove to Millie's house. Inside the car, with only the pale dash lights to soften the quiet darkness, I slipped into a state of tranquility I always felt when the spirit of Arch's dad was near. I liked that he made his presence known when my emotions bottomed out.

"You're here, aren't you Pete, you old goat?" I didn't expect him to answer, but I knew he was there and it brought serenity which allowed me to think rationally and to face the task ahead of me. "Okay, I get the message. You want me to go to M&M with an open mind and listen to what they say. I can do that." I arrived and walked to the front door, all the while talking to my guardian, Pete. "I'm adult enough to handle whatever these nutty buddies have to say."

"Who are you talking to?" Mavis asked.

I jumped about two inches off the porch. I'd been so busy carrying on a one-sided conversation with Pete, I hadn't heard her open the door.

"Uh, no one, but I'd like to talk to you and Millie."

Mavis stepped aside, and I went into their kitchen where I found Millie decked out in mint green, footed pajamas, her hair in curlers, and cold cream slathered on every inch of her face. I stopped short, and Mavis ran into me.

"Don't be frightened," she said. "That's just Millie in her nightly getup. She used to scare me, too, when I first moved in here, but you get used to it."

"Really?"

"Well, unless you wake up in the middle of the night with her standing over you." Mavis closed her eyes and shook her head.

"Hey," Millie shouted. "Scary old woman in the room here. Don't talk about me like I'm not."

Engage brain before mouth. I quickly thought about how Arch and Pete wanted me to handle things. Kindly, peacefully, and without physical contact to inflict pain. *With decorum.* I could do that.

"I'd like to have a little chitchat with you two. Can we sit around the table and discuss the matter of you stabbing me in the back with Booger?"

"I think that's possible, don't you, Millie?" Mavis didn't have a clue of the eruption building inside me, but Millie did.

Softly, she stroked Mavis' arm while looking at me. "Isn't she precious?" Millie then talked slowly and softly to Mavis. "You see, dear, that was sarcasm, and no one does it better than Bertie." Millie motioned for me to have a seat. "Go ahead, say what you have to say."

I yanked a chair away from the table and plopped down. "Okay, I will. If you didn't want me on the council, why didn't you just vote for Booger? Why did you have to make a mockery of my campaign by trying to bribe people to vote for him?"

"Well . . ." Millie said.

"That was the charity you were donating your hard earned money from your peanut business to, wasn't it?"

"Actually, it's your peanut business," Mavis interjected. "Remember, we opened it in your name? So, technically, you banked Booger's barbeque."

"Bet you can't say that three times fast. Banked Booger's

barbeque." Millie took a stab at humor, but all she did was pierce my heart.

"That is not my business. I did you two a favor. And if you think about it, there are very few things you've ever asked me that I didn't do. Yet, you betrayed me. You showed the whole town what you thought of me, and you didn't even respect our friendship enough to tell me you were going to back Booger. But you told everyone else in town. I was the last to know. Do you have any idea how that made me feel?" I was yelling at the top of my voice. So much for decorum.

I got up and paced the kitchen floor.

"I know you said you didn't think I could handle everything on my plate and that you thought my family would suffer, but I knew better. I could have done it all, but you didn't give me the chance to prove it. You tried to take the opportunity away from me. You meddlesome busybodies."

Chilled air swirled around me. I assumed it was Pete trying to get me to calm down. It didn't work. I looked toward a corner of the room. "Mind your own business, you old goat," I shouted at Pete.

Mavis and Millie looked behind them and then back at me. "Who are you talking to?" Millie asked. "Uh, and she says we're crazy," she mumbled to Mavis.

"I'm talking to you. You stuck your noses into my business, but it didn't matter. The results showed I would have won the campaign anyway, if I hadn't withdrawn. So, you wasted your money for nothing."

"Your money, dear," Mavis corrected.

"You're clueless, aren't you?" Millie said to her.

For a moment, Mavis' eyes filled with confusion, but it was quickly replaced with tears. "All I know is that I don't want to go to jail for manslaughter." She buried her face in her folded arms and began to sob.

"Why is that?" I asked Millie.

"Because there are bad people there."

"I mean, why does she think she's going to jail for manslaughter?"

"You see," Millie whispered, "she just can't learn to drive."

Mavis looked up. Tears streamed down her red face. "That's a lethal weapon parked in our driveway. I'm going to kill someone with it."

An instant piercing pain stabbed me in the head and splintered my ability to sort through all the confusion. My brain was crackling like water droplets on a hot griddle. One more item added to it and my brain would be fried.

"Let's back up. Start from the beginning of this whole mess. When did the idea first come into your head that you needed to sabotage my campaign and what, if anything, does it have to do with your car and Mavis' driving ability? But before you answer, I'm going to need sustenance." I sat back down.

Mavis went to the sink and wiped her face on a paper towel.

"Shortly before you decided to run for city council, Mavis and I came to the sad conclusion that we wouldn't be able to keep the Caddy any longer. Mavis couldn't get the hang of driving, and my license was confiscated years ago. You know it; you've been hauling my sorry butt around for years because I'm not allowed to drive."

"Okay, what does that have to do with the campaign?"

Mavis placed a bag of chocolate chip cookies on the table along with glasses and a gallon of milk.

"It's all my fault. The night before the council meeting, I begged Millie to let me quit trying to learn to drive. This old brain just can't get it." She tapped her head with her bony finger.

How sad to reach an age where you had to depend on someone else to take you places. I knew she was a hazard on the highway, but Carl Kelly knew it, too. If he didn't see the need to take the car away from them, I figured I didn't have a right to either. And maybe, somewhere in the back of my mind, I knew that if they didn't transport themselves, I'd have to do it for them. I hadn't thought about it before, but my selfishness could have caused them to be hurt or kill someone.

"I understand what you're saying, but why was my losing the campaign so important to you?"

"It was obvious that with everything else you had going on, you'd have no time for us. If we permanently parked the car, we'd be permanently tied to this house," Mavis said.

"We thought if you lost, you'd have time for us, and we wouldn't come off as selfish. As it turns out, we appear selfish, disloyal, and too old to drive. Doesn't put us in a very good light, does it?"

The heart I steeled before arriving at Millie and Mavis' melted into a pool of compassion for the two ladies. Shame dug deep into my chest. How could I have jumped to the conclusion they betrayed me, when in fact they were trying to survive and still hold onto their dignity? I was ready to battle with them because they tried to keep me from winning a political position I didn't want in the first place. What's up with that?

Get a grip, Bertie. Did I say that, or just think it, or did Pete send it through telepathy?

Mavis' face was blotchy from crying. Millie's cold cream had begun to run. The two of them looked like leftovers from the House of Wax.

"It must be midnight," I said. "My body is beginning to wither. And so is yours."

I stood and stretched. "I understand everything now. You want to get rid of the Caddy because you are dangerous on the highway. You want me free to play taxi for you when you need me. You didn't mean to hurt me, which by the way, you did. And, last but not least, we are all friends again, and I don't have to sit in that infernal council hall and listen to Cy Linder bang that stupid gavel. Am I right?"

"Right as rain," Millie said.

"We love ya, Bertie." Mavis came around the table and hugged me. Millie wrapped her arms around us for a group hug. We were one big happy bag of mixed nuts.

"I love you, too," I said.

At work the next morning, my dad opened the garage and puttered around the office. Since Carrie Sue and Linc were on their honeymoon, Pop had volunteered to be my assistant. I enjoyed having him with me.

He and I were standing at the plate glass window at the front of the building. A group of brightly dressed cyclists rode by. They were a mix of women and men: each wore tight fitting spandex, knee and elbow pads, and a helmet to match their outfit and bikes.

"Where did they come from?" I asked.

"They're from the senior community center."

When I looked closer, I recognized a few of them. They were senior citizens from right there in town. "I've never seen them riding before."

"It's a new club started by Ethel Winchell's daughter. She decided her mom and dad needed something to take their minds off booze."

"Ethel doesn't drink"

"No, but Jacob does. Their daughter feels that if they do something together, he won't drink, and Ethel won't fight with him about his drinking.

"Last week was the first outing. Since no one got hurt or had a heart attack, several others joined. As a matter of fact, your mom and I ordered us some bikes from the shop in Shafer. I'm going to pick them up this afternoon."

"Is this a safe venture?" Inquiring minds needed to know.

"Sure, they do stretching exercises before they start. They only ride on smooth, level roads and a flagman tails them in a car keeping someone from running over them. They only go about three miles a day, but from what I understand, they're having the time of their lives."

"Um, is that so?" I liked the thought forming in my mind. One of the better ones I'd had in a while. "Pop, would it be okay if I go pick up your bikes? I have an errand to run over there, anyway."

"Sure. Everything should be ready. We'd have brought them home yesterday, but your mom wanted a red one, and they didn't have any of them put together."

"Okay, I can be back in about an hour. I'll leave the wrecker and take your pickup."

I made it back to the garage with a truckload of bicycles and safety equipment. Once Pop and I unloaded it, I took the tow truck to Millie's.

"I came to get the Caddy. Come and ride with me to take it to my storage yard. I'll bring you back shortly," I told Millie and Mavis.

While I hooked up the vehicle, they climbed into the cab. All the way to the garage, they rattled off a list of things they would need a taxi for.

"Okay, just remind me of one thing at a time. I'll never remember all that."

We got out at the shop and entered my office. In the middle of the floor sat one blue bicycle and one green bicycle. Next to each was a gift bag of matching safety pads and helmets.

"These little beauties are spectacular. Whose are they?" Mavis ran her hand over the seat of the blue one.

"I bought them for you two."

"For us. For our very own." Millie actually squealed.

"Yes, if you don't like the style or the color, we can take them back to the bike shop and you can pick out another one. They'll also help you with finding the right seat height. And look." I pulled a helmet from the bag. "You each have one that matches the bike."

"Thank you, Bertie." Millie clapped her hands. "I can't wait to get into my bicycle shorts and take this baby for a spin."

One time, I'd seen her exercising in her spandex outfit. I don't know if Sweet Meadow was ready for that or not, but the big wheel was already in motion, and there was nothing I could do to stop it.

"I have a problem." Mavis frowned.

Oh, dear. "What's that?"

"I've never ridden a bicycle."

"Don't you worry about that. It's easy to learn," Millie reassured her.

"That's what you said about driving a car, and we all know how that worked out."

"Don't worry," I said. "I have lots of free time to follow along behind you with my tow truck keeping anyone from hitting you, or I can pick you up if you fall."

As I thought about using my tow truck to wench up one of these dear ladies, if they took a tumble from their bikes, I shook my head. Hopefully, they wouldn't get hurt. I loved them both.

Standing there in my office, I smiled. For all its kookiness, this was my life, and I wouldn't trade it for anything.

The End

Dolores J. Wilson

Dolores J. Wilson's real life is known to be as full of mishaps as her characters'. When she's not writing, she's likely to be cooking up a southern barbeque or creating a theme party for friends and family. She and her husband Richard love to travel in their motor home, where Dolores enjoys one of her favorite past times, visiting and researching historical sites, but she says it's always nice to come back home where she can spend time with her grown children and grandchildren. She is an avid reader, but also enjoys bluegrass music and a multitude of crafts.

Since she and her husband own a body shop and towing service, it was only a matter of time before Bertie Byrd was created. They make their home in Florida, where she's hard at work on the next adventures of Bertie and her gaggle of misfits.

www.doloresjwilson.com

Barking Goats *and the* Redneck Mafia

Chapter 1

I never expected to spend my wedding night in a maternity ward.

"Mrs. Fortney, you'll have to calm down." Dr. Johns mumbled a few more words behind his mask, but I couldn't hear them because my mind was absorbing the *Mrs. Fortney* part.

I had acquired that name a mere three hours earlier in a wedding ceremony that would make any bride proud. Until then, I had been Roberta Byrd, Bertie to my friends. A life-long resident of Sweet Meadow, Georgia. Thirty-two years, to be exact. I'd worked in my father's garage and towing business, Byrd and Sons, since my early teens. A few months ago, Pop had turned the whole place over to me. Its newly painted sign proudly boasted *Bertie's Garage and Towing.*

Since then, my usually dysfunctional life was one pleasantry after another right up to the wedding. I was now Mrs. Arch Fortney. Bertie Fortney. At last, a name I could wear with honor as opposed to the one almost big mistake in my life where I would have married Lee Dew. I shudder each time I realize I could have been Bertie Dew.

Now, a few hours following my and Arch's "I do's," my teeth chattered from the extremely cold delivery room inside Shafer County Hospital. Evidently, my screaming was a little disconcerting to Dr. Johns. He didn't understand this was my first birthing. I had no idea of the pain and agony one experienced to make the wonder of life happen. When I pressed my freshly manicured nails into the flesh of his arm, he ordered the nurse to remove me from the room.

"Out, Mrs. Fortney," the doctor demanded.

"Hey, hey, this can't happen without me." I exhaled an indignant huff. What was he thinking?

While I waited for the doctor to respond, I thanked God it wasn't me who was actually giving birth. It was my best friend in the whole wide world, Mary Lou Jarvis.

Today I married the love of my life, surrounded by my loved ones, and Mary Lou was my matron of honor. It was somewhere in the middle of the conga line she went into labor. Since we were old enough to dream of a husband and children, she and I vowed to be at each other's side when we gave birth.

So there I was, standing in the hallway with my back pressed against the door I'd just been shoved through. Banned from her delivery room because of over-wrought nerves. Running my hand over my beautiful, white satin wedding gown, I brushed away the wrinkles my slouching shoulders had caused. I was Mary Lou's best friend, and I was letting her down.

I'd cracked under the strain. While she showed nothing but the utmost decorum in her last stage of labor, I'd freaked out.

Determination stiffened my spine. I had to get back in there, beside my friend, cheering her on. Someone should knock me on my butt for being so self-absorbed.

I took two steps forward. My veil was caught in the door and sharply pulled me backward. In short order, I landed flat on my backside. I wish God would quit taking everything I said so literally.

Just then, the door opened. "Bertie get in here. The baby's coming," Rex, Mary Lou's husband, called over my head. I scrambled to my feet as quickly as the slipping crinolines, satin material, and highly waxed floor would let me. I swooshed into the delivery room and cocked a half-hearted smile at Dr. Johns. He shot me a full-hearted glare and stuck his head back under a sheet covering Mary Lou's spread legs.

Ten seconds later, he laid an alien on my friend's stomach. I glanced at Rex, who grinned wider than I'd ever seen, except for the time he won a trip to a Trekkie convention in Macon. Had all those sci-fi flicks he watched seeped into his wife's womb?

The doctor gave Rex a pair of scissors, and he cut the umbilical cord. I think he also cut the little fellow free from its mother planet, because, as the nurses wiped away the bloody, ashy covering, a baby boy appeared.

A nurse wrapped him in a paper blanket and stuck him in Mary Lou's arms. She pulled back the covering to look at her naked son.

"Ah, Mary Lou, he has your nose and your mouth and your chin," I said, amazed at how much the tiny person looked like his mom.

"Gee whiz, doesn't he have anything of mine?" Rex whined. Mary Lou stared at her baby. A mixture of fear and joy played across her face. She pulled the blanket further down to reveal his . . . lower parts. "Look, honey," she pointed, "he has your fixtures."

"Okay, we gotta weigh and measure him." A nurse plucked the baby from Mary Lou's arms. She appeared to want to change the subject from Rex's fixtures.

Mary Lou looked up at me. "Thank you for being here with me."

I hugged my dearest friend. "I wouldn't have missed it for the world."

"Now go on your honeymoon." She fluttered her hand in a dismissive wave. "When you get back, bring your daughter over to play with Rex, the second."

My heart swelled to bursting. Mary Lou had a son, and I had a daughter. Petey. She was part of the wonderful package I'd gotten when I married Arch Fortney. His ten-year-old daughter had stolen my heart from the minute I met her. But over the last few months, we developed a mother-daughter relationship, with the extra added attraction of being friends.

I said goodbye to Mary Lou and Rex, aka Mommy and Daddy, and stole one quick glance at Little Rex, who wailed in protest to the sticking and prodding the nurses were doing to him.

Making my way to the waiting area, I found Arch sitting in his tux, leaning forward, resting his arms on his thighs. To the naked eye, he appeared to be in deep, prayerful thought. I knew he was sleeping. With my dress swooshing with every movement, I took a seat beside him. After a few seconds of me staring at his devilish profile, he woke up and smiled at me.

"It's a boy," I said.

"I know. Mary Lou and Rex's family have gone down to the

nursery to wait to see him." He kissed my nose. "You look tired. Are you ready to go home?"

Home. My house was really a home now. "Yeah." He rose and pulled me to my feet.

"Your mom put Petey to bed several hours ago. We'll go by and pick her up in the morning when we leave for our honeymoon."

There was never a spoken decision to take Petey with us on our honeymoon. It was just the most natural thing in the world to include her in the plans. Although we were supposed to leave immediately following the reception to go to Florida, one day's delay wouldn't hurt.

Arch and I headed to the house he'd grown up in. The house I rented after his father, Pete, was placed in a nursing home. The house where Pete's spirit had come to say goodbye the night he died several months ago. I'd been lucky enough to develop a relationship with Pete, the old goat. Although his presence is very strong throughout the house, it only serves to remind me how much I miss him.

But tonight, Arch and I would be home alone to consummate our marriage. Not that we hadn't already consummated it—many times and quite well, I might add—but on this night, Arch wouldn't have to slip out of bed and get home to Petey before she said her prayers. Yes, it would be a night to remember, if I could only stay awake.

ISBN#1932815635
ISBN#9781932815634
Platinum Imprint
US $24.95 / CDN $33.95

For more information

about other great titles from

MEDALLION PRESS, visit

www.medallionpress.com

F   Wilson, Dolores J
WIL   Dolores J. Wilson's Jail Bertie and
        the peanut ladies

30109019659